APES AND ANGELS

APES
AND
ANGELS

PHILIP APPLEMAN

2970

G. P. PUTNAM'S SONS NEW YORK

Published by G. P. Putnam's Sons, 200 Madison Avenue, New York, NY 10016.
Published simultaneously in Canada

The text of this book is set in Janson.

Library of Congress Cataloging-in-Publication Data

Appleman, Philip, 1926-
Apes and angels / by Philip Appleman.
p.   cm.
ISBN 0-399-13379-8 : price
1. World War, 1939–1945—Fiction.   I. Title.
PS3551.P6A85 1989
813'.54—dc19   88-19080 CIP

Designed by MaryJane DiMassi
Printed in the United States of America
1 2 3 4 5 6 7 8 9 10

FOR MARGIE
THIS MOMENT

APES AND ANGELS

I MAGINE.

Not the dark avenues of cities, the long files of traffic lights going green in unison, the throb of the all-night bus at its terminal stop, the lonely cruising taxi; but the moonshadows of maple leaves on quiet sidewalks, the sounds of birds that never sleep, sending their liquid keening into a honeysuckle midnight, and a time, only yesterday, but before television, before jet planes or astronauts, before civil rights, transistors, Xerox, AIDS, the Pill, or the Bomb.

Imagine Kenton, Indiana—according to the 1940 census, a population of 5,342, county seat and agricultural center of Royal County, yet a town so small that it had only one of many things: one high school, one daily newspaper, one scout troop, one regional basketball trophy, one library, one candy-store hangout, one village atheist, one fire truck. And no war.

In the summer of 1941, there was no war in Kenton, only a long progress of sunny days good for the cornfields of Royal County, good for sweltering afternoons of tennis and then a plunge into Long Lake, hitting the cool water with flushed faces. The boys of Kenton roamed the summer streets, tasting the bubbles of hot tar in the pavement, slivers of ice in the splintered oak bed of the ice truck, the stem-ends of grass.

The ice truck is gone now, and so is Jerry Hall, who drove it all summer and played center on the basketball team and graduated in Paul Anderson's class and died on Okinawa two years later. And the ice plant is gone, where the big three-

9

hundred-pound cakes were frozen and sawed into icebox size: driven to extinction by the triumphant new electric refrigerators. The Candy Castle is gone now, too, where teen-age girls spent summer evenings endlessly talking and sipping lemon Cokes and waiting with the patience of predators for the straying boys to put away childish things and get serious about summer.

The popcorn wagon is gone, the crimson and silver cab with golden cartwheels, and gone with it the nickel bag of buttered popcorn, the fresh-roasted peanuts in their warm and brittle shells. And the schoolhouse is gone, the red brick building where Paul and Jim and Betsy and Ruthie learned to read during the great depression, trudging its wavy oiled floors and twice a year, for practice, cascading down the spiral fire escape.

Summers lasted longer in those days, and were a lot hotter. The only air-conditioned refuge in town was the Strand Theater, where grown-ups surrendered a hard-earned quarter, kids a dime, and sat through a double feature and the Movietone News and two short subjects and Merrie Melodies and maybe a chinaware lottery or Bank Night or a sing-along, just to get out of the heat. There was no such cool comfort in the churches, and on Sundays in summer, pious men's suit coats peeled off like scalded tomato skins, and cardboard fans from a local undertaker, featuring a beatific blue-eyed Jesus, fluttered through the congregation like busy butterflies.

From Memorial Day to Labor Day, the summer waxed, ripened, sighed with the burden of its own fullness, and simmered on as if every day were a midsummer dream. But when on Labor Day, September 1, 1941, the President took over the airwaves to speak of "the most brutal and terrible of all wars," "the menace of world conquest," and "insane violence," the dreams of summer ended.

SEPTEMBER

BEFORE THE KLAN came back, and before the Minotaur threatened the local citizens, and before the devastating fires, the events of that autumn in Kenton, Indiana, seemed more or less routine, a little town going about its business as the great world heaved and struggled around it. People set their alarms at night and grumbled in the jangling morning sunshine and endured their cheerful breakfasts and made the beds with the radio braying and got to the factory before the whistle blew and tumbled into schoolrooms bursting with life.

But then odd things started happening inside the heads of the local citizens. It all began with FDR's Labor Day speech and the reappearance in Kenton of Elaine Edelman; and it happened first of all to the respectable family doctor, Thomas Roberts.

Plodding through middle age, Dr. Roberts found himself overtaken by lust. Forty-seven years old, unswervingly faithful to his wife, unofficial father-counselor to a considerable clientele, he was suddenly as lecherous as a sailor.

First it was Millie Burke, early in her initial pregnancy. On September 2, 1941, Dr. Roberts was examining Millie in his office, when, like a buzzing in his ears, he began hearing snatches of Roosevelt's Labor Day speech all over again: *Weapons of unprecedented power . . .*

Alarmed at this strange visitation, Dr. Roberts shook his head sharply to stop the sonorous voice, but it echoed on: *Forces of insane violence . . .*

He had been out late the previous night on an emergency house call and had suffered a touch of vertigo all day, but he doubted if that accounted for the sound, and his medical experience couldn't otherwise explain this odd buzzing in the ears that had turned into FDR's voice: *Crush Hitler and his Nazi forces . . .*

Dr. Roberts was unnerved and certainly could not understand what happened next: Millie's skin turned, against the flat white of his office walls, a shade of pink so alluring that he began to tremble. Hallucination, he thought, and he blinked several times. But the rosiness persisted, and he felt, simultaneously, a pleasant strangling in his throat and tingling in his legs.

Twenty-two years of professional experience are not for nothing. He cleared his throat and laid the disk of his stethoscope against Millie's chest, just below the clavicle. She shrank back a little from the cold metal, and that movement, so graceful, so yielding, paralyzed him. He felt the full arousal now, the visceral tension, the kinesthetic sensations. He pulled the stethoscope away and stared at the pale circle on Millie's epidermis, slowly flushing rosy like the rest. He pressed it against her again, a little lower, and permitted himself to gaze at her small breasts, the dark areolae showing distinctly under her white slip.

It was as if the cars on Main Street, just outside his frosted window, were no longer wheezing and honking, as if Joy Schroeder, his nurse-receptionist in the next room, had stopped typing the monthly statements, as if the rosy hemispheres of Millie's breasts were all the world there was. Little Millie Townsend Burke, whose body he had cured and cared for since she was seven years old . . .

His free hand reached out and cupped her left breast, almost reverently.

The recoil, the sharp intake of her breath, causing the captive breast to flutter like a caged bird, brought him around. He had to get hold of himself. As his eyes began to focus, he realized that his face was only inches from Millie's startled, half-open mouth. He drew back, cleared his throat again, and pressed his fingertips against the edges of her breast, then against the other one, with professional assurance.

"Any . . ." he began, but his voice was thick with phlegm, and he had to clear his throat once more. "Any—discomfort there yet?"

"No, doctor." Her voice was tiny, like her body, Oriental in its delicacy. Did he detect a note of reproach?

"There may be, later." He went to the door briskly. "Well, Millie, everything's normal. Get dressed and make an appointment with Mrs. Schroeder for your next visit."

A casual word with Joy, a nod at the next patient in the waiting room, and Dr. Roberts, stethoscope swinging against his crisp white jacket, stepped into his washroom, locked the door, and masturbated into the sink.

Things didn't get any better that night, or the next day. It didn't help that Dr. Roberts, one of only four MDs in town, was considered fashionable and therefore had as patients some of the most stylish and attractive women in Royal County: Jane Knowles, with the synovitis in her left knee, that happened to be associated with the loveliest pair of legs he had any memory of, and Sally Herbert, with the contusion on her voluptuous hip. There were the alluring stitches in the appendectomy incision of Jeannie Metzger, the bouncy and reputedly promiscuous cheerleader, and the beguiling complaints of fresh-skinned farm girls whose fathers sent him chickens in lieu of cash.

It wasn't that he simply gave in to all that temptation: he did what he could—calisthenics, cold showers twice a day, guilty little attentions to his wife. Faithful by habit, staunchly puritanical, and—he admitted to himself—a little dull, he had never let himself consider infidelity.

Until now. Day after day, without any warning, he would hear FDR's voice again—*weapons of unprecedented power, fight, conquer, crush*—and whenever it happened, he thought of little else except infidelity. Walking to lunch at Mesler's Drugstore, he could not pass a woman on the street without a pang of lust. Endomorphic women like Celia Carshaw, never before attractive to him, now made his mouth go dry whenever they shifted their weight from hip to hip. Ectomorphic women, always attractive to him, became a torment. Joy, his receptionist, a dark-haired woman of twenty-six, was a chronic problem, having what appeared to be a slightly concave tummy. Dr. Roberts, one eye on X rays or lab reports, would study her contours with acute dysphoria. But Joy was off-limits, and not only because of her suspicious husband. Dr. Roberts had not lost all sense of professional duty, after all; Joy was his associate, his employee. Still, he stole peeks at her all day Tuesday and Wednesday. And suffered.

At the drugstore he bought a copy of *Esquire,* sneaking it out in a paper bag. He took it into his office washroom and abused himself over drawings of long-legged lovelies, women with impossible anatomies, too good to be true. It helped, but only temporarily, leaving him feeling soiled and ashamed—until the urge came again.

Between patients, Dr. Roberts considered his appearance in the washroom mirror. He was forty-seven, true, but he was often told he looked younger. Forty, maybe? Thirty-five, even? Not the appearance of an "old" man, anyway: his hair was full and dark; his dress leaned toward camel's hair sport coats, not the gray vested suits of his colleagues; he had always been considered good-looking, in a boyish way. Yes, thirty-five was not out of the question. Eligible.

But eligible for what? For whom?

The Wednesday night after Labor Day, Dr. Roberts woke out of an erotic dream with a stubborn erection and sweating with dread. He got up and studied his old textbooks for some clue to his ailment but found none that satisfied him. On Thursday he threw himself into his work harder than ever, doused himself with another cold shower, and decided to take up golf again. He attended an emergency noon meeting of the Kenton School Board; the presidency of the Board had unexpectedly become vacant, and, thanks to his years of seniority, it was offered to him. He accepted the tedious unpaid job almost with gratitude.

Later that afternoon, trying valiantly to get his mind off sex, he sternly denied himself *Esquire,* hummed loudly to kill the sound of FDR's sonorities, and resolved to do some serious reading: professional literature, nonfiction, nothing even slightly erotic. He visited the town library and turned instinctively to his old hobby, the dry dust of history, checking out books on the Civil War: retired generals' eyewitness accounts of Gettysburg and Appomattox—detailed, authentic. Concentrating, he forced himself to memorize the campaigns, the positions of regiments. The trouble was, he knew that this self-imposed aridity was only a placebo. So as he relived the charge of cavalry, he felt the tingling in his groin. When the cannonballs wrecked barricades and tore into flesh, he felt the pulsing in his member. The aged generals ended their chapters discreetly with the fall of cities, but Dr. Roberts' inflamed imagination always raced on to the inevitable conclusion, the pillaging, the ripping of crinoline . . .

Friday evening, plagued by FDR's voice, he went back to the library. Running his fingers across the titles of old volumes in American history, he came to a gap in the shelves and found his finger pointing through the books at a face a few inches away. A young woman. A very pretty woman. His finger stayed in the gap, as if stuck there. She looked him in the eye for a moment, coolly, then moved to one side, behind the row of books.

Dr. Roberts' heart gave a strange little twitch. He sucked in air, still seeing the face: the wide mouth, the brief green pleasure of the eyes, the red hair. And something else—there was something else in the face, in the eyes. His body felt clumsy with desire. Carrying the book on Antietam he had just picked up, he tiptoed around the bookshelf, turning the corner just as the red hair floated around the next rank of shelves, leaving behind the vision of a blue silk dress and slim hips. Dr. Roberts had a vague sense of recognition: not a stranger. Someone he had seen before. Not one of his patients—he'd remember. But a woman he knew. Where? When?

The library seemed empty except for the two of them—and presumably Miss Froebel, the librarian, who was not visible at the moment. It must be nearly closing time. He rounded the next row of shelves. The red hair, this time, almost brought recollection. Not quite. He approached her, his legs numb. He had no idea why he was doing this, pursuing a woman through an empty library. She was looking at a book, but he knew she could feel him getting closer. A foot away he stopped, and she turned and looked at him gravely, as if waiting for something.

Then he remembered. "You're Elaine, aren't you, Saul's daughter?" She didn't deny it, the green eyes steady, not blinking. What was it in her eyes? "You're Elaine Edelman. Back in Kenton. To teach."

There is no explaining what Dr. Roberts did next. With his

left hand still on Antietam, his right hand reached out and touched her triceps in a kind of accidental caress, then moved over and cupped her breast, as it had Millie Burke's—then slid along her firm pectoralis major and down the intercostals, traveled the transverse muscles of her abdomen, hesitated on the fascia of her thigh, and settled on the mons veneris, which fit comfortably in his palm. This time, though, there was no recoiling, no backing away. She didn't even blink, her green eyes studying his face with that grave, mysterious look. His hand was resting contentedly on her little mound, and he thought: There have been other hands here.

"Doctor . . ." she said, in a voice that sounded dryly clinical.

When she spoke, he recognized the other thing in her eyes. "Hunger," he said, out loud. "It's hunger."

"Doctor," she said again in the clinical voice, "you need professional help."

"Closing time." Miss Froebel emerged from behind the card catalogue files.

The doctor's daring hand slunk away from its bold adventure and slipped into a pants pocket, jingling car keys. Elaine, looking hostile, gathered up her purse and books. Dr. Roberts felt the crushing weight of an irredeemable loss.

Maybe not irredeemable. Doggedly faithful husband, he had no practice in flirtation, no fresh and helpful memory of how he used to proceed when he was young, unattached, and about ninety percent sexual appetite. All he knew now was that he mustn't let her leave like this, offended and hurt.

"Elaine—Miss Edelman—listen. I apologize. I don't know why I did that." She didn't say anything, wouldn't look at him, just started for the door. He followed. "I'm really sorry. I'd like to make it up to you. May I drive you home?"

Passing the front desk, Elaine called out, "Good night, Miss Froebel." The librarian waved from the catalogue file, then stared at the two of them leaving together. The thought flashed through Dr. Roberts' mind: there'll be talk. He didn't care.

Out on the front steps, he repeated, "May I drive you home?"

"Ride with you? I'd rather walk. Ten miles."

"It's early, I'll walk with you. I could use some exercise."

"Suit yourself." She stepped off briskly, down the deserted sidewalk, through a little pool of streetlight, into the shadows of September maples; and Dr. Roberts, god of the consultation room and altogether unaccustomed to supplication, instinctively fell back on his special gift: a reliable bedside manner. Walking half a step behind her, he began talking, and was pleased to find it easy to talk, even without any encouraging response, about their common interest, the high school, about his long service on the School Board, about her new job, about Mr. Graff, the old teacher she was replacing. When he asked her where she lived, she didn't answer, just paused under a streetlight and glanced at him, long enough for him to see the beautiful green eyes again and the hostility still simmering there.

He didn't know where they were headed, how much time he had, but as they turned off of Richmond onto Elm Street, he knew he had to talk fast and be more personal, or nothing would be gained. Casting around, he began to talk about her father, Saul, who was a patient of his, and about Saul's interesting weekly newspaper, and even—with a little twinge of conscience—about Saul's ailments. He knew he shouldn't be doing this. There was something unprofessional about it, possibly unethical; but now somehow that didn't seem to matter.

Where did she live? At any house in any block she might suddenly turn in, dismiss him with her silent back, and slam

a door. Desperate, he began talking about himself, his practice, his life, his home—and finally even about his wife and
their problems, things he had never told anyone: their tough
years in medical school, their not having children, their happiness in spite of all that. And finally, a year ago, the auto
accident that had shattered their pleasant life, put Edna into
the hospital, then in a wheelchair, and then on crutches, and,
when she was finally walking again, had fostered another
condition which she bore with stoic satisfaction. It was something that fed on her while it sustained her, a trauma apparently triggered by the accident but now intensified by her
fervent devotion to good works and her growing obsession
with the austere teachings of the Church of Christ.

Too soon, as he had feared, Elaine stopped at a small white
house and took a set of keys out of her purse. He waited,
nervous as a kid on his first date. When she finally glanced
at him, though, it wasn't a curt dismissal; her eyes seemed less
hostile than before.

"Why didn't you have children?"

The blunt question surprised him, but he was in too deep
now to start being evasive. "Well, in fact, it was my—'fault,'
as they say. Both of us had tests. Edna seemed to be OK, but
I . . . My sperm count was low. Ridiculously low. Bad luck.
Or who knows, maybe good—we had a happy life, just the
way we were. Until a year ago."

She looked at him again, and he could tell she was interested. "Her 'obsession'?" She thought it over for a moment.
"What did you mean by that, what you said about the
church? That your wife is some kind of fanatic? Or do you
mean hypocrisy? Or what?"

He leaped at this unexpected interest, desperately hoping
she wouldn't go inside. "It's not fanaticism, exactly. And it's
not hypocrisy, either. She's the most sincere person I've ever

known. But there's something—well, make-believe about the whole thing, some kind of substitute for real life . . ."

She put the keys back in her purse and started walking again, slower now, apparently waiting for him to go on. Not knowing where they were going, he fell in step, side-by-side this time, and tried to talk sense about his life. But the truth was, he didn't know where his life was going, either. Word by word, step by step, he floundered along.

"Edna and I had always been—not just husband and wife, but friends. Lovers. I don't know what happened in the accident, in her convalescence, but somehow all that got lost. At first it appeared to be just physical. There were a few scars, not huge or hideous or anything, but she seemed to think she wasn't attractive anymore, and wouldn't let me touch her."

Elaine was walking slowly, and he noticed that she glanced at him more often, almost as if she were sympathizing.

"Then it became—what would you call it, spiritual, mystical?—I'm not a churchgoer. Anyway, during that whole convalescence, for months, she spoke every day with Reverend Tucker, sometimes at her bedside, sometimes on the phone. There in her bed, with nothing else to do, she worked endlessly at church activities, talking on the phone from morning till night. By the time she was up and around, she'd become the acting head of the Ladies Aid Society and the Foreign Missions Campaign."

Elaine frowned at him, as though trying to solve a puzzle. Dr. Roberts felt guilty. He knew he shouldn't be telling her this, almost a stranger after all, but he couldn't stop.

"When she came home from the hospital, still on crutches, she used the downstairs bedroom. After she was back on her feet again . . ." He felt foolish saying this. "She stayed there." He felt Elaine's quick glance. "Nothing I could say ever got her back to our bedroom, upstairs. I insisted. Joked. Pleaded.

No good. She was convinced she'd had a religious experience, and had been 'chosen.' For something. Whatever it was, it didn't seem to include me . . ."

Their aimless walk had ended up at Long Lake, small waves slapping at the town pier. They stood there for a few minutes, watching the moon on the water.

Talking it out for the first time, Dr. Roberts felt more and more miserable. "I even tried to get her to see a psychiatrist, but you know how that is—people never think they need one. And for a believer, even the suggestion is a kind of insult. So she wouldn't do it."

He didn't know he was crying until he felt the tears on his cheek. He wiped them away. Who were they for, anyway? Edna? Himself?

Elaine glanced at him, and this time it wasn't a hostile look. Her voice sounded concerned. "Dr. Roberts . . ."

"Please. Call me Tom." And after a pause: "Elaine."

When she looked at him again, he was sure it was tenderness he saw in her face. "It's so dreadful," she said, "when people don't . . . When they can't . . ."

His gesture was a helpless appeal: to what, he didn't know. But she laid her hand over his, and he felt how much warmer her skin was than his. Then she touched his cheek, as if wiping away a tear, and he dared to put his fingertips on her forehead, her temples. And so in the dim moonlight there was a first kiss: tentative, chaste, virginal; a second one passionate; a third one consumed with guilt; a fourth one casting off caution; a fifth one . . .

❦

Kenton was not in the war, but the war was coming closer, the Andersons' crackling radio always threatening disaster. In North Africa, British forces were pinned down in Tobruk, and on the Eastern front, the panzer divisions were pounding deep into Russia, the black arrows in the Kenton *Daily Herald* nearly encircling Moscow and cutting off the Crimea. The week after school started, a German sub attacked the U.S. destroyer *Greer*. Four days after that, an American freighter was sunk, the next day another, and two days later, yet another. For a neutral country, the U.S. was taking a lot of casualties. On September 11, FDR denounced the attacks as piracy.

Home for lunch, Paul, Jim, and Betsy Anderson all spread peanut butter and Miracle Whip on Silvercup bread. Their mother, Nora, called from the kitchen, "Chew every bite ten times, kids." Ravenous, Paul bit off half a slice and washed it down with milk. He and Jim took turns trotting the little red wagon down to Miller's Dairy and filling their clean jugs with skim milk, ten cents a gallon, then stopping by Hollenbeck's Corner Grocery for day-old bread, a nickel a loaf. Being slightly stale, their mother said, gave Silvercup a little character; but Betsy managed to make doughballs out of hers anyway, furtively discarding the crusts, squeezing the flabby white stuff into heavy pellets, and tossing them into her mouth like popcorn.

On the Andersons' little Zenith, FDR was condemning the

German subs, his voice quivering through static. "When you
see a rattlesnake poised to strike, you do not wait until he has
struck before you crush him . . ."

Strike: Paul paused between bites, fascinated by the intense
voice superimposed on the homely sounds of the Anderson
household—Jim's knife clanking on his plate, the rhythmic
tapping of Betsy's feet, their father's heavy stride in the upstairs hallway, his mother bustling at the kerosene stove in the
kitchen.

Crush: basketball practice had started, and he and Jim had
both made the first team. "Unc" Ehrhard, the coach, said
"crush" a lot, as if they were playing football; it always excited Paul.

"The Nazi submarines are the rattlesnakes of the Atlantic.
They attack our most precious rights when they fire on ships
of the American flag, symbols of our independence . . ."

Their mother's voice floated in from the kitchen: "Don't
dawdle, kids, you'll be late. Remember to brush your teeth.
Use salt. Jimmy, come help me with this hot pan."

Despite her severe arthritis, she never stopped working.
She was canning string beans now, jar after jar, two bush-
els of them the kids had picked for free at cousin Harry's
run-down farm. The kitchen was full of green Mason jars,
lids, rubber sealing rings, and great billowings of steam
from the sterilizing bath atop the kerosene burners. All
summer she kept it up: cherries in June, forty jars of them
in the cellar now, waiting to be pies on Sundays and holidays; corn in July, beets in August—and now the beans,
the stringy, despised green beans. Everything was grown
in their own backyard garden or picked up from relatives
or friends, or bought, at a nominal cost, from desperate
farmers, then canned and stowed away in the cellar. "For a
rainy day," she always said.

Meanwhile, FDR's voice went on. "American naval vessels will no longer wait until the Axis submarines strike their deadly blow first."

Strike: the basketball opener was with Fox Lake, rumored to be tough this year. Unc Ehrhard was planning some surprises for them.

Charles Anderson, head of the family, thumped down the back stairs, strode through the dining room, and paused for a moment at the sound of the hated radio voice. "Democrat idiot!" he exploded, and slammed out the front door.

"Hitler's advance guards, not only his avowed agents, but also his dupes among us, have sought to make ready for him footholds and bridgeheads in the New World . . ."

"Wait a sec, Dad, give me a ride!" Paul yelled. "I got to go to Hillmeyer's before afternoon classes start."

"Hurry it up, then!" his father called back from the street. Paul heard the Ford grinding and finally catching. He grabbed his letter sweater. Running for the car, he heard his mother's voice from the front porch. "Charlie, I need three dollars, that insurance man's coming again this afternoon!"

"Tell him first of next week."

"That's what I told him last week!"

Paul yanked the door open as the car eased away from the curb, and jumped in.

"Charlie! When are you coming home for supper?"

"Expect me when you see me!" Charlie called, too far away to be heard. He was all steamed up: "They're doing it piece by piece, step by step! Why doesn't Congress do something about that madman cripple Democrat dictator, wait a minute, I'm running on empty."

At Jed Shinover's Sinclair Service, under a giant brontosaurus, he went on grumbling. "The whole thing is unconstitutional. He ought to be impeached, better yet, run out of Washington on a rail."

"Well, Chuck," Jed drawled, checking the oil in the blue '37 Ford and wiping the stick on the leg of his bib overalls, "you got to admit we can't sit still forever, just taking it and not dishing out anything."

"What do you mean, take it, dish it out—this isn't a kids' fistfight, he wants a war! Just like the Wilson war—re-elect him as a reward for keeping us out of it, and right away he shoves us into it. Democrat wars, Jehosaphat!"

In the front seat, Paul was getting nervous. "Let's go, Dad, I've got to be back in class by one o'clock." He understood next to nothing about the war, but ever since the President's Labor Day speech, he'd been thinking about it a lot. *Insane violence. Rattlesnakes. Strike. Crush.* He was looking forward to basketball practice.

"Yeah, I know, Chuck," Jed persisted, carefully cleaning the windshield. "Still and all, you gotta admit we're getting stabbed in the back."

"Why are our backs out there with all those knives? We're neutral, remember? They want to stir up a war every twenty years over there, let them do it, it's not our business. Keep our noses out of it, like George Washington said."

"Yeah, something to that, all right."

"Dad, I'll be late!"

"OK, Paul. Lindbergh's on the radio tonight, Jed. He'll tell 'em. Put this on my tab, OK? I'll take care of it first of next week."

"I'd appreciate that, Chuck."

Paul's father always bought five gallons of gas, an even dollar's worth, and he always drove faster after talking politics, the little sixty-horsepower Ford bucking and coughing at being prodded so savagely.

❦

THE KENTON DAILY HERALD

Des Moines, Iowa, Sept. 11, 1941
Col. Charles A. Lindbergh said here tonight, "The three most important groups who have been pressing this country toward war are the British, the Jewish, and the Roosevelt administration."

Col. Lindbergh added, "It is not difficult to understand why Jewish people desire the overthrow of Nazi Germany. The persecution they suffered in Germany would be sufficient to make bitter enemies of any race. But no person of honesty and vision can look on their pro-war policy here today without seeing the dangers involved in such a policy. Their greatest danger to this country lies in their large ownership and influence in our motion pictures, our press, our radio, and our government."

THE DAILY HERALD WORLD NEWS ROUNDUP

WENDELL WILLKIE: "Lindbergh's speech in Des Moines was the most un-American talk made in my time by any person of national reputation."

THOMAS E. DEWEY: "It was an inexcusable abuse of the right to freedom of speech."

PAUL V. MCNUTT: "The voice is the voice of Lindbergh, but the words are the words of Hitler."

❧

Miss Edelman, the new teacher, was quite a change for Kenton High School. Everyone had taken Biology I from old Mr. Graff, who had postponed his retirement beyond all reason. Although officially younger, he was rumored to be well over seventy by the time he retired last spring, and he had developed a tendency to lose track of things—chalk, books, his own questions. On warm days he'd often drowse off at his desk, halfway through class.

The kids would usually just fool around quietly and let him sleep. Avid for basketball season, some of them would arch big paperwads from their desks up to the teacher's wastebasket, littering the floor with their misses. Laura Hill would sneak up to the blackboard and draw an authentic Bugs Bunny with the caption, "What's up, Teach?" And Walter Stone, relying on Mr. Graff's notoriously defective hearing, would do his Spike Jones imitation, full of squeaks, honks, and grunts. Once Terry and Al had done a whole minstrel show routine, Al's knit cap pulled low for blackface, and once they had joined Scrap and Gopher for a reprise of their big hit in the Friday auditorium program, a barbershop quartet. They got all the way through "The Banks of the Wabash" before the high wail of their special coda broke the old man's slumber.

But nobody, after five minutes with Miss Edelman, would have dreamed of horsing around in her biology class. She was the youngest and prettiest teacher at K.H.S., but she was also the toughest, firing hard questions when they were least expected, when kids were staring out the window or sneaking notes to each other. She was even stricter than Miss Eva, the intimidating but popular English teacher.

She was a Democrat, too—unusual for Kenton, where Democrats were considered less than respectable, and Democrat schoolteachers, if there were any, kept quiet about it. Not Miss Edelman, though. She sometimes mentioned FDR in the classroom, with obvious approval. Daring.

In the second week of school, she startled the class with a peculiar question. "All right, how many of you listened to the President's speech yesterday noon? Hands."

Paul's hand went up, and Jim's and Ruthie's, and one or two others. Miss Edelman looked annoyed, though she must have known that most of the juniors and seniors had their pushbutton radios set, day and night, to Benny Goodman and Artie Shaw and Duke Ellington, not to politicians. But ever since FDR's Labor Day speech, Paul had been listening to the war news a lot, dialing in WLW, WOWO, WGN, the Blue Network.

"All right, class, I'll tell you something the President said that applies to what we're going to be studying in here. He said the Nazi subs are the rattlesnakes of the Atlantic Ocean, and he said we're already in a war. Did you read the chapter on adaptation last night? Hands."

A few more hands went up this time.

"Good. Now listen to this. 'The state of nature is a state of constant warfare, and from that warfare, from famine and death, come all the plants and animals on earth.' Do you know who said that?"

The class looked blank.

Warfare. Rattlesnakes. Strike. Crush. Paul thought of Unc

Ehrhard, and his mind wandered off to basketball practice.
Miss Edelman's sharp voice brought him back quickly: "It
wasn't in your chapter, was it? Well, you're going to find out,
anyway."

Mr. Graff had never said anything even distantly connected to the real world, and he stuck strictly to the book,
assigning the chapters in order and then paraphrasing them
in class. Miss Edelman assigned chapters, too, but didn't always refer to them directly.

She balanced a large photograph on the chalk tray. "This
is the peppered moth, seen against its natural habitat, the bark
of an oak tree."

The photo was nothing but a pattern of light and shadow.
Most of the kids stared without interest.

"It's all right, you're not supposed to see it at first. But now
follow the pointer." She traced a circle, and suddenly there
it was, inside the imaginary circle, a light gray moth sitting
on the gray bark. "That's what's known as protective coloration. If a bird can't see you, it can't eat you. You survive, you
propagate, and you win the war, the struggle for existence—
the death-and-starvation war. So color can have survival
value—got that? All right, now look at this next photo."

It was a similar picture, but the tree trunk was darker,
nearly black, instead of the light gray of the previous one.

"See the moth now? OK, look—it's here—right here." She
drew another circle, and it emerged, like magic. "It's the
peppered moth again, but now it's black. *Why is that, Bill?*"

Bill had been whispering to Connie, which is why Miss
Edelman called on him. Of course he hadn't the slightest idea.
Neither did Connie, or Ethel, or Paul, or anyone. A teacher
wasn't supposed to ask questions that didn't have answers in
the book.

"I'll give you a hint, and you can figure it out. The first

picture was taken out in the country, no factories around for miles. The bark of the tree is light gray, as it should be, and the moth is gray, as it always had been. The second photo is from a different place, near a factory town, where smoke-stacks have been pumping grime into the air for years and years. The trees—not to mention people's lungs, that's an-other story—have all been sooted over. OK, now you know all you need to know. What's the explanation for this brand-new moth?"

Everyone sat mute, edgy at another question that wasn't in the assigned reading. Thinking, thinking: it was uncomfort-able.

"Terry? . . . Pat? . . . June?"

Finally Jim's hand went up, a little tentatively. Paul sighed. Of course *he'd* figure it out, infallible big brother.

"Jim?"

"Is it because after the factories came, I mean after the trees got black, the color gray wasn't, what you said, protective anymore?"

"Good. And not being protective, it . . ."

"Didn't help the moths survive?"

"Right. Gray loses its survival value, and black takes on survival value, and as a result?"

"The moth has to become black, too. Or else."

"Or else not survive. The moths have to change—mutate, it's called. So those moths that do happen to mutate and evolve into darker varieties end up as the winners in this war we're talking about, this struggle for existence—and then go on to propagate the next generation of black moths. Do you understand that, everybody? It's the key to what we'll be working on this semester—organic evolution, the key to un-derstanding all of biology. OK, let's begin with our planet, the earth. Does anyone know how old it is?"

Nobody moved to answer, most of the kids looking bored. Paul thought Jim might know, but he wasn't paying attention, either. He was leaning close to Ruthie Peters, their bare arms just meeting. Jim was a big success as always, a classroom triumph, survival of the fittest.

"Two billion years, that's the answer—a minimum of two billion, maybe more. Try to imagine what two thousand million years is like. Well, you can't really imagine it, can you? But look at this."

She drew a straight line across the blackboard, all the way across the room, left to right.

"Say that line is two billion years long. On that scale, how long is a human lifetime?" Rhetorical question, no pause. "If the right end of the blackboard is 'now,' and I tried to draw a human lifetime on this scale, you wouldn't be able to see any space between the chalk marks on the right end—that's how small it would be. Even if we mark the whole million years that some kind of human or nearly human animal has walked upright, look how small it is, compared with the age of the earth."

The mark was only a fraction of an inch from the right end of the board, the gap barely visible.

"That fraction of an inch is the whole history of human existence. So we're really Johnny-come-latelies in biological history, aren't we? Long before us, the dinosaurs came and went—about here." She drew two lines, a little farther to the left. "And before that, there were fishes—and arthropods—and invertebrates. And way back here, there were primitive forms of marine life for millions and millions of years."

She had been hash-marking vertical lines over her horizontal line, farther and farther left across the board, but she was still not halfway across the room. On the left side of her time-line, the primitive earth sat vacant, inert, and sterile.

Time schemes were always frustrating: Paul was a year younger than Jim, and all his life he had felt stifled by that cold fact. "These days," his mother would say, "we have to economize." So Paul wore Jim's cast-off clothes, played with his cast-off tennis racket, followed him grade by grade, hearing from his cast-off teachers how bright he was, and hearing from his scoutmaster how Jim had rocketed through the merit badges to Eagle Scout. Jim kept a rabbit's foot hanging around his neck for good luck, and it always seemed to be working.

In high school, once or twice, Paul had caught up to him, like now. Bored by Mr. Graff, Jim had put off taking the second semester of biology; now he was a senior and had to have it to graduate. Paul, a junior, was taking it now, too. So here they were, the two of them together; but it was still Jim—"Ace," he made his friends call him—up there, up front, answering the tough questions, and rubbing arms with cute Ruthie Peters.

"You don't last for a million years without the equipment for survival. If you look at human beings as we are now, you'll see we're not very well equipped for survival in a jungle, for fighting, for the war of nature—compared, say, to a tiger, or even a wolf. Suppose you found yourself in a cave, naked and surrounded by the dangers of the forest—how would you go about getting food, raising a family, defending yourself against cougars or grizzlies?"

Jim could manage it, Paul thought bitterly. *I'd* never make it, but *he* would.

"Of course, at first you wouldn't have *been* naked. The animals we developed from, as Charles Darwin said, were undoubtedly hairy, hairy all over, like apes. If we saw one, we'd probably say it *was* an ape. But it had something special about it just the same, that the other apes lacked, some kind of genetic good luck that its biological cousins didn't have. And eventually—meaning in the course of millions of years . . ." She ticked a couple of places on her time-line, very close together. "Its skull got bigger, the brain became more complex, more convoluted, the big toe lost some of its articulation, allowing the animal to stand upright—and little by little the creature developed into a new thing, a sort of man-ape, the earliest one we know about—Java Man."

When she mentioned Darwin, Fat Emmert had twitched, as if he'd been pricked with a pin, and he began paying attention. The only time anyone heard the name of Darwin in Kenton, Indiana, in 1941, was when Emmert's father, the Reverend Dobbins of the Pentecostal Church, or one of the other preachers, denounced him from the pulpit.

She drew another line across the blackboard. "But suppose, now, that this new line represents 'only' a million years, the time since Java Man. Then look how briefly true humans—*Homo sapiens*—have been around." She drew a mark near the right end of the line. "Look at the gap between Java Man and us. Well, what happened in all those hundreds of thousands of years?"

Paul tried hard to imagine it, that chasm of time. It made him feel dizzy, like standing on the edge of a cliff.

"The truth is, we don't yet know the whole story of that huge gap. There must be a lot of so-called 'missing links,' fossils, buried in the earth somewhere, but so far we've found only a few of them—Peking Man, Heidelberg Man, Neanderthal, Cro-Magnon—enough to give us a pattern, but not yet enough to show a neat form-series of skeletons. Still, given the pattern, reason tells us that the fossils must be out there somewhere—in Asia, or Africa, maybe. Darwin thought we'd find them in Africa—just waiting for some lucky paleontologist to dig them up."

Fat Emmert had twitched a few more times, and Miss Edelman apparently noticed it, gazing at him while she talked, as if she knew what was on his mind.

"But think about Java Man for a minute—big-toothed, long-nailed, hairy, muscular—as compared to ourselves. Think of the frailness of our naked bodies."

For the first time, Paul thought about Miss Edelman's naked body. He had imagined a lot of naked bodies—Ruthie Peters', mostly, and Sally Crothers', and even Mildred Fox's—but he had never actually seen a naked woman. Occasionally that thought depressed him. Right now, though, it was very nice to imagine Miss Edelman's body, and the more he thought about it, the more clearly he could imagine it. He began to think that he could even smell it—a seductive, musky smell that grew more intense as she went on talking. "Miss Edelman," he said to himself, "Elaine."

"We can't run as fast as leopards, we can't slash like bears or pounce like panthers or poison like snakes or dive like hawks. We're not as strong as lions, or armor-plated like rhinos. And yet, the softer we've become over the course of human evolution—the less clawlike our nails, the less dagger-like our canines and incisors—the more dangerous we've become. So that now we—the small, soft creatures—are killing off some of the biggest and fiercest animals, exterminating them. Why is that? How did it happen?"

Some of the kids seemed to be paying attention for a change, and this time it was such an easy question that Paul caught on right away. But Jim's hand was up first, and Ruthie blurted out the answer without even being called on.

"Tools," she said. "Weapons."

Jim and Ruthie, the smartest students at K.H.S. Paul knew they'd always be a jump ahead of him.

"Tools are part of it, yes." Miss Edelman stalked along the blackboard without pausing again, slashing an occasional mark on the time-line. "The hand ax, an ordinary rock chipped away to a sharp edge, is perhaps the most important tool in the history of human evolution, and it survived for hundreds of thousands of years—from *here* to *here* on the time-line—helping to protect the soft human body in the war, the war of famine and death." She was talking so intensely that she wasn't watching the class much anymore. *War. Famine and death.* Paul squinted. Some of the kids' chairs seemed to be inching together, and Walter Stone had reached out his leg until it touched Sally Crothers' bare knee.

"But look here—*here* at the very end of the time-line— by now three great ice ages have come and gone, and here is where human beings, real human beings, enter the scene: *Homo sapiens,* 'smart people,' Cro-Magnon. Outside their caves there was always the terrible cold, and also, of course, the hairy mammoths, the saber-toothed tigers, the bears. But the Cro-Magnons had tools, yes, weapons, and they had something else that no other animal had, something more dangerous than fangs, more important than the hand ax . . ."

Her voice was a throbbing, husky contralto. Paul looked around and blinked. Was Jim's hand stroking the small of Ruthie's back? And was Bill's elbow touching Connie's waist? Boys all around the room had slid their chairs closer to nearby girls, and the smell of Miss Edelman's naked body was stronger now, a sultry perfume that made it hard to breathe.

"And that 'something' they had was *mind.* Brain. The ability to think, to remember, to plan, to imagine. It didn't really matter all that much that they—we—had lost our claws, because we had something much more powerful, and with it we could make murderous weapons for the war of nature: spears, stone-headed axes, snares, bows, flint-headed arrows.

"But even more special than that—*here,* on the time-line,

twenty thousand years ago, give or take a few thousand, something happened that had never happened before. Here on the map, where it's now southern Europe—those people did an absolutely new thing." Miss Edelman took a deep breath. "They invented art. Back in the dark corners of those caves, they scratched and painted animals, beautifully drawn animals, mammoths and bears, bulky red bison, ocher horses, bulls, and running deer."

The cloying odor had grown more powerful; Paul was so dizzy he had to hold on to his desk. The classroom was a steam bath—someone should open the windows. Miss Edelman's naked voice became slow and dreamy, and to Paul it seemed unbearably erotic. He began to itch all over.

"Why did they bother? What was it all for, all that effort? We don't know, and we probably won't ever know. But the paintings are evidence, anyway, of something important that had become part of our lives, a way of searching for what we *are* as human beings. Charles Darwin never saw the cave paintings, but he obviously understood what inspired them. We're all in this thing together, this thing called life, he said. Listen to this."

She picked up a worn old book, not their textbook, and read: " 'Animals, our fellow brethren in pain, disease, death, suffering, and famine, our slaves in the most laborious works, our companions in our amusements—they may partake from our origin in one common ancestor, we may be all netted together.' *All netted together*—one of Darwin's wonderful perceptions, that helps to explain why we are what we are . . ."

Looking sad, Miss Edelman gazed out the window. "What we are right now—two-legged featherless creatures in Biology II at Kenton High School on Friday, September twelfth, 1941."

She turned and tossed her chalk into the tray, and, as if she had willed it, the bell rang. Chairs began to scrape and bang. The strange perfume had completely disappeared. Jim and Ruthie were sitting a foot apart, as if nothing had happened. So were Walter and Sally, and Bill and Connie. And the others. Paul couldn't believe it. What was going on?

He grabbed his books and started for the door. *Strike. Crush.* Starvation and death. He headed for basketball practice.

Fat Emmert was leaving just ahead of him, his eyes wide, his face sort of crumpled. "That wasn't Christian," he whispered, sounding as if he'd been choked. "That wasn't Christian at all."

YOU NEED PROFESSIONAL HELP: her diagnosis was just what the doctor ordered, and Thomas Roberts prescribed for himself decisively. Elaine Edelman, K.H.S. Class of '35, BS (Purdue), MS (Indiana U.) turned out to be the only professional help Dr. Roberts needed. He lay in her wrinkled sheets, marveling. If it was hunger he had seen in her eyes, she must have seen starvation in his, and she had fed him, carefully at first, then fully, then recklessly. Contemplating a return to thirty-five, Dr. Roberts had become twenty again.

"It was fate," he called to her, "destiny, our meeting like that in the library." Twenty-year-old performance, twenty-year-old philosophy.

She appeared in the bathroom doorway, naked, so beautiful he stopped breathing. She was brushing her red hair. Had he not studied her face so thoroughly, he wouldn't have known she was smiling. "If you believe in fate for the good things, you have to accept it for the messy ones, too."

Granted, but he wouldn't accept it. "I'd rather pick and choose, thanks."

"Eat your cake and have it." The subtle smile again, complicating her cool gaze. "You're spoiled, Doctor."

"I have a lot of time to make up for. I've only been spoiled for eight days."

Eight days since that lucky meeting in the library. Twelve days since Labor Day, since the insane violence, the rattlesnakes. He still heard the President's buzzing voice from time to time, but, thanks to Elaine's magical remedy, it didn't scare him anymore.

She sat down beside him. "Look, I'm twenty-four, pushing twenty-five, so I know some things you don't even remember. Stick with me, kid. You're a young man, but you've been living an old life." Her breasts swayed as she reached across with her brush and stroked his pubic hairs.

Hands under head, he looked down and beheld the miracle. She played the brush softly around the insides of his thighs, and his brand-new twenty-year-old member responded sturdily, standing like a tower. Again. "You're a conjurer, a sorceress. A few centuries ago they burned people like you at the stake."

The brush paused and her face came around to him slowly. She stared at him, the green eyes gone opaque. "It may not be too late," she whispered.

Unaccountably, he contracted with fear. What did *that* mean? He thought of Edna, and withered.

She slapped his thigh with the back of the brush. "We talk too much. *You* talk too much. You've got this gorgeous body, why do you have to talk so much? It's bad for the glands, take it from your local biologist."

She tossed the brush away and straddled him, massaged his arms, his throat, his chest, his belly. Her fingers trailed across the insides of his thighs, and he closed his eyes, heard himself groaning somewhere far off, felt her lips, her tongue, gently gliding. He lifted her head and she slid upward across his chest and kissed his open mouth, and he tasted his own body, and then they rolled over and he slid down and kissed her warm places, playing gently with his tongue until she rocked slowly back and forth, her hips swaying, and then he entered her. He felt her tears on his cheeks.

Somewhere beyond those drawn blinds it was still a bright Saturday afternoon, and young women in white skirts were swatting tennis balls around grassy courts, and middle-aged men in white undershirts were forcing lawnmowers through tough crabgrass, and Edna Roberts was lying on her white bed, phoning instructions to the Sunday school teachers at the First Church of Christ, and white phosphorus artillery shells were whining into Kiev, exploding showers of spectacular fireworks into the Russian night. But in Elaine's darkened room, only lavender shadows rippled on gray walls. Nothing else stirred.

Later, later—how much later? Had they been asleep? He stroked her hair. Her eyes opened and she smiled her half-smile.

"Tom," she mumbled.

He kissed her. Absolute peace.

"Tom," she murmured. "Don't ever desert me."

❧

P AUL ANDERSON was born on December 10, 1924, and his memory began functioning just in time to record the 1929 stock market crash and the beginning of the great depression. By September, 1941, when he was nearly seventeen years old and already contemplating the new peacetime draft, he could remember no time, no time at all, that was not the depression. Everyone he knew had always had to hustle, and they hustled for peanuts, so it was no particular disgrace for a high school junior to spend Wednesday afternoons hiking the *Saturday Evening Post* to lonely women in porch swings at five cents a copy, the penny-and-a-half net profit squirreled away, shiny dimes in his dime bank. Paul's most frequent recurring dream was of finding money. Never paper money, always the real thing: quarters, half-dollars—bright, provocative, mockingly beautiful.

One of Paul's *Post* customers was Mr. McGraw—or anyway, someone in the McGraw mansion, that formidable brick house with tall white pillars, surrounded by a city block of well-tended gardens and a high iron fence. The McGraws owned the biggest factory in Kenton, a plant that turned its billboards toward the New York Central tracks to proclaim the World's Largest Manufacturer of Windmills and Pumps. It was intimidating to walk up that long driveway, deliver the *Post* at the back door, and collect a nickel from an aproned servant, but it was the high point of his route, Paul's weekly connection to the great world of wealth and power.

Another factory, in a loft above Hillmeyer's butcher shop,

belonged to Paul's father, and it was probably the world's smallest producer of insecticides. Small but mighty, it produced the devastating Slayzall.

Slayzall was the most diabolically poisonous concoction ever invented in the endless war against bugs. "100% Active," it was absolutely guaranteed (or your money back) to kill moths, bedbugs, roaches, flies, mosquitoes, and, in fact, just about anything that crept or crawled. The factory, or "lab," as Charles Anderson called it, was a sort of combination alchemist's den and Detroit production line. Big cans of carbolic acid sat in boiling water atop lurid kerosene flames; gallon jugs and five-gallon cans full of chemicals marked DANGER and POISON cluttered the dingy room.

Anderson padded along a high catwalk, emptying poisons into a big mixing tank. The basic ingredient was kerosene (called, on the label, "mineral hydrocarbon oil"), which alone would kill most insects; and into the kerosene, Charlie poured a lethal dose of liquefied phenol, a jug of oil of mirbane, and several other ingredients, anonymous "essential oils," all of them toxic, the combination a very scourge to life. He had bought the secret Slayzall formula from someone else years before, and only he knew what baleful mentality had dreamed it up in the first place. At any rate, Slayzall fit right in with the malign decade of Stalin, Hitler, Mussolini, and Hirohito.

Charlie talked while he worked, talked while he drove, talked while he ate, talked in his sleep. The rest of his family fell out of the habit of talking when he was around. He was, people said, a natural-born salesman. He was also the owner and proprietor, and, except for Jim and Paul, the only employee of the Slayzall Manufacturing Company, an enterprise that he believed in with the passion of a visionary, and an enterprise that had kept his family in humiliating poverty as long as Paul could remember.

"Carl Potter," he was saying, "used to pay his clerks at

Potter's Hardware fifteen dollars a week. For that terrific prize we worked nine hours a day, Monday to Friday, and eleven hours on Saturday. At inventory time we worked eleven hours every day, doing our tallies of nuts and bolts long after the store was closed, every night for a week."

He was a handsome man, with powerful legs and huge biceps. To show off, sometimes he'd grab the rear end of the Ford and lift one wheel right off the ground. Now he took a big can of warm phenol off the kerosene stove and balanced it carefully on one shoulder, then stepped gingerly up a ladder to the mixing tank. With tight-jawed precision, he poured it in, and its vapor slithered into the closed room, making noses prickle. Jim, at the automatic bottler, sneezed three times but didn't slow down. Paul felt woozy but kept on labeling bottles.

"There's nothing easy about the hardware business. Long hours, sometimes heavy and sometimes dirty, fooling around with pipes and blacking, dressed in your white shirt and necktie. It's tough even to learn it all. Somebody comes in, asking for a certain size nail, a plumbing fixture he can't quite name or even describe, a certain size washer or screw or bolt, you've got to be able to put your hands on it, right now."

When the oil of mirbane hit the tank, Jim sneezed again.

"So, after three years in the store, all those fifty-six-hour weeks without a vacation, I'd finally worked my way up to seventeen-fifty a week, and then what happens? That idiot Roosevelt comes along with his 'minimum wage,' fourteen bucks a week, and Potter sees his chance, his excuse, and right away drops us all back to fourteen! Two bits an hour—that's when I quit him. Now he says I was the best clerk he ever had, and he wants me back. But I'll never work for him again, or anyone else. You work for another man, you'll never amount to anything. You go into business for yourself, you can *be* somebody, remember that, Jim. You, too, Paul. Even when times are bad, like this lousy Roosevelt depression, you're better off taking a chance, giving it the old one-two— and then you just keep on, keeping on."

He was stirring the venom in the mixing tank now, back and forth with an old canoe paddle, its varnish long since dissolved in the brew. The smell was heavy and pungent, but Paul was used to it. Jim was still working the automatic bottler, a complicated gadget Charles Anderson had invented. From high up on a scaffolding, a valve at the base of the mixing tank released the Slayzall through a two-inch pipe into the filling tank just below. The filling tank was long and flat, and Charlie had equipped it with eight nozzles, all with float valves, so you could shove eight bottles under the noz-zles at once and they'd fill to just the right place and shut off. The trick to being a good bottler, Charlie said, was in getting the bottles filling at eight different levels, so you could be constantly changing a bottle, never having to wait, and never having to hurry and maybe spill the stuff. Jim was good at it, moving rhythmically along the row of nozzles, the full bottles sliding regularly down a smooth plank to the capping and labeling table.

"Never make the mistake of working for someone else," their father called down to them. "Get them working for you, instead. Show me a man who works for someone else, and I'll show you a failure. Larry Butz is still down at Potter's Hard-ware, still making fourteen a week, and he'll always make fourteen a week. You know why? Because he's got a fourteen-a-week mind, that's why, he was a failure in school and he's a failure today, and he'll die a failure. If someone showed him how to be a success, laid it right out there under his nose, he'd back off like a crab, scared to death."

Paul kept on labeling, wondering what it would be like to

know that every single week of the year you'd have fourteen dollars coming in, free and clear. He couldn't remember Charlie's hardware days very well, but nothing had ever seemed free and clear since the coming of Slayzall. It sold for a prohibitive price, compared to the other insecticides that were mostly water: $1.75 a quart, a small fortune. But after the 40% discount to the retailer and sometimes another 20% to a wholesaler, there wasn't much profit in it for the manufacturer unless he had a big volume, which his father, running the business on a single shoestring, could never manage. His mother complained that any money Charlie made was always plowed back into supplies and advertising. Slayzall was a rathole as far as she was concerned, always had been and always would be. Charlie said reinvesting profits was the way you built up a business, made it a success.

Success. Failure. The words were never off his tongue for long. He had his standards, rigorous ones, all codified in dollars of net income. Anyone else, using those standards, would immediately have declared Charles Anderson a failure in 1941, as he had been in 1940 and 1939 and on back. But he never lived in the past or even the present. His orientation was stubbornly toward the first of next month, the second half of the year, the first of next year—periods near enough to seem relevant, far enough in the future to allow for vision.

Paul's mother had never resigned herself to it. Pretty Nora Jerrold was valedictorian of Kenton High, Class of '20, and the yearbook declared her Most Likely to Get Hitched to a Star. A week after graduation, she married Charles Anderson, who was tall, bright, hustling, manifestly Nordic, and a strong candidate for Most Likely to Succeed, if he had ever finished high school and seen his photo in a yearbook.

Charlie had a large capacity for understanding how things worked and for charming the people who worked them, and he found it much easier to step into a junior assistant plant manager's job at age seventeen than to stay in a classroom and read American history. From that time on, he called himself a self-made man, and he spent the next twenty years engaged in a series of ambitious and failing enterprises.

To Nora, all of this mattered in ways Charlie seemed impervious to. The collapse of a pancake-mix business or the foundering of a bedside-table enterprise was a mere episode to Charlie—a learning experience, something to build on. To Nora it was an emotional debacle, wreckage in the viscera. She rarely received a phone call that wasn't a challenge, a crisis. Is Mr. Anderson there? When will he be back? When can we expect payment? This matter will be turned over to a collection agency. Four months overdue. Something on account. Eviction proceedings. Garnishment. Paul watched her whenever the phone rang: a recoil, a drawing back, four rings, then finally a shaky hello. He felt so sorry for her that he took to jumping for the phone himself.

Like rads from a hundred X rays, the result was cumulative, and Nora Jerrold Anderson, after twenty-one years of penetrating stabs from the telephone and doorbell, had become edgy and defensive. Worse, something—perhaps the constant glandular turmoil—seemed to have stimulated the growth of calcium in the joints of her fingers and knees, and by age thirty-nine, her beautiful hands had knotted like the branches of an old tree. On humid days she had to be helped in and out of bed, her face twisting with pain. Whenever that happened, it always hurt Paul too, jabbed him in the same places where Nora hurt. When they list the fallen victims of the great depression, he thought, my mother will have to be named.

Fighting off depression, fighting the great depression was everybody's job, and the Anderson family and Grandma Jerrold and the various aunts and uncles all pitched in, making do with next to nothing, but partying as best they could. No birthday went unnoticed, anniversaries were always proclaimed, holidays celebrated: little gatherings at Grandma's with supper and games, bingo and keno and beano, and penny prizes on long strings pulled out of Grandma's big kitchen kettle.

The focus of every party was a poem, or two, or several, depending on who had time to write them. Mere doggerel, Miss Eva would have called them in English class, but brothers, sisters, aunts, and uncles were all disappointed if their presents didn't come wrapped in verse. Paul's memory had retained snatches of them, sometimes in spite of himself, until they became a little family anthology in his head. Great Aunt Sally in 1936, writing a poem to herself as widowed matriarch:

> *Hardly a man is now alive*
> *Who knows or cares that I'm 75.*

And little sister Betsy, that same autumn, picking up both family habits and ancestral politics:

> *Mollie Mae Jerrold is 63,*
> *And she does lots of things for me.*
> *Even if I do tell stories,*
> *She lets me know I'm hunky-dory.*
> *Happy Birthday to my Grandma,*
> *Be sure to vote for Alfred Landon!!!!*

Paul himself had written them for years, dozens of them, scurrying off with a gift-wrapped present to bend over the table in the living room and scribble quickly:

> *Mom, exchange these if your stomach churns,*
> *And you will get your many happy returns.*

or:

> *For the man who now has everything,*
> *This after-shave has quite a zing,*
> *Oh, dad, where is thy sting?*

You could even say "love" in a birthday card, something the entire Anderson clan avoided saying otherwise; but bitter-sweet, sweet-and-sour, and never sticky was the unwritten rule. Self-mockery was best, and Paul's favorite was his mother's little ditty, discovered under Charlie's dinner plate on their twentieth anniversary, which began:

> *They say that love is blinder than a bat,*
> *And I love you, so put that in your hat . . .*

Put that in your hat, Paul recited to himself whenever things got tough: put that in your hat.

"You'll never catch up to me at that rate," Jim laughed. Paul jumped, startled, into the present. He realized he had stopped working altogether.

"What's the matter, Pug?"

Why, Paul wondered, do guys like Jim always have nick-names like Ace, and guys like me get stuck with Pug? Why, for that matter, did Jim look handsome and mature, a local Robert Taylor, while Paul, frowning at the bathroom mirror, always saw a baby-faced kid? Put that in your hat.

"Let me show you, you're going at it backwards." Jim did everything better than anyone else. People would see him skating, or swimming, shooting baskets, dancing with Ruthie Peters, bottling Slayzall, and they'd almost always comment: talent, they'd say, that kid's got natural talent.

It wasn't just that he was a year older than Paul; he really was better at everything. And to make matters worse, he was probably the most generous person in town, always helping somebody out: teaching Paul and the other tenderfoot scouts the tough knots, bowline and sheepshank; coaching them on the junior lifeguard techniques, with dozens of surface-dives in Long Lake; forever correcting Paul's serve, backhand, and volley; helping with his magazine route in bad weather; tutoring him for his algebra exam.

"You don't have to do this, Ace," Paul would protest, sagging under the burden of yet another spontaneous kindness.

"Come on, Pug, you're my brother. Someday you'll do *me* a favor. Money in the bank."

Paul didn't feel like a cashier, or even a teller; he felt like a debtor teetering on the verge of bankruptcy.

Jim showed him again, as he had before, and when he made the deft moves, they worked: brush into the pot of gum arabic, just the right amount spread thinly across the porcelain slab, both ends of the label neatly touched into the glue, label in the left hand, bottle in the right, two quick sealing gestures, and a bottle of Slayzall was identified, the bright yellow label perfectly straight, and as smooth as the bottle itself. He did two more, a lot faster than the first one, just to show Paul how it was really done, something to aim at.

Paul tried again, and did better, but when he hurried, labels went on crooked or wrinkled and had to be torn off and thrown away. Waste. The Saturday morning slid by, Jim working circles around him, getting way ahead on bottling and capping, then coming over to help label for a while before going back to the bottler, like a guy playing both sides of a Ping-Pong game. Depressing.

Wednesdays before basketball practice, Paul walked and jogged the whole town, covering his far-flung *Saturday Eve-*

ning Post route, from the Mintons' house on Main Street, up to the Longs' on North State, across the tracks to the McGraws' on Mitchell, and so on east, south, west, and back to Mesler's Drug, where he'd started.

It was always the McGraw mansion that set Paul to brooding. The Andersons had rented a series of old, slightly rundown houses, and they moved from neighborhood to neighborhood every two years, like some kind of recurring ritual, two years apparently being the maximum time Charlie's fluent promises could keep an unpaid landlord mollified. It was a little unsettling for the kids, but also fun, in a way, because every move was an adventure, nomadic. Nora hated it. She wanted to settle down in a place she could call her own. Had anyone been keeping a medical history on her, it would have shown that with each move, her arthritis became worse.

The McGraw mansion had always belonged to the McGraws and only the McGraws, and it always would. There were three of them, the two parents and a college-age daughter, and Paul had never in his sixteen years actually seen any of the three. They spent a lot of time in Europe and Florida. The daughter, whose name Paul never knew, had been sent to private Eastern schools, then to an Eastern college. Any family member who was in town entered and left the mansion gates in a long black car. Paul wondered, sometimes, if any McGraw had ever literally set foot on a Kenton street.

And every week he walked that long drive and rang the back doorbell. It seemed the longest part of his route, that driveway, and, though right down the street, the distance from the McGraw mansion door to the nearby Anderson front porch was immense. Paul's house was shabby and small, a view from the wrong end of a telescope. It was disturbing, living so close to the McGraw mansion, getting by on navy beans and five-cent stale bread bought sometimes from his dime bank. It made Paul think too much. His sister Betsy's cut-down dresses evoked the McGraw girl's lavish wardrobe at her expensive Eastern college. Charlie's shiny double-breasted blue serge suit conjured up rows of worsteds and pinstripes in Mr. McGraw's capacious closets. Nora's arthritic joints brought on envious visions of Mrs. McGraw: youthful, perpetually tanned, and a tiger on the Palm Beach tennis courts.

Success. Failure. By Charlie's standards, Mr. McGraw was a prodigious success, and Charlie himself, in spite of his ambitious schemes, undeniably a failure. Did that mean that Mr. McGraw was "better" than Charlie? Smarter? Or was he just luckier, having had a head start in the big game that grownups played? Was there some kind of protective coloration that saved Mr. McGraw from disaster, while his father, a gray moth on black bark, was forever being skewered by hostile beaks?

Why did Mr. McGraw have, say, twenty pairs of shoes, while Charlie had to keep buying glue-on half-soles for his one ratty pair? Did Mr. McGraw work harder? But he was hardly ever in town, let alone at his office, whereas Charlie worked virtually all the time, never took a vacation or even time off for hobbies or recreation, spent his days and nights cooking up the deadly Slayzall, creating Slayzall road signs, persuading retailers to share the cost of Slayzall radio commercials, and traveling, in his sixty-horsepower Ford, through the whole tri-state area—those little two-lane roads sizzling between the cornstalks all summer and covered with ice half the winter—giving his Slayzall pitch to wholesalers and retailers, talking nonstop, running his repertoire of scandalous Roosevelt jokes, persuading, wheedling, somehow occasionally and improbably conning tight-fisted, depression-scared drugstore and hardware store owners into stocking the expensive stuff. Nobody could possibly work harder than he did.

What was it then, Dad? What was it, Mr. McGraw?

Unc Ehrhard, the coach, had taken sick after lunch and canceled basketball practice, so after the *Post* was delivered, Paul stopped by the lab to see if there was anything he could do to help his father.

The stairway to the second-floor lab was outside, near the back door of the butcher shop. That was where the Hillmeyers, father and son, took deliveries, and in that same back room they did their own butchering. As Paul was about to start up the stairs, there was a rumpus of chicken protest going on inside, so he stayed to watch for a minute.

Tag Hillmeyer waved at him and went on dragging the reluctant chickens out of a wooden pen. He was hooking them by their fettered claws to a long wire. When he had about twenty chickens on it, he tugged on a pulley rope, and they all jerked off the floor, upside down, and into the air like a flag up a flagpole, fluttering and screeching. Tag put on rubber boots, rubber gloves, and a big rubber apron and picked up a long, thin knife with a sharp hook on the end of it. Then he grabbed the neck of the lowest chicken, shoved the knife up its throat, and ripped the hook of the knife downward to the head, opening a slit about two inches long in the chicken's neck. The blood flowed like a spigot, splashed on the cement floor, and ran out a drain. Tag grabbed the next lowest chicken.

By the time he was halfway up the string of white chickens, the lower ones were all bright red, soaked in the blood of the others. When he finished the whole string, he waited until the bleeding slowed to a small drip, then swung the whole string over to a big vat of steaming water and dunked them. They came out of the hot water nearly white again, and there were no more twitches. The smell was worse than brewing Slayzall. After the water drained off, Tag grabbed the top one and tore away feathers in big handfuls.

It doesn't take long to pluck a scalded chicken. It's all in knowing how, Paul thought, remembering his struggle with the Slayzall labels.

At the other end of the room, Tag's father, Wilhelm Hill-meyer, in his white shirt and polka-dot bow tie, was cooing at a calf tied to a pipe. The calf was ignoring him. Wilhelm obviously wanted to get it just right. He held the flat edge of an ax just above the calf's head and crooned: Heeer, calfie, heer, yess, yess, ooop, now, just a leetle mooore . . .

The calf finally lifted its head, the big brown eyes gazing into Wilhelm's. The ax came down, just right, and the calf fell instantly, like a dropped puppet. Wilhelm grabbed it by the hind legs, dragged it to the floor drain, and slit its throat. The sewers of Kenton, Paul thought, the streets of Leningrad. The war of nature, famine and death.

The smells were making him sick. He waved at Tag, covered now with blood and white feathers, and went up the stairs to the lab, thinking, How about that, Dad? How about it, Mr. McGraw?

❧

D R. ROBERTS eased his green Nash up to the curb, gunned it a couple of times to encourage the aging battery, and cut it off to a chorus of bird sounds. The starling swarms were beginning to invade the neighborhood trees for the evening, twittering and squawking. A long Monday at the office.

The birds had already made a mess of the sidewalk. He picked his way up to the front porch and retrieved the *Herald* from the mock-orange bushes, where Joey Prentiss invariably tossed it. He was going to have to speak to that kid. Glancing at the headlines, he stopped, halfway up the steps: SHOOT ON SIGHT, SAYS FDR, and, in smaller print, "Nazi Subs Hunt at Their Own Peril."

It didn't matter that he had already heard it all on the radio. It jolted him, anyway, recorded there in stark black and white, and he began to feel the buzz of Roosevelt's radio voice and the inevitable excitement in his groin. A hazy vision of Elaine Edelman hovered in the evening air. He folded the paper inside out, turned around on the porch steps, and closed his eyes for a moment. Shotguns exploded two doors away—the Cassel boys out front again trying to scare off the pernicious starlings. *Shoot on sight.* Dr. Roberts got a stern grip on himself, and went inside.

Lowell Thomas was saying, ". . . and so long until tomorrow." He was even later than he thought; Amos and Andy were coming on. Putting down his bag, he snapped off the radio, tossed the paper on the couch, and listened. Edna was on the phone in the parlor.

She was always on the phone in the parlor. He hated the ugly feeling in the pit of his stomach whenever he thought of that black instrument, as if it were some kind of malignant presence: a rival, a competitor. At his age he should have more control over those irrational sensations. He tried to concentrate on the pleasant smell of pot roast and onions, stared into the round hallway mirror, and forced a smile. There, that's better.

Holding the smile, he opened the parlor door and poked his head in. "Home," he said softly. "At last."

Edna looked up and waved, but absently, and didn't interrupt her sentence. Tom could always tell when she was talking to Reverend Tucker, a certain tone of voice she saved for the minister, deferential but suspiciously sensual, as if her lost sex life had been transfigured into these busy conversations.

Her concentration was remarkable: she went on talking steadily, as if he weren't there. At a moment of emphasis, she lifted her eyes to some sympathetic heaven, a lifelong habit of hers. Tom remembered the first time he ever saw her do it—in college, in a math class—and how it had captivated him. Prettiest girl at I.U. It captivated him now, and he ached for her, for the loss. She was still a beautiful woman, but after twenty-four years together, he realized he didn't know her anymore. He formed her name in his mind, and the word "wife."

He closed the door. Those were always long talks, endless scheming on behalf of the church, the Reverend Tucker a man who never failed to express himself fully. Tom felt the ugly sensation again, but he knew it was coming, and suppressed it.

Dusk: he turned on a floor lamp in the living room and switched on the chandelier in the dining room. The tablecloth was full of good intentions, all china and silver, but still in heaps. He smoothed the cloth, put two place settings neatly in order, and sifted the extra pieces into the silver drawer and the china cabinet before checking the kitchen.

The supper smells were making his stomach growl. He lifted the lid of the big kettle and inspected the simmering pot roast, potatoes, carrots, onions. Almost dry. He took a big bite of pot roast, added some water, and turned down the gas. By the sink, lettuce and scallions, washed and laid out on a dish towel, had gone limp. Hunger, and that other feeling—anger? resentment?—mingled in his belly as he broke the lettuce into the salad bowl, covered it, and put it in the refrigerator.

She must be finished talking by now. If not . . . He thought of how it used to be with them, before Edna's obsession, her only noble work in those days being the annual drive for the Community Chest, and both of them constantly grateful and pleased to be alive, to be in love, to be a household, a family: his return from the office a daily celebration, sometimes with a bottle of wine, sometimes an impulsive shedding of clothes . . .

He shook off that memory; it was too painful. Back at the parlor door, he could still hear her Reverend-Tucker voice, and with a noisy rattling of the knob, he thrust open the door. She glanced up, frowning, waved him away, and went on talking: "You're right, yes, try something less traditional, get the Board to thinking for a change."

"Edna . . ."

She waved him off again, closed her eyes, and concentrated on Reverend Tucker and the Building Fund. But an imp of stubbornness sat on his shoulder and refused to move, so he stared at her until she felt it and opened her eyes. She talked for a moment more before finally giving in: "Well, I'll have to stop now, Reverend Tucker . . . Yes, we can manage the rest tomorrow . . . Thank *you* . . . Yes, good night."

She hung up and glared at him. "Well, where's the fire?"

"I guess you don't know what time it is."

"I can see the clock."

"Dinner was ready to burn."

"Did you turn it down?"

"Of course."

"It wouldn't have burned." She got up. "Well, come on, then, since you're so hungry."

"Starved. Aren't you?"

"I never get hungry." It was one of those things she had taken to saying, like "I never get sleepy."

She didn't seem to notice what he'd done in the dining room. They served the meal together and ate for a minute in silence. Then came the moment he realized he had been waiting for, and dreading. Her voice was a weapon: "That moron Kirkland! He did it again today."

What could he say, that he wasn't interested, that he knew what was coming, that he wasn't going to play this game anymore? But he finally asked, "What is it this time?"

"You know how Mrs. Buckwalter is—touchy about everything, but especially about the church reading room."

"The one on South State?"

"Of *course* the one on South State, how many are there? When she gave that house to the church, it was supposed to be a parish house—a kind of monument to the memory of her husband, whose memory could use some cleaning up. The worst mistake that stupid Board of Elders ever made was when they turned it into a Church of Christ reading room that nobody uses. She's never been quite so generous since then."

Her knife handle rubbed patterns in the tablecloth. "You've got to be *practical* to run a church—how many rich Mrs. Buckwalters do we *have* in our congregation?"

"Hey, don't get sore at me, I'm not on the Board of Elders."

"I *know* you're not. *You* never do *anything* for the church, you don't even *go,* the whole place could just cave in, for all *you* care. You and Kirkland, two of a kind."

What ever happened to the notion that it took two to make an argument? Out in the street the shotguns blazed away. "I believe it was Kirkland you were talking about."

"He's an *idiot.*" Rage: it had become her sustenance, bread and water.

"Anything specific?"

"Do you know what he did today? Do you *know* what he did today?"

"You haven't told me yet."

She glared at him. "Two of a kind!" It took her a moment to control her voice. "That fool actually proposed to the Board of Elders that they tear down the old place and turn it into a parking lot! Imagine! A parking lot!" She choked, and Dr. Roberts rushed around the table to help, but she shrugged him off and finally cleared her throat.

Her reproach embraced mankind: "Oh, dear Lord, do you know what that would mean? In this everlasting depression, and hard times . . . And Mrs. Buckwalter all furious and tight-fisted . . . What would happen to the Foreign Missions Fund, the Building Fund?"

He knew she would cry, and wasn't surprised at the bitterness of her tears or the racking sobs, but he felt desolate, anyway, helpless. He knelt by her chair and put an arm around her shoulders. She flinched away as if it burned her.

"You don't care!" she sobbed. "Nobody cares!" She ran to her bedroom sanctuary, where Tom knew better than to follow, and soon he heard water running in the bathtub. A hot bath was her own prescription for despair.

Feeling drained, he began to clear the table. He knew Edna hated it that she needed him, but they had been together too long; she was stuck with him, couldn't get along without him. And Dr. Roberts marveled once again at the obstinacy of the human spirit: despite her hostility, despite the sexual famine, despite even the bright vision of Elaine Edelman, he knew he was stuck with Edna, too—his partner, his past, his life. He loved her.

❧

OME PEOPLE complained that the Reverend Stephen B. Tucker didn't *look* like a preacher. With his neat mustache and wavy brown hair, he looked, in fact, a little like Douglas Fairbanks. But there was no doubt that the Reverend Tucker was a man of the Lord, deep in his faith, passionate in his ministry. He presided over the parents and schoolteachers who taught the Sunday school classes at the First Church of Christ, baptized the young when they reached the age of reason, personally instructed girls and boys of high school age in their Christian duty, and united in marriage all those in his flock so inclined. He came calling upon the birth of every new soul in his congregation, counseled erring husbands, consoled abandoned wives, visited the sick and the shut-in, and at fresh graves in the Riverview Cemetery, spoke nothing but good of the dead.

In addition to those pastoral duties, the Reverend Tucker preached a lengthy sermon on Sundays and a briefer one at Wednesday-evening prayer meeting, met with the Board of Elders to decide policies and discuss budgets, dropped in on the Thursday Quilting Club, faithfully attended meetings of the Kenton School Board, and, constant as the sunset, sat in on the weekly choir practice, always dressed in his black double-breasted suit, summer and winter, white shirt buttoned up, black necktie as neat as a Sears, Roebuck illustration.

Paul Anderson at age sixteen could hardly remember a

time when FDR was not President of the United States and
Reverend Tucker was not pastor of the First Church of
Christ. And as long as the voice of the President had soothed
the citizens of Kenton with promises of recovery, so long had
the voice of Reverend Tucker exhorted them to virtue under
the stern threat of hellfire. But as the voice of the President
grew more and more brusque with the accents of war, the
Reverend Tucker began to linger sensuously on labials and
sibilants.

Paul sang a clear and natural tenor, a rare asset in a small-
town choir. So, in spite of his complaints that he had no time
for it, he obeyed his insistent mother and dutifully attended
choir practice every Thursday and sturdily performed the
choral anthem every Sunday, working virtually alone against
a phalanx of basses and a shrilling of reedy sopranos. Thursday nights were a torment—the chaos, the cacophony, the
general horsing-around. So Paul, when he wasn't horsing
around himself, passed the time observing the really serious
business of those unruly sessions: how Bill Heit, the harried
director, found new and tactful ways of tempering Celia
Carshaw, the off-pitch soprano; how Willy James, one of the
teen-age basses, managed to keep the sideways attention of
pert Julie Campbell; and how the Reverend Tucker's eyes
maintained contact, in the organist's mirror, with the pale
blue eyes of Miss Huron.

Miss Huron taught music at the high school, and she was
a good organist—far too good for this choir, Paul always
thought; what kept her coming? She was loyal to the weekly
caterwauling, and on Sundays she always saved the anthem
by opening up a few more stops to give guidance to the
sopranos. But why did Miss Huron—such a stickler for per-

fection with the high school chorus—let herself be tarred by association with all this dissonance? Paul wondered about her constant blue-eyed gazing at Reverend Tucker in the organ mirror, but it never entered his adolescent mind that a respectable woman like Miss Huron—let alone the central pillar of the First Church of Christ—could be sitting there, in the very sanctuary, entertaining impure thoughts.

By bad luck, Paul was held by the shirtsleeve after choir practice, on the night of Thursday, September 18, by Earl Offstender, a middle-aged baritone with bad breath and a fondness for high school boys, who breathed at him the heady news of blitzkrieg, German tanks going for the jugular of Mother Russia, FDR's disastrous billions for Lend-Lease, and the boss of the American Legion, down in Indy, swearing to back the President to the hilt. Finally Paul saved himself from his own politeness by pleading algebra homework and breaking loose into the fresh night air. Jogging the long way home to avoid any further contact with Earl Offstender, he found himself coming up behind a brisk figure wearing a black Homburg, who looked, from a distance, like the Reverend Tucker, and who, at the next streetlight, turned out, in fact, to be the Reverend Tucker, far from his parsonage and headed in the wrong direction. Paul slowed to a walk.

He was not inclined to melodrama, but the purposeful gait of the preacher intrigued him, and every step Paul took became more stealthy than the one before, until he realized he was sneaking down the sidewalk, easing along in the concealment of elm trees, avoiding the occasional streetlight, even doing an Indian walk, edges of the feet first. As the preacher came close to Oak Street, Paul held his breath, and when he made the right turn that led to Miss Huron's house, Paul's throat made a little gasp.

Tracking like a Stone-Age hunter now, Paul kept his shadowy prey just within eyesight, and as Miss Huron's house loomed ahead, the living room lights burning behind drawn blinds, he slunk along, darting quickly from bush to bush. In front of that house, Reverend Tucker paused for a moment, looked about, then slipped around to the backyard. Paul didn't follow, but he listened carefully and heard the sound of a back door being pulled shut.

There in the warm September night, he watched and waited while the living room lights went off and the upstairs lights went on, and he thought of Miss Huron's curly brown hair and Reverend Tucker's arching eyebrows and Mrs. Tucker, at home alone; and he stood there blushing, and stared at the drawn blinds in wonder.

When he finally got home, his mind was still troubled by the thought of Reverend Tucker, upstairs at Miss Huron's house.

"Why so late, Paul?" his mother called from the dining room. Before she went to bed, she always mended clothes and darned socks, sitting at the dining room table, listening to Wayne King or Paul Whiteman on the radio. She looked over the top of her reading glasses as he came in, and turned down the volume.

"Mr. Heit kept us. A tough anthem on Sunday." It was true, though not the whole truth.

"Jeepers!" Betsy called from the kitchen. "That choir can't even do the easy ones!"

"That's enough, Betsy." Nora didn't like to hear criticism of anything connected to their church, especially if it was true.

"You know I'm right, Mom. Last week they barely made it through 'The Old Rugged Cross.'"

"I said that's enough." Nora was darning again, her arthritic hands curled around the darning ball, working slowly. "You can get just as much good out of a nice hymn sung by our own choir as you can from those fancy anthems at the M.E. Church."

Betsy came in, eating bread and honey. She was always eating something. Her pretty face was a bit cheeky, and she complained that her legs were too thick. But she kept her strength up and usually had the last word. "Mom, what about that fat Celia Carshaw? Don't you just cringe when she tries to hit a high note? That awful wheeze, sounds like a broken saxophone."

"Betsy, if you don't stop that, you're going straight up to bed. As a matter of fact, it's your bedtime right now."

"Bedtime! Why isn't it Paul's bedtime? And how about Jim? He's not even home yet."

"You're only fourteen. You'll have your turn later."

"It wasn't so bad," Paul said. "Celia had a cold, or laryngitis or something, and wasn't really singing, just mouthing it."

"If we're lucky, she'll still be sick on Sunday."

"All right, young lady, that's it." Nora put down her darning, a sign that she was serious. "You march right upstairs and wash your face and get to bed. *Now.*"

There was a certain tone of voice that made things final around the Anderson house, and Betsy recognized it when she heard it. There would be no reprieve now, but at least she had the last word. "For a *month* of Sundays!" she called, climbing the front stairs.

Nora opened her mouth to reply but stopped herself. She knew, Paul thought, how to be a good winner. Would he ever need to learn that?

The amber lampshade with beaded sides hung directly over the round oak table, casting a tent of yellow light over his mother. She was slumped over her sewing again; the cotton housedress looked discouraged. Paul hated the thought of her crippled hands, and yet this was such a peaceful moment that he wanted to stop time for a while. Upstairs there was a gurgling of water in the sink. He closed his eyes for a few seconds.

"So, then, where were you tonight, Paul?" She hadn't been fooled by his evasion, and she hated having anyone lie to her. He knew he'd have to tell—he always did—but he was too embarrassed to begin.

He stalled. "Where's Dad?" He knew where Jim was: studying with Ruthie again.

"It's his night with the America First Committee in Fort Wayne, you know that. Answer my question."

"Well, I got stopped by Earl Offstender after practice. And then, to keep away from him, I came home the long way."

"Yes?" She had cringed at the mention of Earl, a constant worry to the mothers of teen-age boys.

"And I ran into Reverend Tucker. I mean, I saw him, going out of his way, too, so I—well, I guess I got curious. And I followed him."

Nora gave him a quick look out of the corner of her eyes. He had a feeling that she knew what was coming.

"He, uh—went to Miss Huron's house." Nora had stopped darning and was staring at the table. Paul felt his ears burning, as if he himself had been caught in Miss Huron's bedroom. "I didn't want to tell you, Mom."

She was having trouble speaking. "There's been a lot of talk."

As usual, he was the last to know. He felt like a dunce. And pain—how could you feel so much pain, he wondered, over something you weren't even involved in? Inherited from his mother? Can you inherit pain?

They sat quietly for a moment.

"Sometimes the vessels of the Lord are chipped, but that doesn't spoil the water they carry."

He didn't know what to say. "I guess maybe I'll go to bed, too. I feel kind of sick to my stomach."

"Better take an Alka-Seltzer."

On the stairs, he heard his name, and he paused. "Paul—we mustn't judge, lest we be judged."

Paul felt lost, as he often did these days, bewildered by events he had no control over and couldn't even understand: the war, success and failure, Reverend Tucker and Miss Huron, FDR and Lindy, Ruthie Peters, *Homo sapiens.* Life is a jigsaw puzzle, and the pieces don't fit. No, it's a story, a long, long story, and some days he felt he was just a reader, but other days he was actually in the story himself, an essential part of the plot, and it was all coming to a climax, the decisive battle, survival of the fittest. It scared him. Maybe, he thought, it's better to be just a reader after all.

Betsy was in bed, but not asleep, her white streamlined portable turned low so Nora wouldn't hear the sounds of "Blue Champagne." Passing her half-open door, Paul heard her loud whisper. "Squeaky! Wheezy! On the high notes, she sounds like a screech owl!"

THOUGH IN KIEV the German assault had reached blitzkrieg tempo, the Nazi lightning and thunder couldn't stop the K.H.S. Fall Carnival on Friday afternoon or the frank-and-bean supper or the

opening basketball game with Fox Lake that night. The smell
of burnt cork at the carnival was familiar, the high school
grads come back to sit on the stage at the end of the girls' gym,
exchanging old minstrel songs and ancient jokes. Paul
watched the respectable local men, Mr. Potter, Mr. Mesler,
Mr. Hillmeyer, Jed Shinover, and Mr. Hedges, all with kinky
wigs and blackened faces and big white grins painted over
their mouths. In the center of the row of ebony faces sat Mr.
Merwin, the portly superintendent of schools, his lone white
face gleaming and benevolent.

"Mr. Bones," he called out, "how are you getting along
with your wife these days?"

"Had a awful argument with her, Mistuh Interlocutor."

"What about?"

" 'Bout a month."

"I mean, what was it over?"

" 'Tain't over."

"What I mean is, what were you arguing about?"

"About the baby we was expectin'. I wanted to call it
Rufus, and she wanted to call it Rastus."

"Well, when the baby came, what *did* you call it?"

"Liza."

"Oh, it turned out to be the contrary sex."

"Contrary? Downright stubborn."

Paul slipped out the back door. Everyone was obviously
having a good time, but for some reason that he couldn't
put his finger on, he was uneasy. The game with Fox Lake
was only hours away, and a breath of fresh air would feel
good.

There were no Negroes living in town, because back in the
twenties the Ku Klux Klan had fixed the moral tone of many

Hoosier communities. "I am the law in Indiana," quoth the Grand Dragon in 1925, speaking a kind of truth.

Sixteen years later, the Klan was no longer so high and mighty, but it had touched the Hoosier character and lived on in the backs of people's minds: no dark skin had ever been seen after sunset inside the lily limits of Kenton.

The Klan was not much fonder of Jews than of Negroes, and in 1941 only three Jews had settled in town, struggling to survive in that alien soil like flowers in a desert. Two of them long ago had gone into the junk business, competing, as destiny would have it, not against the goyim but against each other. Both men did well in the business, and the classier one began to call himself a scrap broker. He imported a wife from out of state, and in due time his sons and daughters went off to Eastern colleges and became doctors and lawyers, serving more promising places than Kenton.

The townspeople accepted all this with the smugness of the deserving poor confronted with the undeserving rich, treating them with Anglo-Saxon indifference. The third man, though, a Jew with different intentions, was viewed with perpetual suspicion. His name was Saul Edelman, but he was always called, behind his back, Old Saul, perhaps because his beard—the only beard in Kenton in 1941—was almost entirely gray. His hair, however, was as red as October maples. His business in the community was never clear—or rather, it seemed clear to different people, from time to time, in confusingly different ways. He ran a newspaper, for one thing. Not a respectable paper like the *Daily Herald*, but a meager little weekly called *The Hoosier Rationalist*, an exotic plant indeed in Kenton, but one that had survived there for six years. It was said that its readership was statewide, even nationwide, and that it carried influence in certain progressive groups in Washington. Maybe so, but it had a very limited circulation

in Kenton, subscribed to by a few schoolteachers, certain city
fathers who didn't want to miss a trick, and a number of
busybodies whose stock of gossip always needed replenish-
ing. Certainly it carried no local advertising.

The *Rationalist* was not a local paper at all, not like the
Herald: no news of births and deaths in Royal County, no
church activities, no arrests or auto accidents, no high school
basketball scores, no marriages or divorces. It was a mishmash
of things that most people in town would as soon not have
had to think about, and, except for Edelman, wouldn't have—
how the poor of Kenton were symptomatic of our nation,
wrung and depleted by the great depression; how the inade-
quacy of Royal County poor-relief was an inevitable conse-
quence of our corporate state; how the unorganized workers
at McGraw, Inc., drudging for a better life for themselves and
their children, would never succeed without solidarity. There
were occasional news items concerning such subjects, but
mostly the paper was a string of what amounted to editorials.

Union organizer, that was the suspicion of some barbershop pundits and of occasional innuendos in the *Daily Herald*.
Hadn't Edelman arrived in town just a few months after a
radical Democrat congress passed the Wagner Act? Old Saul
was obviously a paid agent of that pinko new CIO and probably a hireling of the NAACP.

The red and the black: neither sat well with the local au-
thorities, civic or clerical. Even the name of Saul Edelman
was unwelcome in respectable circles. One sensed, in the
furtive gossip about him, the aroma of brimstone and the
suggestion of cloven hooves.

The *Rationalist* had a formal opinion page, on which were
printed think-pieces from extremists like Walter Lippmann,
John L. Lewis, and obscure, know-it-all college professors.
Every week for six years, the little press in Edelman's base-

ment had clacked out these poisonously provocative essays, until at last Kenton came to accept them and even to take a sort of perverse pride in them. You got nothing like this in Auburn or Goshen or Warsaw, buddy. Smell the brimstone? That's *our* brimstone cooking.

But a pointy-bearded heathen with cloven hooves, even with the dispensation of six years of tolerance, can go too far, and when "The Labyrinth" appeared on the opinion page, Edelman had clearly stepped across the line. The piece was a deadly affront to local sensibilities.

The Hoosier Rationalist came out on Fridays, and this Friday morning, everyone in town was talking about the Fall Carnival and the Fox Lake game and the battle at Kiev. But carnival or no carnival, before the day was out, it was "The Labyrinth," borrowed copies passing quickly from hand to hand, that occupied the people of Kenton.

THE LABYRINTH

The simpler the society, the cruder the problems: we can imagine Neanderthals crouching in fear—of the tiger, of the dark, of thunder—but we do not suppose that they had the leisure for exquisite neuroses.

We have changed all that. Disillusioned with our lives, discontent with our civilization, lost in a maze of neurosis, we wander a labyrinth asking ourselves: What went wrong?

The answers must begin with our expectations. What is it we want? And why? Who are we?

A beast condemned to be more than a beast: that is the human condition. In the course of Darwinian evolution, we developed a large brain and routed our natural competitors, because brain proved to be the ultimate weapon.

Every gain carries loss on its back: the brain that could imagine a useful tool could also imagine a "divine" creation. In this primal fiction, we presume to sovereignty over every living thing that moves upon the earth. But that fantasy of Divine Right is so dissociated from reality that it sows the seeds of neurosis, and when they bear their bitter fruit, we run for the mind healers.

The mind healers remind us that we begin our lives in total helplessness but with boundless desire; that this stark contradiction persists for many years; and that we cannot outgrow it unless we teach ourselves to deal with facts, not fantasies. Life is a series of tests, and if we fail this very elementary one, we must take the penalties: anxiety, neurosis, and fear. Not fear of tigers or thunder now, but something far more alarming: the terrors of the imagination. The large brain is the ultimate weapon, and sometimes it is aimed at us. It imagines all sorts of useful and pleasant things: wheels, houses, poems. But it refuses to stop before it is too late and proceeds to invent devils, and hell, and God.

God is an unnecessary hypothesis, but for some people, suffering the terrors of the imagination, a seductive one. We are always tempted by easy answers. God is an easy answer.

God is also a convenience. "What is the meaning of life?" "Where shall we spend eternity?" The unanswerable question is referred to the undefinable Being, and lo, we have the impression of an answer, though in fact we know no more than before. This soothes some minds temporarily, as an empty bottle may temporarily soothe a crying baby; and the nourishment from each is the same.

And so, shuffling through the tangle of our lives, pretending that we have heard answers to our awesome questions, we refuse even to look at the painful truth: by worshiping a God who is a figment of our own imagination, we ourselves have become the Labyrinth.

—The Minotaur

❦

Fox Lake is a town so small that nobody even slows down for it on the road; compared to Fox Lake, Kenton is a metropolis. But it had its own high school, and so here they were, the Fox Lake Raiders, out on the hardwood, opening the basketball season against big bad Kenton, the county seat.

Ordinarily it wouldn't have been a contest, but back in the twenties, the farm folk around Fox Lake had, by some genetic fluke, conceived what was to become, in due time, a tribe of giants. On the Friday that the Wehrmacht blazed into Kiev and the Minotaur outraged the local citizens, the Raiders invaded the K.H.S. gym: the Hosler twins, Peewee and Tiny, both 6′5″ in their bare feet; their cousin Slim Black, 6′3″; their second cousin, Tarzan Stokes, center of the team, 6′8″; and the team midget and scoring star, Speedy Spencer, a mere 6′1″. Beyond the starting five there were three on the bench over six feet and a freshman nearly seven feet tall. And at the moment they were beating the sweatsocks off the Kenton Comets.

They were brutal under the boards. Husky and aggressive, they had, out there at those barn-door hoops, developed ways of elbowing and gouging that the refs didn't seem to see. Paul saw them, all right, or anyway felt them, the bruises purpling under his crimson and gold shirt—and K.H.S. tempers were beginning to fray. Eight points behind Fox Lake in the last quarter, or in any quarter, was humiliation enough, without adding injury to insult. Unc Ehrhard, the Comet coach, was spending a lot of time jumping off the bench to bellow at the refs, and Kenton's Jerry Hall, 6'5", hot-tempered, and accustomed to being the biggest man in sight, was doing some complaining of his own. Guarding Stokes, he yelled, loud enough for the other players to hear, "One more elbow like that last one, Tarzan, and I'm going to loosen your teeth."

Stokes grinned down at him. "What's the matter, shorty, can't take it like a big boy?" He turned his back on Jerry, and Peewee Hosler stepped directly into his tracks, blocking Jerry out. Stokes dribbled around them and went up for a lay-in; Paul switched off and went up with him, but all the action was a foot above Paul's flailing hands. Coming down, Stokes elbowed him in the belly, leaving him gasping. Stokes trotted off, smirking.

Ten points behind: the whistles blew. Unc had called time, and the team walked wearily to the bench. Jeannie Metzger and Chuck Green, the Comet cheerleaders, were bouncing and cartwheeling, trying to work up some enthusiasm— *Rickety-rax! Give 'em the ax!*—but the crowd was gloomy. Even the K.H.S. band, desperately honking away at the fight song, sounded forlorn.

"You're playing good ball," Unc said, "but they're too damn big for us. So listen, what we're going to do now is, play ball that *isn't* so good—just go for broke. I want a fast break *every time* you get the ball, OK? *Every* time, even when there's no sense to it, even when you think it's dumb. And on defense, I want a tight man-to-man, full-court press, *every second* they have the ball, you got that? They won't lose you, you're faster than they are. Stick to them like horseflies, worry them, hassle them right to the point of fouling—but *don't* foul. Not yet. Jerry, I saw that bad time you were giving Stokes. Lay off it, you got three fouls, we need you in there.

Pug, *you* give him an elbow or a knee if you get a chance, you've got only one foul, and you owe him one. So *crush* the bastard!"

Paul owed him more than one—but he always felt itchy when Unc talked dirty ball like that, which in a tough game was pretty often.

"One more thing. Whenever a fast break doesn't produce, Jim, you and Paul switch, and you drop back to guard and try some outside shots, loosen up that zone. Oh, and listen—the Hoslers are both sloppy passers, and they're getting tired and getting worse. You ought to be able to pick one off, watch for it. Now get out there and give 'em hell. Pug, get those elbows and knees working."

Those crisp October nights, the smell of burning leaves hanging in the air, Jim and Jerry and Paul doing two-on-one, or horse, or sudden-death at the basket on Jerry's garage, going high for rebounds, giving it the old hip, shooting till long after sunset under the corner streetlight, the dark ball whooshing the shadowy net, attack, shoot again, strike . . .

And now Jim would switch off with Paul for the outside shots, because Jim, a senior and high-point man, was older, taller, stronger, better.

The fast break was pointless at first, because after the time-out, Fox Lake was already down there, waiting. Paul and Scrap came at them fast anyway, passing hard, then working the ball crosscourt, back and forth, harrying their massive zone defense. They couldn't get it through to Jerry, though, and soon Jim came outside, so Paul went under for him and waited. Two passes later, Jim was open for just a moment. He pushed his favorite two-hander from eye level: it floated and scored, hitting nothing but net, a beautiful swishing. Eight points behind. Paul could hear his father's jubilant yell from the sidelines.

Kenton was on them, tight, hustling and feinting. Fox Lake had trouble getting it to the ten-second line, and just as they made it, Tiny Hosler bounce-passed to Stokes, not quite hard enough, and Jim was there, charging downcourt the minute it touched his fingers, passing it up to Scrap, who took two long strides and went up for an easy lay-in. There wasn't a Fox Lake man within five yards of him. Six points, two minutes on the clock. Chuck and Jeannie were dancing and clapping, and some of the Comet fans were believers again, cheering. Jim was wearing his rabbit's foot around his neck, as usual; Paul saw him touch it.

Hassling them, giving it the old chatter, Kenton almost caught them on the ten-second rule, but not quite; Stokes lobbed a long one downcourt to Spencer, who had no chance at it—out of bounds.

The fast break started from scratch, the ball zipping up to Jim without trajectory, like a baseball. Jim didn't even bounce it, just whipped it on to Scrap, like an infielder on a double play. Scrap bounce-passed to Paul, who picked it up a step ahead of Stokes and slipped it in off the backboard, just as Stokes came down on top of him, the heel of his big hand like a bludgeon, paralyzing Paul's right shoulder. The whistle stopped everything. Four points behind, two minutes still showing on the clock. Through the roar of approval, the band blared out the Comet fight song. Fox Lake called time.

Unc was fever-eyed, a festering of nerves. He erupted in a sonorous belch, as he always did in the final minutes of a tough game. "It'll go on working if you can keep them off balance, but they'll stall now, for sure. You're going to have to be even faster, cagier. Keep up the press, even closer, keep up the fast break, *every time.* You'll get a few plays, with any luck at all. The official time is one minute forty seconds. Listen, this is important. *Don't foul till the last thirty seconds.*

Keep an eye on me, I'll give you the sign, one finger—and if you have to foul, try to foul Stokes, he's the worst shot on the team. Pug, make that free throw, we need it. OK, get *in* there!"

The whistle blew and they lined up at the foul line. Paul was worried. Stokes had chopped him right across the shoulder muscle, and his right arm was quivering. Stokes, under the basket, smirked at Paul as if he'd pulled a fast one. Paul hated that look, and, as the pain burned in his shoulder, began to hate Stokes, too, looming there like a dark tower and waiting for Paul to fail so he could grab off another rebound. Paul bounced the ball a couple of times to loosen up the shoulder. He was the most consistent foul-shooter on the team, and he hoped, despite the bad arm, that he could still make it.

He bounced the ball twice more. The roar of the Kenton crowd quieted; the pause was a vacuum.

November afternoons at Jer's garage, the pavement crack for a free-throw line, the gray winter clouds . . .

It wasn't clean, it bounced off the front rim, hit the backboard and fell in. Paul finally breathed again, and the roar, a roar like airplanes, began and didn't, wouldn't stop. Three points behind.

Fox Lake tried something different this time, Black holding the ball out of bounds until all four teammates were down the floor, close together, then lofting them a long pass. Spencer took it and bounced to Peewee Hosler, and Jim, running alongside him, got a hand on the ball but couldn't control it. Hosler tried to dribble it ahead of him, but he lost control of it, too, and in a moment it was out of bounds, Comets. Jim dove into the screaming fans and grabbed the ball. The ref happened to be right there, and touched it, and almost in the same movement, Jim threw it downcourt like a football pass.

It all happened so fast that only one man in ten was down there, the crimson and gold of Gopher Starr, who leaped high and caught it, dribbled twice, and laid it in.

One point behind. How many seconds left? The big clock was unreliable, only the officials' stopwatch counted.

Unc was right: the giants were getting tired, and getting sloppy. When Tiny passed in the ball, Jim raced over and picked it off, snaked it out of Spencer's grasp, right under the K.H.S. basket. The home crowd went crazy: SHOOT, SHOOT, SHOOT! But three of the giants were on Jim, burying him in enormous hands. He saw Paul at the side, all alone, and passed it, deflected by Black. Paul sprawled for the ball, saved it, and set to shoot, but the stretch, the wrench, had finished his right arm; he knew he wouldn't make it. He managed to heave it back to Jim, who dribbled once and, as the buzzer sounded, hooked a fall-away shot, and scored.

Pandemonium! The Kenton crowd was jubilant. Jim was on someone's shoulders and the band was squealing away happily.

But there was an angry shrieking of whistles, a hand-waving discussion at the center circle, ref and ump excited, pointing here, pointing there. Unc waddled out on the floor, and then the Fox Lake coach, and the hand-waving got violent. The four men proceeded to the officials' table, and the argument went on. Both teams stayed on the floor, watching. The crowd, sifting down from the bleachers, sensed there was something amiss and slowly quieted. The band fell silent, instrument by instrument, until only the bass drum was still at it, hump, hump, hump.

It wasn't long before someone asserted his authority. The PA system crackled. "Ladies and gentlemen," came the mechanical voice, "the officials have ruled that the last goal came after the end of regulation playing time. The winner of this game is Fox Lake."

The collective gasp, the chorus of outrage, as the Fox Lake players bounced around the hardwood and carried their coach off to the locker room. Making his way through the crowd, Stokes looked back at the Kenton team, gloating, and Paul felt a boiling of hatred. Unc, looking drained, came back from the officials' table and slapped his players on their crimson shirts, halfheartedly. They started off the floor. Paul felt as if he were sneaking out.

There is no Hoosier disaster like losing a home game. The booing kept on, louder and louder, and as the Kenton players walked to their locker room, it began to sound as if it was meant for them.

Paul carried a burden of guilt into the shower. His not taking that last shot had cost them the game. Would it always be like this, his whole life a string of near-misses, all of them his fault? Under the scalding water, he relished the hurt in his shoulder, a good, clean, uncomplicated pain.

The team showered in their private silences. Losing the close ones hurts the most, and getting one yanked right out of your fingertips hurts worst of all.

If only, if only, if only . . .

The weariness wore off in the shower, and the hot water made Paul's shoulder feel better, leaving him with only that peculiar basketball pain in the soles of the feet, as if they'd been scrubbed with steel wool. When he finally came out, toweling, Jim was already in his Jockey shorts. "Sorry, Ace," Paul said. "But I knew I couldn't make it if I shot. After I went for that pass, I could barely hold the ball."

If only . . .

Jim's greenish eyes looked as if they had melted, turned to water; it was his only way of crying. "Not your fault, Pug."

He grinned, a bent grin. "We'll get 'em next time. Thanksgiving. In the tourney." Automatically, he touched his rabbit's foot.

"When we get to the county tournament," Jerry spoke up, "I'll know how to handle that Stokes son of a bitch." His voice broke; it often embarrassed him like that. To cover it up, he sort of yipped: "Come on, you bastards, anyone needs a ride, the train's leaving."

Jerry's dad had been office manager at McGraw's right through the depression, a good job for a small town, so Jer had always had things the others didn't: at age ten the only regulation basketball on the block, then a genuine Boy Scout uniform, and now a car—just a '34 V-8, but it ran like a jackrabbit. Jer was generous with it, taxi driver for the team. He loved driving and wheeled the V-8 around town like a barnstorming biplane. In the winter, he'd speed down a snowy street, hit the brakes in a sharp turn, spin the old tub completely around, and keep on going as if nothing had happened.

After the home games there was always a dance at the Kenton country club, where the Melodaires, a K.H.S. group, did earnest if understaffed versions of current Glenn Miller and Tommy Dorsey favorites. On the way to the dance the V-8 swayed through town, the "Hut Sut Song" blasting from the radio—a jocular chariot, as if it were bearing victors, not chumps. Everyone began to cheer up.

When they went inside, the Melodaires were playing "The Things I Love," and Ruthie Peters was waiting at the door. Jim's hand went out, she took it without a word, and they went to the dance floor without pausing: graceful, as if Jim's entrance were a team play they had practiced. As they moved onto the floor, Ruthie looked back at Paul and smiled, a bright smile that he took to mean, "Not your fault, Pug, you'll get 'em next time."

Sure, sure—but maybe she meant, "Close only counts in horseshoes, kid."

Jerry whistled, a low whistle that sounded like a sigh. "Jesus, those legs. I wonder if Ace is getting any of that."

Paul was surprised to find himself offended. He realized that he didn't like to hear Ruthie talked about like that.

"Come on, Jer, let's get a Coke and see who's here."

Ruthie was either the prettiest girl at K.H.S. or second-prettiest to last year's prom queen, Sally Crothers, depending on what type you went for. Paul went for smart girls, so Sally, notoriously scatterbrained, didn't interest him. Ruthie was so bright that she scared people, and Paul found that exciting. She was a senior like Jim, a year older than Paul, and consequently out of reach—boys sometimes dated younger girls, but never vice versa. Still, Paul envied Jim his steady dating of Ruthie more than any of the hundred other things he envied his big brother, and sometimes he even let himself imagine what it would be like to talk to her, dance with her. And yes, sure—to neck with her, too.

She was a pretty blonde, with wondering deep blue eyes, and at school when she wore the orange dress that quit well above the flex of her knee, there was very little reading done by any boy in the study hall; nobody wanted to miss a single step of her occasional trip to the pencil sharpener. Ruthie was probably the cause of more adolescent self-abuse in Kenton than Betty Grable and Ingrid Bergman combined.

What made her really fatal, though, was that she didn't seem to be aware of her effect on boys. She exuded innocence, shyness even—that exciting combination of provocative body and absolute purity that can drive decent men to the breaking of commandments. When the guys at K.H.S. talked dirty, it was almost always about Ruthie Peters.

And it was Jim, of course, who had her, and deserved her, because Jim was older, smarter, better-looking, more talented . . .

There is just so much poetic justice that a person can stand. Paul made up his mind, resting there at the counter, with his sore feet and his aching shoulder and his lukewarm Coke, that he was going to find out what it was like to dance with Ruthie Peters. Tonight.

The Melodaires kept playing bouncy new tunes that Paul didn't feel like dancing to—"Take the A Train" and "Chattanooga Choo Choo"—but finally, to his relief, they eased into "Stardust." "The immortal Stardust," it was proudly called on the Fort Wayne radio stations, since it was written by a Hoosier and had been around for a while. Paul was as nervous as before a big game. He decided he'd better be fast, or he'd never have the nerve to do it at all. He poked Jerry, to make his challenge irreversible. "Watch this."

He squeezed past two or three couples and tapped Jim. "Hey, there, Ace, could I dance with your girl? If you can spare her a minute?"

Jim was surprised and glanced at Ruthie, who stood there, innocent, neutral. Then he smiled a little, an amused look. "Sure, Pug. Have fun."

Paul couldn't tell if the last remark was for her or for him. Ruthie's right hand, still warm from holding his brother's, came into Paul's, and she smiled up at him with a shyness that was unbearably exciting. Paul had had no intention of "dancing close" with Ruthie; she was his brother's girl, after all. But as soon as his arm went around her, she snuggled against him, warm and slow-moving, and Paul wasn't sure how it had happened, and he didn't care. He had never really enjoyed dancing, but then he'd never danced with Ruthie Peters, out there on a dim floor in the sweet fatigue of a hard game, her warm breasts against his shirt, a smell of Ivory soap and baby powder, her movements so gentle, so intimate that it was—he imagined—like sex itself.

He was getting an erection, and ordinarily he would have been embarrassed and tried to back away from his partner; but there was a fine recklessness about all this that changed things. He didn't back off, and he didn't even fight it by trying to think pure thoughts. He just let his arm and his chest and his legs feel Ruthie, and it was the sweetest erection he could possibly imagine, and Ruthie didn't back off either; she accepted it, or tolerated it in her invincible innocence. They danced that way, neither of them saying a word, until "Stardust" came at last to its muted, heartbroken ending.

When the music stopped, they didn't change position, just stood there hugging and swaying, until "Night and Day" began, and Paul said, "May I have this dance?" and they both grinned because there could be no question of not going on.

Let Jim do his own worrying, let *him* cut in if he wants to. Paul relished the thrill of wickedness.

So they danced some more, and Ruthie seemed contented, and Paul was half delirious, and they went on dancing until Jim finally did have to cut in to get his girl back. But she must have seen him coming and whispered, just before he got there, "You were wonderful tonight."

Paul turned her loose when Jim tapped him, and tried to imagine what she meant. He had to stay on the dark floor, standing alone among the swaying dancers for a while, until he had relaxed enough to be seen in the light again. And he wondered if she meant his basketball playing, or his dancing, or what.

Wonderful? Pug Anderson? Wonderful?

It didn't seem real, but she'd said it all right, he didn't dream that one up. He didn't make up the way her hand tightened on his just before they had to quit.

Something had happened out there, and now everything was changed. Something had started that would never stop.

Jerry would have given him a ride home, but he didn't want to see anyone, talk to anyone, or ride prisoner in a car. In pure joy, he skipped, then jogged, then finally slowed to a walk on the long stretch of West William Street, under the dim arch of maple trees, brightened periodically by small yellow streetlamps. It was that odd time, between summer and fall, when you could smell both seasons in the air, mellow summer still hanging on, the cool tang of autumn hinting at big changes.

Something had happened. He knew what it was by definition—in book language, in movie terms. He knew he was "in love," as much in love as Romeo or Mark Antony, as much in love as Tyrone Power or Robert Taylor had ever been. But what did that mean, that little phrase everybody took for granted?

In the yellow circle of light from a streetlamp, he picked up a maple leaf, an early victim of the dead season. It hadn't turned color but had somehow lost its grip on summer, and fallen. He examined the leaf, its splendid construction: the sturdy stem, the seven branching veins, the network of capillaries. "Bilateral symmetry," Miss Edelman would say. Paul touched the leaf, ran his finger along the veins, then felt his own face, the division at the tip of his nose, the upper lip, the cleft in his chin, the notch in his breastbone. Symmetry. He put the leaf in his shirt pocket and moved on, from streetlamp to streetlamp, down the little cracked sidewalk, past the sleeping houses.

By the time he got home the house was dark and everyone was in bed, but he knew the front door would be open. You could try every door on the block, day or night, and never find a locked one. He tiptoed in, up the stairs, down the hall to the bathroom. Peeing quietly against the porcelain, he gazed at his penis, the pitiful little waterspout that so recently had raged against all those layers of clothing between it and Ruthie Peters' skin. The memory stirred him, and the waterspout instantly swelled again. He wanted to masturbate, but resisted, afraid of spoiling it all.

In the bedroom, he glanced at the other twin bed: Jim wasn't home yet. Still out there, somewhere, in that cool mysterious night, with Ruthie. Paul wondered what they were up to, right this minute. Not actually doing it, like Walter and Sally or Bill and Connie, he was sure of that. Not Ruthie. But they were probably necking, maybe on her front porch swing, or just standing there in the dark of that big porch, hidden by forsythia bushes. The thought was an exquisite torture. His penis squirmed, an independent presence in the small room. As he got into bed, he held it gently, trying not to excite it.

He thought of Ruthie's warmth, the softness of her breasts against him, her slow movements on the dance floor. Nobody else ever danced like that, her body a fragrant cascading liquid music. His penis throbbed and ached.

And her eyes glancing up, shy and amused, a ceaseless provocation to the world, and her lips . . . Paul's left hand grabbed for his handkerchief as his right hand moved slowly, up and down, once, twice; and at only the third stroke, his poor penis, teased and denied for hours, was finally content. Thinking Ruthie, Ruthie, Ruthie, Paul fell asleep.

❧

THE KENTON SCHOOL BOARD met every other Monday night in the Home Economics room at K.H.S., the only room with long tables in it. It was never easy to get new volunteers to run for the Board, so the same people kept being elected to it year after year, and by now they were used to each other's idiosyncrasies. Dr. Roberts had long since resigned himself to breathing Carl Potter's foul cigar smoke and to hearing Joe Berry's chronic cough. Berry sold real estate, was outdoors a lot, and from November to March seemed to live on licorice cough drops, filling the room with a medicinal smell and giving him a black tongue that showed when he laughed at his own frequent jokes. In every discussion he was a loose cannon, veering into uncontrollable anecdote. Potter, on the other hand, was a stickler for relevance, bulldogging every issue to the ground, but he had never, in Dr. Roberts' judgment, been on the reasonable side of any issue. Wendell Keller, the local district attorney, had the irritating habit of rotating his little finger in his left ear when he was talking, but he usually spoke so cogently that Dr. Roberts forgave him his little quirk. Millard Stackmore, a well-to-do retired farmer, rarely said much, but occasionally brought meetings to a dead pause by clearing his throat resonantly and opening his mouth—and then not saying a word, just gazing into open space. Lucinda Jacobs, an alert and rather nervous former schoolteacher, never missed a word, and punctuated everyone's comments with little interjections: *"Hm!" "Ho!" "Mm-hm!"* Reverend Tucker drummed on the table constantly when anyone else was talking, implying a certain impatience at these digressions from his own considered wisdom.

When their deliberations became unbearably frustrating, Dr. Roberts would squint around the table and imagine everyone with chalky-white faces and big red sponge-rubber noses. What in the world, he sometimes asked himself, am I doing here, surrounded by gas burners, sewing machines, and clowns? He had run for election, years ago, for the same reason he joined the volunteer firemen: because Wendell, one of his patients, had badgered him into being a "good citizen." He had stayed on as much out of habit as out of fear that things would be worse without him. Inertia is a great decision-maker.

But how much worse could things get? He had been trying for an hour and a half to bring the Board to a vote on three budget items, and so far they had managed to pass only one of them. The second one was his own pet project, rejected by the Board two months ago on a close vote: a five percent raise for the teachers. He knew it wouldn't be easy this time, either, and had introduced it with some high-minded exhortation about the desirability of quality education, the necessity of competing for good personnel, and the dismal salaries in the Kenton schools. But ever since he made the proposal, Carl Potter had held the floor with a cocklebur voice that emerged in one continuous sentence, uninterruptible, his cigar waggling for emphasis.

"Let me make it clear," he was saying, "I'm all for quality education, I mean, we want the very best for our kids here in Kenton, but we have to be practical, too, don't we, I mean, a five percent raise, across the board, that'd be the straw that broke the back for our taxpayers, what they need in these hard times is a little relief, not sky-high tax increases from some gang of bureaucrats who want to solve every problem by tax-tax, spend-spend . . ."

Dr. Roberts tried to break into Potter's steady drone but was pre-empted by Joe Berry, a salesman who was used to interrupting people.

"*We* heard about this last week, down at the Realty Association, and believe me, *nobody* there was too tickled about it." He popped another cough drop onto his black tongue. "My cousin, Steve Grote, over at Garrett, *he* says they tried to put through a raise like this, and they had a taxpayers' revolt. They just wouldn't *stand* for it. There's a lot of coloreds living over there, you know, and those jigs said if the pay came up to their standards, *they'd* take all the teaching jobs!" Berry's metallic laugh ricocheted around the walls. "Say, speaking of jobs, one of the darkies was reading the want ads down at the station, and my cousin says to him, 'Rastus, why are you reading the female want ads?' And he said, 'For a job.' And Steve says, 'You're not a female.' And Rastus says, 'No, but my wife is!' "

This time Berry's guffaw was echoed by Carl Potter's cackle. Even Millard, usually poker-faced, snickered.

"*Hm! Ahem!*" Mrs. Jacobs said.

Dr. Roberts squinted at their whiteface, their big painted grins. "Gentlemen!" he called out, "And lady. We have a proposal before us."

"And I'm for it." Wendell Keller put his little finger in his ear. "I don't know how the hell—excuse me, Lucinda. It beats me how those teachers can live on nine hundred, a thousand a year, some of them with families, kids to put through school. They haven't had a raise since before I came on this Board, and that's over five years. I say they need a raise a lot more than the rest of us need the penny or two off our tax rate."

"*Hm!*" said Mrs. Jacobs. "Well, I may be prejudiced, having been a teacher myself, but I agree with Wendell. You can't expect to have good morale in the classrooms when the teachers are worried sick about how to pay their bills."

"Now, now." When the Reverend Tucker stopped drumming his fingers, everyone braced for the long haul. "Let's not go off the deep end, here. Our teachers' salaries aren't as bad as all that. Many others in this county and this state, and I dare say all over the country, are just as low. We're not exactly in a boom period, remember, we're just trying to hold the line, hold that line, until things look up a bit. Meanwhile, our teachers can surely get along on their nice steady income—rent more modest homes, maybe, get summer jobs with the local stores or farms instead of always running back to college for master's degrees and such, cut out some of the luxuries . . ."

Berry took a quick cue: "There's this Jewish fella, name of Abie. He wants to live in luxury, see, but all he's got is his pushcart. 'Papa,' he says, 'I want to marry this Gentile girl, she's loaded with money!' His daddy looks at him like he's crazy. 'Abie, you should live so long. Now listen to me, you marry a nice Jewish girl and settle down.' 'No, no, Papa,' says Abie, 'you marry a poor girl, you settle down. Marry a rich girl, you settle *up!*' "

Berry and Potter guffawed and Stackmore snickered again. Dr. Roberts squinted at them, buffoons swatting each other with inflated bladders.

Reverend Tucker wasn't used to being interrupted, and obviously didn't like it. He picked up his argument as if he hadn't been stopped: ". . . cut out some of the luxuries, live a simple and wholesome life, they'd be better off. I have it on good authority that some of our teachers, far from being threadbare, have all the money they need to go out to that liquor den on Road Six and buy themselves bottles of booze."

Everyone looked grim: that was a startling charge, just short of treason or homicide. Dr. Roberts intervened. "Reverend Tucker, whether or not certain teachers have an occasional drink, well, that's their personal life, a private matter . . ."

"I don't mean 'certain' teachers, I mean a specific teacher, namely that new woman we hired to teach biology."

"Miss Edelman?"

"That one. Not only do I have it on good authority that she drinks, but now it turns out her father is a sworn enemy of religion and morality. It looks to me like we've made a serious mistake."

"Reverend Tucker, I've spoken to the principal about both our new teachers, and he says they're doing a fine job in the classroom."

"The classroom, unfortunately, isn't all we have to think about. We have other obligations here. What kind of example does that woman set for our youngsters? A drunkard and an atheist!"

"Reverend *Tucker!*" Dr. Roberts heard the anger in his voice, and toned it down. "We'd better be careful about the kind of allegations we make, even behind closed doors . . ."

"Closed doors, that reminds me of a story, . . ." Berry began.

In the end, Dr. Roberts was almost relieved when they tabled his motion and went on to discuss at great length the elegant new shower rooms for the basketball team: the color of the walls, the size of the tiles, the type of shower heads, the placement of lockers, and other significant matters.

S UMMER AND WINTER, in school and out, Jim and Paul worked in the Slayzall lab, bottling, labeling, packing, invoicing, shipping. They didn't know how to concoct the wicked stuff. Only Charlie knew that secret, and he wasn't telling anyone, as if he meant it to die with him— which might not take too long, Paul often thought, watching him up there on the catwalk, in the swirling fumes of the mixing tank, stirring away.

In the summer, when Jim and Paul were younger, Charlie sometimes took them along when he drove out of town to badger his old customers or beat the bushes for new ones, in the drugstores and hardwares of Decatur, Indiana, or Three Rivers, Michigan, or Bryan, Ohio. Before they got the sixty-horse '37 Ford, they had an ancient Essex, a pusher. Charlie had paid only thirty dollars for it, so it wasn't surprising that they used to spend about half their time shoving it along, trying to get it to stir itself into action. Also, it was a boiler, a tricky performer in the summer sun, blowing its radiator cap without warning, and spouting steam. Whenever that happened, they had to bring down the open windshield in a hurry to keep from getting scalded. But the old square crate got them around, somehow, and they chugged across the corntasseled flatlands of the tri-state area, the hot mohair upholstery prickling their skin.

So Charles Anderson carried his magic brew out into the great world, a chalice borne against vermin: not only the little bottles, to be sold to housewives at their favorite pharmacies, but gallon jugs and five-gallon cans, enough poison in the back of the old Essex to wipe out hosts of enemy insects, moths, bedbugs, roaches. He took the stuff everywhere: to neighborhood living rooms, where Jim and Paul helped him mothproof rugs and sofas, and also to factory foundations crumbling with termites, to furniture warehouses imperiled by silverfish, to meat-packing plants writhing with cock-roaches.

It was a brave sight, Charles Anderson on a demonstration tour of a meat-packer's infested establishment, pump-sprayer strapped over his starched white shirt, neat necktie pulled up tight, his narrowed eyes darting along cracks and crevices. When the plant manager indicated the worst site in the build-ing, the little entourage of clerks and straw bosses would stop and wait, and Charlie would unsling the sprayer, give it a final pump or two to make sure the pressure was up, adjust the nozzle to a fine stream, sling the sprayer again, and go to work.

He knew from experience where the enemy was hiding out, waiting for dark and the midnight feasting. He aimed a silver stream of Slayzall accurately, and suddenly the still, expectant room was aswarm with life, and with death, cock-roaches and water bugs streaming out of the crevices, fleeing the spray. But too late: the taint was on them. They hit the floor with a steady crackling sound and lay there in heaps, kicking and twitching. If roaches had had voices, the room would have shrilled with their torment.

Sometimes the plant manager was skeptical. "Maybe that stuff is just scaring them."

Charlie sniffed his disdain—the only man alive who was sufficiently immunized to be able to sniff, in the presence of Slayzall fumes. "Keep an eye on them," he gritted. "They're done for." And sure enough, there were never any miraculous recoveries. The little beasts lay there in their hundreds and their thousands, belly-up, twitching for a while, then not at all.

Charlie was a talker and a seller, and these two things were inseparable in his life. He took it for granted that most of his retail customers, Midwestern small-town businessmen, were Republicans, and Slayzall was a supremely Republican insecticide: proud of its conspicuously expensive price, proud of its 100% active ingredients, its money-back guarantee, and its defiance of FDR. Charlie had been taken to court by the Democrats' Pure Food and Drug Administration and was finally forced, after a legal skirmish, to increase the type size of the POISON warning on his label, to clarify the lethal nature of its contents, and to delete the claim that Slayzall was a "deodorant," lest some halfwit use it the wrong way.

But Charlie's dislike of FDR went far deeper than that little fracas. He distrusted FDR's New Yorkishness, detested his Harvard cronies, disapproved of his pinko Social Security Act, despised his cozying up to the labor bosses, was offended by his soak-the-rich taxation, and was furious when FDR had the gall to run for an unprecedented and unconstitutional third term. And then won, hands down. Would the man never have the decency to die or give up?

"If this kid," he'd tell a pharmacist, putting a hand on Paul's head, "couldn't run a government better than that jackass in Washington, I'd tie him in a gunny sack and drown him in the river."

Paul, ten years old, would blush and grin at that, and scuttle off and read the comic books, and Charlie would make a sale or not, usually not. When he could fill an order out of the stock in the back of the car, they'd go home happy, with money in pocket, pleased and ready for another trip next day, to Coldwater or Edgerton or Berne. When nothing went right anywhere, they would drive home glum and hungry, hoping the radiator cap wouldn't blow.

By the summer of 1941, Jim and Paul rarely went along on the trips anymore. But one hot day in July, when Jim was caddying at the country club, Paul impulsively jumped in the Ford to keep Charlie company.

It turned out to be one of those tough days, in Payne, Ohio. Charlie talked and sweated his way through all the local hardwares and drugstores, bad-mouthing Roosevelt, repeating his best jokes, and hustling, hustling, hustling Slayzall. But after so many years of the depression, the shops of Payne were as hard to penetrate as fortresses. Charlie was still batting zero as the heat began seeping out of the stores on the west side of the street. Under the big ceiling fan at Wilkens' Drugstore, Paul suddenly shivered, remembering Mr. Brandt, his Sunday school teacher, telling him after class, "Your daddy's got guts, Paul. He's been up against it. You don't know what it means to have guts yet, because you've never had to have any. But your daddy knows—I tell you, son, he's been up against it. And he's never quit. You hear that? He's never quit."

Paul walked around, looking at things in the drugstore. The display of tennis rackets was irresistible. His own racket, Jim's castoff two years ago, was ratty: no leather on the grip anymore, and one string broken, it met the ball with a mushy sound. But it wouldn't have occurred to Paul to ask for a new one, and at a penny-and-a-half profit per *Post*, he never could have afforded the classy $12.00 Don Budge model he was holding, cautiously sweeping through the air, avoiding the greeting card displays.

Charlie must have been making a pretty good deal with old

man Wilkens. After a lot of persistent talking and laughing, Paul saw him go out to the car and get a carton of Slayzall from the trunk, then put the bottles where they belonged on the counter display.

Paul helped him arrange them. Charlie said goodbye to Mr. Wilkens.

"OK, Paul, let's hit the road." He grinned. "Oh, and bring that Don Budge racket with you."

At first Paul couldn't believe it, but his father's broad grin convinced him. Charlie had made a trade! The most beautiful, most expensive racket in the store was his. He knew Charlie didn't have two dollars in his pocket. Better than a birthday present, more unexpected, it was the truest kind of gift: someone giving you all he's got.

An hour later Charlie was driving the Essex along the narrow Ohio road that led west, straight as a pencil line through the July corn and soybeans, toward the setting sun of Indiana. He stopped at an intersection. The county roads crossed, every mile, perpendicular and absolutely unswerving, to the north and south. "Look, Paul, this is the flattest county in Ohio. You can see nine miles in any direction from here."

The limp corn glistened to the north, east, south, west. Holding the racket in his lap, Paul had a bursting sensation in his chest which he recognized as that rare thing: happiness. Red barns and tall silos shimmered in the distance. It seemed to Paul that he could see a lot more than just nine miles.

❧

HEN "THE LABYRINTH" appeared in *The Hoosier Rationalist*, it was quite a shock, and at first no one knew how to react to it. Even the town preachers, usually so nimble in squelching the ungodly, let a Sabbath opportunity slip by while they pondered their response. By Sunday, September 28, they had caught their breath, held a meeting of the Ministerial Association, and with a single will released broadsides into their expectant congregations. In sanctuary after sanctuary, there were special prayers for the souls of heathen, and pastoral indignation at the sins of pride and blasphemy. At the Methodist Episcopal Church, there was a final, militant rendering of "Soldiers of the cross, arise, gird you with your armor bright!" At the same time, the Missouri Synod Lutherans were concluding with "A mighty fortress is our God!" And Reverend Dobbins and the Pentecostals in their homely frame chapel were singing "Fight the good fight with all thy might!"

At the First Church of Christ, however, nobody was singing yet. The Reverend Stephen B. Tucker, strong in the service of the Lord, was only now reaching the culmination of a lengthy sermon that had already dealt severely with doubters and disbelievers from Thomas the Apostle to Robert Ingersoll; and his ringing voice called upon sinners to witness, heathen to renounce, and heretics to believe.

"God is not an 'easy answer,' but a mystery," he called out, his earnestness reaching the hard-of-hearing in the farthest row. "God is not a source of neurosis, but of lasting peace. He is the ultimate will, the omnipotent force of the universe. And yet, because in all His might He is also love itself, He counts every hair on the head of mankind, Matthew Ten, and for that reason, has given mankind rightful dominion over all creation, plant and animal, stream, rock, and forest."

Reverend Tucker's right hand felt for the knot of his black necktie, and his voice lowered half an octave, his eyes darting around the sanctuary. "But today in our community there are teachers in our schools and scribblers in our midst, who turn the truth upside down, who try to make bad arguments defeat good ones, and who are steadily and willfully corrupting our youth. If man was descended from a monkey, they say, then the Bible is not true, and what Moses wrote about the Creation is a mere myth. This is an out-and-out attack upon religion, and therefore against morality, and when Christians of all denominations fully understand that a war has been declared against them, right here in Kenton, they will, to a man, rise up in arms in the defense of their faith.

"The first shots have been fired. We have fought this foe before, and we will stand to do fair battle today. The call to arms is made, and we shall not fail."

Miss Huron, with her usual prescience, had slipped over to the organ and was already on the bench when the Reverend Tucker's expressive eyebrows lifted and his eyes met hers in the mirror over the keyboard. There was a moment of expectant silence as they gazed at each other, the Reverend Tucker breathing heavily from his long peroration. Then Miss Huron struck the first chord with an ear-splitting diapason and the choir and congregation all rose and sang, "O watch and fight and pray! The battle ne'er give o'er!"

Paul sang loudly, relieved that the sermon was finally over; but it was unclear to him, at that point, whose side he was supposed to be on.

OCTOBER

⚜

THE KENTON DAILY HERALD

Fort Wayne, Ind., Oct. 3, 1941
Heated arguments developed among partisans outside the
Gospel Temple here tonight as Charles A. Lindbergh made
an address for the America First Committee rally. Inside, an
audience of 4,200 gave the flier applause mingled with scat-
tered boos.

Outside, about 3,000 persons heard the speech over an
amplifying system. A considerable detail of police, with two
armored cars, was on the alert.

At least half the throng came from outside Fort Wayne,
and their automobiles choked the area around the temple.

⚜

JIM HAD A DATE with Ruthie, and Nora was taking Betsy
to the Ladies Aid mother-daughter banquet, so Paul was
the only one who rode along with his father to Fort
Wayne. They got there early, but the crowd was ahead
of them, and they ended up in the last row, a disappointment.
So at Charlie's suggestion, Paul sneaked down the aisle to get
a better look at the famous man. It wasn't easy. The ushers
kept trying to stop him, and he had to insist that he'd already
been seated up front.

Finally he made it, but he still couldn't see very well. A grim line of tall men standing along the platform blocked his view. Paul stepped around the platform and up three steps at the right side, into blue velvet curtains, and ended up in the very wings of the giant stage. Perfect.

There was a nervousness about the occasion that Paul could feel like a coming storm, but when the hero stood up to speak, it was a stilling of the waters. Tall, slim, boyish, as handsome as his own legend, the Lone Eagle spoke slowly, choosing his words with care. As he continued, however, Paul felt the uneasiness in the hall again: the unprecedented power of Roosevelt, the one-man rule, dictatorship, the loss of freedom, the censorship, the undeclared warfare. "They have been treating our Congress more and more as the German Reichstag has been treated under the Nazi regime. Congress, like the Reichstag, is not consulted."

An eruption of applause: Lindbergh looked startled and shifted his shoulders. Paul imagined his father out there in the back row, clapping till his palms stung.

"We must face the fact that you and I and our generation have lost our American heritage. It is no longer simply a case of defending it. It is a case of rebuilding it."

A standing ovation. Lindbergh awkwardly smoothed the lapels of his single-breasted suit. Paul clapped silently, not wanting to draw the attention of the guards. He remembered playing with Jim in the backyard, waving at airplanes in the summer sky and calling to every one, "Hi, Lindy!"

"What if there are no elections next year? The time has come when we must consider even that. I can only say that there is still, deep within this country, the spirit that built America; and on that, in the last analysis, we must rely. That spirit burns in men and women like you here tonight; and that spirit is the strength and hope of our nation."

The hero's arms went up in a salutation, a plea, a farewell; and at that signal the four thousand throats in the Gospel Temple roared gratitude and love. The meeting was over, but the standing ovation went on and on, a thunder to resound in the ears for days afterward.

With no hope of finding his father in the thousands of jostling bodies, Paul knew he'd have to work his way back to their rendezvous, the blue Ford. This was the biggest mob Paul had ever seen in one place, bigger even than the Royal County Fair, so he looked backstage for an exit, and found it. Soon he was in the rear parking lot. As he walked around the temple, a side door opened and two burly men in dark suits and snap-brim hats came out, looking around quickly—and then, in the dim light from the door, there was the aviator himself, just a few feet away. Paul never expected to find himself this close to the hero. He blurted out, "Hi, Lindy!"

The two men in dark suits whirled and put their hands inside their jackets, but the flier waved and smiled his famous smile. Paul felt silly, too silly not to go on, so he said, "That was great tonight, Mr. Lindbergh." The bodyguards relaxed, and as Lindbergh got into his limousine, he called back, "Thanks, son. God bless you."

The car moved off, turned into Rudisill Boulevard, and headed west in the heavy traffic. Paul was stirred, as if he'd just stepped into history. He stood there a moment, savoring the feeling, then began walking down Rudisill to South Harrison Street, turned left, and found the Ford at the curb where they'd parked it, behind a shiny new maroon Buick.

His father wasn't in the car, though. He was sitting on the lawn, talking in quick bursts to a white-haired man and a pretty young girl. He was like that, always talking to strangers. The two men were obviously in sympathetic agreement with everything Lindbergh had said, and "that idiot in the

White House" was taking a lot of heat. When Paul arrived, Charlie got up, patted him on the back, and introduced him to the white-haired man and his daughter, a long German-sounding name that Paul didn't quite get. The daughter, Charlie said with a touch of formality, had just been named the Typical American Girl, and was going to be on the cover of *Life* magazine on December fifteenth. Paul was impressed. History was shaping itself all around him.

The Ford took a little coaxing, but finally started up, and Charlie made a U-turn, heading back to Kenton. As they pulled away, the white-haired man and the Typical American Girl with the German name stood together, waving goodbye. Under the dim streetlight, they looked like a Norman Rockwell cover on one of his *Saturday Evening Post*s.

THE DAILY HERALD WORLD NEWS ROUNDUP

Berlin, Oct. 3, 1941
Adolf Hitler declared today that a "paralyzing blow" had been dealt the Russians, and that they "never again will rise up." The Russian forces he called "not human beings, but animal beasts. That's what Bolshevism has made of them."

Washington, D.C., Oct. 3, 1941
Senator Claude Pepper (D, Fla.) said that the address of Charles A. Lindbergh in Fort Wayne, Ind., tonight made clear that the flier proposes to be the "Fuehrer of the United States."

Washington, D.C., Oct. 3, 1941
Paul Vories McNutt, former governor of Indiana, made public today a plea for American unity, addressed to Dr. William L. Bryan, President Emeritus of Indiana University. The letter concludes: "I share your deep concern over the persistent efforts of a small group to cast discredit on the Government's defense program. The toleration of opposition, even

in the face of grave danger, is the very essence of democracy. However, the insistent exercise of the right of opposition at such times is a complete misconception of the duties of democratic citizenship and one which may lead to tragic consequences . . ."

Indianapolis, Oct. 3, 1941
The Commander of the American Legion said in a speech here tonight, "Lindbergh and all traitors have got to be stopped. The time for freedom of speech is past."

Miss Edelman's Advanced Biology labs were unlike anything else at Kenton High, because she insisted on absolute discipline and tolerated no sloppy work. She used professional terminology—"phenotypic differences," "mean number"—and expected the students to understand them. She used adult words—"fertility," "sexual selection," "copulation"—and expected teen-agers to accept them without snickering or nudging. No one in the class was accustomed to this treatment, though Jim rose to it quickly as a matter of pride, and Ruthie acted as if it, like everything that brushed against the surface of her life, was perfectly normal. Paul had a little trouble, though, and Chuck Green, his lab partner, had a lot more, grinning and flinching nervously every time he heard the word "copulate."

For the students, fruit flies were just plain flies, pesky little gnats in the apple barrel. But in Miss Edelman's class, they became the invaluable Drosophila, and were elevated to heroic roles in the history of biology; they were protagonists with Morgan and Muller at Columbia, and with her own professors at Indiana. She had done her master's at I.U. with Alfred Kinsey, and could draw compact lessons from mutations of Drosophila or the behavior of gall wasps.

So every Tuesday and Thursday afternoon, in the formaldehyde reek of biology lab, the class warily entered the Lilliputian world of the fruit fly, tolerated that busy microcosm for two uneasy hours, and finally escaped to the familiar expanse of basketball and bebop, as if released from a dungeon. Too many nagging issues emerged from those stoppered bottles of tiny insects and Miss Edelman's running commentary: race, normality, evolution, sex, survival. Students at K.H.S. were not accustomed to such relentless relevance in their schoolwork.

By Tuesday, October 7, they had been foster parents to three generations of Drosophila, holding them at twenty-five degrees centigrade, forty hours to the hatching of eggs, five days as larvae, five more as pupae. Then, two days after emergence, they became sexually active, and the cycle repeated itself.

"At this stage," Miss Edelman lectured, "they live for about three more weeks. The mean number of eggs per female is about two hundred. Copulation is repeated and frequent."

Predictably, Chuck Green flinched, nearly upsetting Paul's open bottle. Paul held everything steady: with concentration, anything is possible.

Miss Edelman brought in bananas and ripened them in glass-stoppered bottles. Control cultures were carefully kept. Flies and food were sealed in meticulously washed glassware. Pedigree work had to be pure.

The egg-laying females were given a new piece of banana, always at the same stage of rottenness, every two days. Pupae were picked out of the larval dish and placed on moist blotting paper in a small vial, from which adults could be transferred when they emerged. Students were required to come in once a day, in addition to the regular Tuesday and Thursday lab sessions, to maintain the process; Miss Edelman oversaw it, but the students had to do the work. She went around the lab, occasionally quoting: "Sexual selection, Darwin said, is a struggle of one sex, generally the males, for the possession of the other sex. The result to the unsuccessful competitor is not death, but few or no offspring."

She walked between the long lab tables, observing, correcting, always talking, an education machine that never rested. "The power to charm the females, Darwin said, is sometimes more important than the power to conquer in battle."

Tanks closing in on Moscow. Paul squinted, trying to concentrate. His biggest problem in biology lab was not his clumsy partner, but Ruthie Peters. She was Jim's lab partner, but they worked at the sink next to Paul and Chuck, disconcertingly close. She was a natural at lab work, deft and precise, and as she moved briskly around the table, Paul kept smelling her freshness through the prevailing formaldehyde, that special perfume of Ivory soap and baby powder, so innocent it was maddening. Ever since the Fox Lake postgame dance, she always smiled at Paul when they came close, a smile too open to be an invitation, too shy to be meaningless. Paul had a lot of trouble focusing on fruit flies.

"Sexual selection, Darwin said, acts on human beings as well as other animals. What we call racial differences—in color, hairiness, shape of features, and so on, may be partly the result of thousands of years of sexual selection."

When they were ready for mating, the sexes had to be separated before they were a day old. No female that was more than twelve hours old before it was isolated from the males could be used as a parent. Parents were killed after one hundred offspring had been produced. The students were looking for mutations, a classroom full of small-game hunters, and Paul got excited each time the wings of a new generation went under the microscope.

"Bateman calls the selective females 'discriminatingly passive' and the males 'indiscriminately eager.' The control of sexual selection by one sex, the females, and its operation on the other sex, the males, was clearly known to Darwin."

Mr. Hedges, the principal, swung into the room on one of his inspection tours, looking with overt suspicion at these goings-on, so remote from his own chosen profession in health and phys. ed.

"The normal venation of Drosophila," Miss Edelman said, ignoring the principal's presence, "is extremely simple, the costal vein reaching to the fourth of the five longitudinal veins . . ."

Mr. Hedges, unaccustomed to finding a classroom of such order and industriousness, stomped away, frustrated. Going out the door, he snapped off the overhead lights. "Waste not, want not, Miss Edelman," he called. "Don't you know there's a war on?"

The smell of Ivory soap and baby powder drifted across Paul's consciousness again. Without planning it, he eased over to the right, and his elbow touched Ruthie's bare arm. A current of joy pulsed in his arm, his shoulder, his chest. Neither of them moved for a magic moment, the current, Paul imagined, throbbing in her, too. On the table in front of them, Drosophila copulated repeatedly.

Jim, impatient with anything short of perfection, needed his partner. "What's the matter, Ruthie?" He sounded irritated, his voice breaking the magic spell. "Come on, we've got to get these crazy bugs separated before they louse up the whole experiment."

Miss Edelman flipped the overhead lights back on, and the smell of formaldehyde triumphed.

"This is another example of behavior at the mating site, the lek," Miss Edelman announced, showing Paul's table a bottle with a leaf in it. On the leaf, a male fly was depositing a liquid film. "He'll defend that lek, a good example of territoriality. This intensifies sexual selection, since the males have to attract the females to the lek. Defending their territories, they become belligerent and posture aggressively."

When the bell rang, Jim grabbed Ruthie's arm, pulling her toward the door. "Come on, let's get out of here and find some fresh air."

Paul stayed behind, still separating bottles. Miss Edelman spoke to the emptying classroom: "The territorial Drosophila verify Darwin's observation that, even in insects, the more 'attractive' individuals are preferred by the opposite sex."

H E REFUSED to consider it at first, but as the feeling became stronger and stronger, Paul finally had to admit it: he lusted after Ruthie Peters. He knew it was supposed to be a sin. He puzzled frequently over Jesus' stern teaching: if you do it in your heart, it's as bad as doing it with your thing. A hard saying, as Reverend Tucker would put it, and Paul tried to find a loophole. But there were no loopholes for Protestants, no Jesuitical traditions, no easy mechanical dispensations. He had to face the fact, the cold letter of that moral absolute.

And yet, somehow, he didn't really believe it, not even if Jesus did say it, right out, in the plain English of the King James Bible, Authorized Version. Like the skeptical grown-ups who somehow hoped that Chesterfields and Lucky Strikes weren't really killing them, even if they did call them "coffin nails," Paul clung to a desperate hope that lust in the heart wasn't a sin, after all.

In any case, it was true: in his heart, he lusted after Ruthie Peters. And so, without quite realizing what he was doing, Paul had begun a furtive pursuit of her. Had anyone asked him—had he consciously asked himself—he would have in-dignantly denied any such thing. She was his brother's girl, after all, private property. He wouldn't dream of stealing her, even if he could. And yet, again and again, he found himself trying to catch up to her, on the streets, in the school hall-ways, at the Candy Castle.

All of her places had become magic: the front porch on Elm Street; the Methodist Episcopal Church, where the Peters family went every Sunday; her study-hall desk, anonymous as lumber but always breathing her presence; the streets she took to school, dangerous with promises. Paul walked her neighborhood sidewalks in a perpetual state of alert, wanting so much, fearing so much, that he constantly rang up false alarms: the wrong girl in the next block, the wrong blonde in a shop window.

Not every apparition was a false alarm. He would see her sometimes at a distance, the electric shock of her reality al-ways jolting him. But she was rarely alone—a maiden sur-rounded by dragons: her mother, her sister, Jim. Hopelessly inaccessible.

After she smiled at him on Tuesday in biology lab, Paul

managed to drive himself more than a little crazy, and by Thursday he decided to risk being obvious. He got up half an hour early and dressed more neatly than usual, white shirt under his red letter sweater with its big yellow K. He dutifully downed a bowlful of Post Toasties and answered his mother's questions minimally but politely: "Yes, I did." "Just a little." "I will." "The usual time, I guess." "OK, Mom, so long." Then off to his adventure.

He knew she walked down Elm Street to Main and turned left on Diamond. The trick was to get down Mitchell and turn right on Main, arriving at the corner of Main and Elm from the other direction at exactly the right moment, not so early that he couldn't wait for her casually, not so late that he couldn't casually catch up.

But at the first corner, he could see that he was too late: a flash of orange dress a long block away, she was almost out of reach. He ran down Mitchell to Main, then sprinted the two blocks from the popcorn wagon to city hall, and pulled up at the corner of Elm, breathing hard, hot and itchy under the wool sweater. She wasn't there yet, not yet. And then she appeared, materialized at the corner of the building, walking in that deliberate, innocent, somehow sexy way, her body leaning slightly back, arms clasped around her books.

Waiting for her, expecting her, Paul was nevertheless unprepared. "Going to school?" he blurted, and instantly cursed himself for a jerk.

She smiled, but didn't laugh at him. "Hi, Paul." Nothing ever seemed to surprise her. They walked down Main to Diamond Street side by side, not saying much. Ruthie smiled at him now and then.

"Did you read 'Lancelot and Elaine' last night?" she finally asked.

"Yeah, *all* night. 'Tirra lira by the river, sang Sir Lance-lot.' "

"It is kind of long. But Miss Eva sure likes it."

Miss Eva had taught English since Paul's mother was in high school, and no one left her classes unchanged. An older version of Miss Edelman, she ran a tight classroom, and there were certain things her students always learned to do: to read the assignments on time, to memorize poetry, to explain motivations, to read aloud with feeling.

Paul reflected. "I think maybe Miss Eva still believes in knights and ladies."

"Well, don't you, young man?"

Banter, he knew very well, was her normal mode of conversation. That was OK for Jim, who was quick and could spar with anyone, but Paul always felt self-conscious with that Candy Castle teasing. Still, he had to try, or the game would be lost before he started.

"Oh, I believe in ladies. That's a matter of faith."

"You mean, not a matter of reason? Shame on you."

"Knights are matters of reason. That's why they're extinct these days, while ladies multiply." How long, Paul thought, would they keep this up? Five blocks to go. Tirra lira.

"No knights? No knights? You're walking me to school just to tell me there are no knights?"

"Don't make them like they used to. Sorry." With an uneasy transition, he hummed a few bars of "Night and Day," hoping to evoke that country club dance so long ago, three weeks into ancient history, no home games since then. Would she remember?

"We danced to that." But she said it casually, as if it weren't important.

"We danced? When was that?" Paul made big innocent eyes.

She turned to him abruptly, looking hurt, then quickly

laughed. He'd managed to catch her off guard, and it worked: the dance had really meant something to her. Two points for him. Four blocks to go.

She smiled sweetly. "Oh, maybe it wasn't you, after all. Maybe it was Chuck. Or Tim. Or Jerry. How can I keep you all straight?" Two points for her.

"Or Jim?" No score.

"Oh, no, I'd remember Jim." Two more points for her.

She was ahead now, and Paul didn't know how to get out of this. He cursed his inexperience. "Thank God tomorrow's Friday—another home game, another dance."

"Who'll you forget you danced with tomorrow night?"

"Listen, I never forget a face. Will you put me down for the immortal 'Stardust'?"

"Maybe I'd better ask Jim."

"Jim who?"

She sighed dramatically. "You're right, there are no more knights."

Three blocks to go. "Maybe there are no more Elaines."

"Only Gueneveres, you mean? Naughty boy." She skipped a few times, getting ahead of him, and he trotted to catch up. She smiled. "I forgive you, my son." It made a big difference at sixteen, her being a year older.

Paul recited, with feeling: "Even as immortal God forgives?"

She stopped walking, and they were facing each other. It was so abrupt, and her smile was so pretty, pink and white in the October sunshine, that Paul felt his heart play a little trick on him, and he sucked in a quick breath. She declaimed, "I am not King Arthur, nor was meant to be."

"You don't look a bit like King Arthur." Paul was suddenly so violently in love that he lost control and dropped the game. "You look like an angel."

That caught her off guard, too, and her wide eyes stared

at him wonderingly. If they weren't carrying all these books, Paul thought, what would they be doing with their hands?

The dangerous moment finally passed. She pulled back from the abyss, chattering, "Angels, immortal God, the immortal 'Stardust'—maybe you didn't mean it, Paul—maybe chivalry isn't dead."

"Speaking of 'Stardust,' maybe we should try it again tomorrow night—just to see if we got it right last time."

"Hmm. Well, these things are complex and difficult, young man. I mean there are all sorts of implications. You don't 'Stardust' with just anyone."

"I don't mean with just anyone, I mean with that smart, tough basketball star you know."

"Oh, that's sweet—you really do admire your big brother, don't you?"

"This side idolatry, as Miss Eva says. And 'Stardust'?"

"Well, maybe as a reward, say, like Lancelot in his tournament. If you score, uh, twenty points against Huntington tomorrow, and do it wearing my green sleeve in your helmet . . ."

One block to go. Paul felt the frustration building in him, the jealousy. "And Jim? Does he have a quest too? A challenge?"

"Oh, Jim. He's so strong, he's beyond the challenging of silly girls in ivory towers. Jim's independent, isn't he? And smart, isn't he? And always right, isn't he?"

Paul knew this catechism by heart. "Oh, yes, King Arthur himself, trustworthy, loyal, helpful, friendly, courteous, kind . . ." Infallible big brother, Eagle Scout with Silver Palm, his merit badge sash loaded with trophies.

They were almost at the school entrance. Ruthie stopped and turned to him again. She looked unhappy, and when she spoke, her voice was apologetic.

"I'm sorry, Paul. It's just that . . . Well, it's been a long time, Jim and I, and, whether you think so or not, there's a little Elaine in everyone. You see?"

They walked up the steps to the school door.

" 'Stardust,' then?" he asked.

All around them the October maples blazed and shimmered. She smiled, and slipped into the bustle of hallways, her orange dress clashing with crimson letter sweaters.

"Tirra lira," she called back.

❧

I T HAD BEEN three weeks since "The Labyrinth" appeared in Saul Edelman's paper, and after the first startled fuss, and the broadsides from the town ministers, Kenton gradually absorbed the heretical episode into its easy forgetfulness and its considerable capacity for avoiding hard thoughts. Even the Thursday Quilting Club had found other things to gossip about. So by Friday, October 10, when another "Labyrinth" appeared, it was received with a sense of shock almost as profound as the first one.

It wasn't as if people didn't have other weighty issues to think about. On October 1, Frank Knox, the Secretary of the Navy, had come to Indianapolis to tell Hoosiers that they must now police the world. Two days later, Paul had heard Lindbergh in Fort Wayne, insisting on the opposite. Now everyone was taking sides and squabbling in public. Meanwhile, the Royal Air Force was battling the malevolent Luftwaffe; U.S. ships were being torpedoed; and Moscow, Leningrad, and Rostov were all in grave danger. On October 9, FDR called upon Congress to arm U.S. merchant ships.

At such a time, the local citizens might have been excused for being too preoccupied to think much about God. Yet that seemed to be all that Old Saul Edelman and *The Hoosier Rationalist* wanted to talk about these days, as if God were somehow a part of the overall problem. Nobody in town cottoned too much to that idea, but nobody wanted to miss a good piece of local gossip, either. When the second "Labyrinth" appeared, people discovered that they could buy it at the drugstore. Bob Mesler, sensing a quick buck in these hard times, had made a retailing pact with the devil.

By the time school let out that Friday, people were already standing in groups on street corners, holding copies of the *Rationalist* and shaking their heads. And sometimes their fists.

THE LABYRINTH

The Lord thy God is a jealous God. And that's not all. Judging from His own written record, He is also vindictive, tyrannical, narcissistic, bloodthirsty, bigoted, and irresponsible. It is hard to imagine why anyone would kneel to such a moral degenerate.

Unfortunately, we are beset by priests and preachers who promise us that if we do kneel, we will be rewarded with an eternity of infinite delight—precisely the prospect we have been weaned away from in our infantile years. Now, once again, the shamans deliberately tempt us with these blandishments, urge us to desire eternal life, and even try to make us feel guilty if we do not. No wonder so many people become confused and even mentally ill, trying to be something they can never be.

Religion is not simply a maladaptive compulsion in

our lives: it is intentionally maladaptive, charging us to abjure "this world." Preoccupation with an after-life necessarily reduces our interest in this life, but the problem goes deeper than that. The glittering mirage of Paradise breeds actual contempt for "this world," thereby encouraging antisocial tendencies, including the seductions of fanaticism.

Religious fanatics without power are only a bore, but fanatics who somehow gain power are murder-ous, as history constantly reminds us. To the fanatical mind, the act of pure religion is an act of pure vio-lence: the hanging of "witches" by pious Protestants in Massachusetts; the massacre of Huguenots, Incas, and Albigensians by pious Catholics; the massacre of Hindus by pious Buddhists (and vice versa) in Cam-bodia; the slaughter of Moslems by pious Hindus (and vice versa) in India; the starvation of Armenians by pious Moslems in Turkey; the slaughter of Midianites, Amalekites, and Philistines by pious Hebrews, from Genesis to Judges; the slaughter of Jews by pious Christians throughout two thousand years of West-ern "civilization." Religion stalks across the wastes of human history, knee-deep in the blood of innocents, clasping its red hands in hymns of praise to an ap-proving God.

And now the new religion of Nazism, with a follow-ing as rabid and brutal as the most fanatical Moslems or Christians who ever lived, is flaming across Europe, leaving in its wake charred corpses and rub-ble. We have known for years what these thugs are capable of. We have stood by and watched as they persecuted their own countrymen: sealing them in ghettos, stealing their livelihoods, destroying their shops, burning their homes, and arresting them with-out charge—whereupon the victims disappear into prisons of a barbarity we can only imagine.

But who are these people, these victims? Why, of course, they are Jews. They are *only Jews.* And where has organized religion been hiding all this time? Where is the outpouring of righteous indigna-tion over the harming of one hair on the head of a child? Where is that oracular voice from the depths of the Holy See in Rome? It speaks not. At the breaking of families, it is mute. At the destruction of synagogues, it finds no voice. At the disappearance of thousands, and tens of thousands, and hundreds of thousands of human faces, it is silent.

Why? Because the victims are *only Jews*. Persecuted for centuries by that same "eternal church," why should anyone expect the Vicar of Christ to risk anything now, for the sake of mere Jews? If you prick a Jew, will he bleed? The answer is, Who cares?

And so last week our Aryan hero aviator stood up with his Iron Cross in the Fort Wayne "Gospel Temple" and addressed the overwhelming moral challenge of our time: what should be done about Hitler, about jailings and beatings and torture and mass murder?

The hero's answer was, Pass by on the other side.

—The Minotaur

IT WASN'T EASY, but on Friday night, the Kenton Comets, undefeated since the Fox Lake game, knocked off Huntington in overtime, 53–52. Unc Ehrhard, belching profoundly, managed to hold himself together through one more threat of apoplexy; Gopher Starr broke up a last-minute Huntington stall without fouling; and Jim had been set up for his favorite outside shot in the last ten seconds: *swish*.

Winning again felt good, and the team showered with bravado, towel-snapping, cussing, and horsing around. Nobody said it aloud, but everyone knew they were building for the Thanksgiving tournament and a return match with the giants from Fox Lake.

Paul hadn't scored his twenty points for Ruthie, but Jim had, touching his rabbit's foot each time, a little caress. So where did that leave Paul, who was heading for the after-game dance?

Out in the cold, Pug. Way to go, Ace.

The Melodaires were working hard when Jerry's Ford swung up to a gravelly skidding halt at the country club door, disgorging the young victors, locker-room fresh in their yellow cord pants and crimson sweaters with the big yellow K's. Jim had borrowed the family car for his date, so he was already there, dancing with Ruthie, jitterbugging to "In the Mood," a reasonably faithful reproduction of the Glenn Miller original. Paul watched them with a sinking feeling: the way they moved together, knowing from experience how to maneuver through a tight squeeze of bouncing bodies and find a little space where they could execute some fancy dip or turn. Ruthie's sexy legs made even these frenetic movements look graceful, and her long blond hair swung in slow motion on the spins.

Watching that perfect combination in the dusk of blue lights and the flash of revolving mirrors, Paul fell victim to his customary lust and despair, and felt like a traitor and a sneak thief. Why was he doing this? She was Jim's girl, his brother's girl. But guilt or no guilt, he was determined to dance with her again. He was going to feel again the intoxicating warmth of Ruthie Peters' body.

And he did. When "In the Mood" finally ended, Jim left Ruthie at their table and headed for the rest room, and just then, miraculously, the Melodaires' clarinets began the slow whine into "Stardust." Paul pushed through the crowd of slow-dancers and edged up to the table.

She saw him coming: "What *is* that funny tune they're playing?"

"I've heard it somewhere."

She took his hand, looked around warily, and gradually, as they moved onto the floor, let her body fit into his.

"Even if you didn't get your twenty points tonight."

"Well, we didn't really need that many, and I didn't want to show up my elderly brother—over the hill already."

"He's my age, kid."

"I like older women. Can't you tell?"

"No—you didn't even wear my green sleeve tonight."

"I wasn't wearing my helmet."

And then they didn't talk anymore, just moved slowly together, and Paul got excited again, and Ruthie ignored it again, and they moved with a rhythm like sex, until a muted trumpet pronounced the end of the song. Ruthie didn't go on dancing this time, but stopped and backed away.

Paul ached with the sudden loss. "Next dance?"

She looked away. "Not this time, Paul. Jim will be back by now."

"He'll survive for five minutes. Or ten. Or twenty."

She smiled, but nervously. "We . . . I have to be—careful, now."

"Be careful with him. Be reckless with me."

She smiled again, then blinked and brushed a hand across her eyes, and walked back to the table. Paul followed, mystified.

Jim was sitting there, watching, a tight grin on his face. "Can't turn my back a minute, someone runs off with my girl."

You're my brother. Someday you'll do me a favor . . .

Paul wiped his brow dramatically. "It's a jungle out there."

Ruthie made gorilla sounds, and Paul laughed.

Jim kept on grinning that taut little grin, and pushed a Coke across to her. "All's well that ends well . . ."

He had made that sound like a question, Paul realized, slipping off to the company of wallflowers, but harboring a naughty little bubble of happiness.

❧

D R. ROBERTS, satisfied, nevertheless flopped restlessly in Elaine's tousled sheets. Abruptly, she sat up.

"All right, Tom, what is it?"

"What is what?" All innocence.

"You know."

He didn't look at her. "I was just wondering—are any of your old friends still in town?"

Her eyes widened, then narrowed. "Friends?"

"From high school."

"Not really. We moved to Kenton halfway through my senior year—you can imagine how happy I was. So even by the time we graduated, I was still 'the new girl.' Why'd you ask?"

"I just wondered."

"Tom, you're sidestepping. Ever since you came in to-night, you've been wanting to tell me something."

"What makes you think that?"

"The way you hold your hands, making fists. The way you just made love—abstracted, a hundred miles away. I feel like I've been had by a robot."

"I'm sorry."

"I'm not blaming you. I'm not even complaining, really. I'd just like to know what's bothering you."

"Well—it's complicated."

"I have plenty of time." She turned on the bedside lamp and lay on her side, facing him, a cool, patient look.

"OK. It's the Board. We met this afternoon. As usual."

"Yes?" The same composed look, but Dr. Roberts noticed a shadow in her eyes, something he had seen before.

"Well, to make a long story short, there's some trouble."

"That's *too* short." She waited.

He felt his hands, under the sheet, making fists again. He forced them to stop. "It began with Dobbins."

"The Pentecostal minister?"

"He has a son in your class."

"Emmert."

"Fat Emmert, yeah. Well, his father, Fat Emmert, Senior, the Very Reverend Dobbins, wrote me a hot letter, insisting that the Board prohibit all teaching of evolution. He also demanded your resignation."

"And?"

"We ignored it. Or I guess I should say I ignored it. Just quietly kept it off the agenda. Finally Dobbins phoned me and yelled for a while. I just told him that you were the biology expert, not me. If he wanted a pill for his nerves, I said I could help him."

"You didn't."

"From the tone of the Reverend's voice, he wasn't pleased. He's a natural heroic tenor, did you know? Anyway, after that he apparently went under my head, so to speak. To Hedges."

"If you can't get the Board to do your dirty work, try the school principal, is that it?"

"That's it. So it took the matter out of my hands for a few days. But Hedges didn't know quite how to proceed, or even whether to proceed. It's unusual. No precedents. Apparently nobody's ever so much as mentioned Darwin before in any school in Royal County."

"They mention him in the Sunday schools, I'm told."

"In the same breath as the devil, sure. They say *you* talk about him as though he practically invented biology."

"Which is accurate enough."

"Well, your principal formally requested that the Board advise him. So I had to bring it up at this meeting."

"And?"

"A lot of talk. They're such clowns, most of them. But they think they know their Bible, and they do know how they *feel.*"

"Yes?"

"I finally told them what *I* thought, too—that you're the biology teacher, you have excellent credentials, and you're undoubtedly teaching good biology. That if they started poking around in subject matter, we'd end up arguing about Euclid's shortcomings as a mathematician or Shelley as an atheist or Ben Franklin as a philanderer. And you know what?"

"What?"

"When I put it that way, some of them looked as if they wanted to do it."

She laughed, but nervously.

"These 'Labyrinth' articles haven't helped any. Your father's zinged into a hornet's nest—the way he goes on about Darwin and biology in the same breath with atheism and sacrilege—well, it makes it all very sticky."

"Tell the truth, no matter how much it hurts. That's my dad."

"This time it may hurt his daughter. Sometimes people with high principles leave a lot of wreckage around them."

"Don't they, though." She ran her fingers through her hair.

"The rest of us, we play the game, we compromise, we tell people what they want to hear. But people like my father, they stand toe-to-toe with the dragon and slug it out. Of course, they always lose. And when they go down, they take some of us with them. That's just the way it is."

He knew she wasn't finished.

"I love him," she said.

He kissed her. "Well, they finally took a vote, Potter insisted on it. He wanted you reprimanded and dismissed, then and there. Half the Board were for it, Potter and Tucker and Berry. The other three all voted nay. That left me with the tie-breaker, so we stopped it."

"This time."

You'll probably hear from your principal about it anyway, when he gets word of the meeting, and the split vote."

"Oh, I'll hear about it, all right."

"What worries me is the intensity." Dr. Roberts deliberately unclenched a fist. "Fanaticism. You had to be there to appreciate it. I'll hear more about it, too."

She looked at him quickly, and he saw again the shadow across her green eyes. Had he been wrong, back there in the library, thinking it was hunger?

Was it fear?

She slipped an arm under him and hugged him around the waist, hugged him so hard he had to fight for breath. Her warmth along his body, from chest to ankles, inflamed him. They made love again, better this time.

❧

B<small>Y THE TIME</small> basketball practice was over, it was getting dark. Paul slammed his locker and snapped the padlock.

"Going my way, Pug?" Every way was Jerry's way. He was the class jester, and he'd give anyone a ride, just to keep an audience; but Paul had something else on his mind. "Got a few things to do upstairs."

"See you at Mesler's?"

"Maybe." But Paul wasn't in for pinball, not tonight.

Ruthie's part-time job in the principal's office coincided with basketball practice. Paul hadn't known that until yesterday, when Jim happened to mention it. So that's what got Paul out of the showers first, out of the locker room first, and upstairs two at a time: he didn't want to miss her. Jim had a bad cold and had cut practice; the coast was clear.

It took some acting talent to be there at the right time without making it obvious that he was waiting for her. He checked his desk in study hall, went to the rest room, walked past the principal's office twice, furtively checking through the glass door to make sure she was still there. Finally, from the end of the hall, he saw the light go out. He trotted down the hall, hoping to get there just as she emerged, and did, scaring her.

"Paul!" She gasped, then tried not to show he had startled her. "I didn't recognize you in the dark."

"It's not so dark. Your eyes aren't used to it yet."

"You finished with practice?"

"Just out. Had to get a book from my desk." He hoped it sounded plausible.

"Going home now?"

"Yep." Paul would have taken much less for an invitation. They walked toward the stairs. With a chest full of feelings, his head went blank; he couldn't think of a thing to say. She was walking cautiously in the gloom of the hallway. At the edge of the stairs she paused and her arms went out, one to the railing, the other vaguely in Paul's direction. Without thinking, he took her hand, and instantly he was dizzy with love, literally dizzy. He stopped.

She turned her head, and was smiling. "Did you forget something else?"

So she hadn't been fooled. Paul felt his whole face, his ears, burning bright. "No," he muttered, and dropped her hand.

"Paul," she said softly, as if pitying him, and took his hand again, pulling him forward. As they went downstairs, Paul was giddy again, in a bewilderment of feelings: embarrassment and pride and fear, and guilt at touching his brother's girl—and love, love, love, love, love.

Her hand. Her skin. Paul was constantly thinking about Ruthie Peters' skin. It wasn't like ordinary mortals', it was so lovely that he could hardly bear to keep his hands off it. He ached to reach out and run his fingertips over its surface. Ruthie's arms were slim and dimpled at the elbows, and pink, pink all year, even in the summer when she was suntanned a little—and nobody could have looked at those arms and not wanted them close to him, accidentally rubbing his forearm in biology class, softly around his shoulder at country club dances. Ruthie's arms were almost as seductive as her legs, and a lot more available. Moving slowly down the stairs in the dusky October evening, Paul let his bare arm slide against her bare arm and felt electricity pulsing at every step.

Downstairs, he had no more excuses. He let go, but the feeling stayed with him. Paul and Ruthie, Ruthie and Paul, two walking electrodes, a lesson in physics.

As they walked out the door, a light drizzle was sifting down, and they put on their jackets. "Do you want to wait till it stops?"

She was already down the front steps. "What's the matter? Scared of a little rain?"

The game again, it had to be played; anything to avoid the perils of sincerity. Paul followed her, caught up, took her books. "Galahad," she murmured.

"There are no more knights," he insisted. He knew he was blushing. They walked along, silent for a moment, the gentle rain dampening their faces and clothes.

"Were you high-point man again tonight?"

"One of my off nights. Thirty, forty points, I lost count."

"Thanksgiving tournament, here comes Pug!"

Paul didn't want to talk about basketball. "Are you trying out for 'The Snow Goose'?" The Thespian Club was going to do a dramatization of the popular war story next semester. She would be just right as the girl: pretty, lost, bewildered, tragic.

"Only if you do."

Paul was ecstatic. The two of them at rehearsals together, running lines together, walking home together . . . He whooped. "I'll play the cripple! How's this for a limp?" He hammed it up and she laughed, coming to his aid, propping him on one arm and holding his hand. But that magical skin—did she know what she was doing to him? He could have sworn sparks flew when she touched him, their bare hands in the October drizzle a veritable magneto. They walked like that for a moment, and he breathed with difficulty.

"Ruthie," he said, but his voice broke, so he cleared his

throat and trumpeted like a goose, *oo-hoo, oo-hoo,* and she trumpeted with him, and they decided right then that they'd both try out for the play.

But he didn't let go of her hand. They walked along Oak Street slowly, neither of them in a hurry, as if the only place to be was right where they were. They went a block without talking, but it didn't seem to matter that they weren't talking. Eventually, though, she gently removed her magical skin from his touch, leaving an ache in his hand that circuited through his chest.

At her house, behind the friendly screen of forsythia bushes, they dropped into the big porch swing. It bounced and squealed, then eased into a gentle creaking. Ivory soap and baby powder wafted through the October dusk. Paul took her hand again, but she pulled away and sat up straight in the swing.

"Hard to get?" he grinned.

"I have to tell you, Paul. You'd better not walk me to school anymore. Or come home with me." She kept her eyes on the floor.

He was stunned. After all that euphoria, those eight blocks of pure joy? "But, Ruthie! . . ."

"Please. Just help me."

"Well, sure, that's what I want to do, always . . ."

"We're in trouble, Jim and I. We've got to the point where we don't know what to say to each other anymore."

Jim? Ace? In trouble? "What's the matter?"

"Don't you know?"

"It's too important for guessing."

She paused. "You, Paul. You're the trouble. Jim is—well, he's jealous of you, I guess."

Of Pug Anderson? Paul found this thought so original that he couldn't absorb it.

"And I don't want to cause trouble with you, to come between you. You've always been so close."

Paul nodded. "Like brothers, you might say." He was in a daze, couldn't take it all in. "You mean—just because we danced a couple of times?"

"It's more than that. Jim understands."

Understands? Paul was out of his depth, caught between the joy of some revelation he didn't dare hope for, and the terror of exile, of sudden banishment. "Understands what?"

"You know." She wouldn't look at him.

"No, I don't know. Tell me. Come on, Ruthie, what is this?"

She touched his hand briefly, a twist of the knife. "I'm sure it's for the best, for all three of us. I know it is."

Time stretched out ahead of him: an hour without Ruthie, a day without Ruthie, a week without Ruthie: torture. "I can't. I can't stop seeing you. Wanting to see you."

"For a while, at least. Please. We have to get through this. We're still friends. We'll always be friends."

"We're more than that! Aren't we? Otherwise, what's he so scared of ?"

At last she turned toward him. "Help me, Paul. Help me." The pleading eyes.

There was only one answer to that. "OK . . . All right." He couldn't believe what was happening. "I'll back off, if you say so." He grasped at a straw: "But I'll be around."

She looked grateful, and the slight easing of her shoulders filled him with love and anguish. A wet maple leaf swirled in on the cool breeze and landed in her lap. She picked it up and looked at it in the dim streetlight, its red-gold, its symmetry. "They're starting to fall already."

What could he say? October sixteenth, the most beautiful

day of the year. He felt death in the rustling forsythia bushes, fear in the smell of wet leaves.

"There'll be snow on the Moscow front," he mumbled, and felt like a blockhead. He stared at the streetlight through the drizzle.

He didn't want to see Jim, but he had to go home, he was late for supper. As he opened the front door, his mother's voice keened through the house.

"We can't! We can't *do* this anymore, I can't *stand* it!"

The tone of her voice, the familiar desperation, tore at the ragged edges of his pity, self-pity, the pain of being alive.

"Isn't it bad enough, the phone calls, the collectors at the door? Now I have to be insulted in public, by women and kids?"

So far into despair, what did he have to lose? Paul crept through the house. In the living room, Betsy crouched on the floor by the old radio, Tommy Dorsey's "I'll Never Smile Again" turned up loud, her hands over her ears, eyes squeezed shut.

"From across the tracks, from Sunnyside, she comes with her runny-nosed kid and bangs on the door, and screams at me, they want their money, they want their money, we're cheating them, her husband did the work, fair and square, they've got to have it, her kids are hungry! *Her* kids!"

Jim slipped by, sneezing twice. Forgetting where he'd just been, what had happened, Paul grabbed his shirtsleeve. "What's going on?"

Jim blew his nose. "Groudy, trucker, delivered some stuff, took a check, it bounced, his old lady did some yelling." He climbed the stairs: escape.

Paul hesitated. He was already dead, what did it matter? He went into the dining room. His father had his back to the wall, keeping an eye on Nora's storm, the limping about, her painful hands attacking the air.

"What are we going to *do?* It's been like this for twelve years now—out of this, none of that, cut down, make over. I'm *sick* of it, Charlie—nothing in the cupboard, the kids need warm coats, everything coming due today, tomorrow, the next day—what'll we *do,* what are we going to *do?*"

Charlie played it softly. "I'm making Grand Rapids next Monday, big wholesaler there, hardware, good for a dozen cases, at least, maybe some gallons . . ."

"Next Monday, next week, next month—my God, what good is that? We can't wait to eat till next Monday! Why isn't there ever a *today* in our lives? It's your smelly bug-killer, that's why—that nasty stuff is driving us out of house and home—oil, rent, advertising, trucking, bills, crazy women dunning me on my own front porch, *in front of the neighbors!*"

Paul sat down at the empty table, his stomach in cramps.

"Look at him, Charlie, your son—all three of your children—home for supper and there's no supper, just canned beets and beans again tonight, rickets tomorrow, and it's *your fault!* Why can't you go out and get a steady job at Potter's or McGraw's or the foundry or anywhere there's a paycheck, something coming in, like other people, instead of everything going out that rathole!"

"Mom," Paul said quietly, half afraid to speak up. "I've got something in my dime bank. I'll go to Hollenbeck's, they're open late."

"In your bank? *Look* in your bank! Your father got there first, he knows you deliver the *Post* on Wednesday."

Paul stared at his father. It had happened before, but he couldn't help feeling betrayed.

"If you'll quiet down, Nora—I've got twenty cases made up, plus the gallons, I'll do Ligonier tomorrow, Nappanee, Goshen, maybe . . ."

Nora's gnarled hands grappled with empty air. "Ligonier, Goshen! Good God, you've been at this forever—and year after year it's always the same, they all buy that cheap stuff instead, and in the meantime we need coats and boots, I'm tired of stuffing cardboard in their old shoes! We take care of everything so it lasts, I patch and darn and make over, and it's never, never enough, we can't go *on* like this!"

"Well, the damn depression can't last forever. Unless that idiot in the White House thinks it'll get him elected again."

"*We've* had a depression since 1929, nothing *but* depression! Fred Jensen has been in it just like us, but he kept a job at McGraw's, a steady job, and now Thelma has a home of her own."

"That shack?" Now Charlie was indignant. "You wouldn't live there, not even overnight, you wouldn't even consider it."

"It's *theirs,* it's *something,* the landlord can't kick them out tomorrow for not paying the rent!"

"We're only two months behind, he's not complaining. Much. Anyway, McGraw's isn't so terrific, they've been laying off again. Fred was laid off for almost a year, maybe you forgot that, but I'll bet *he* never will. His kids were eating turnips and dandelions all last summer, and last winter they were burning old packing cases from the McGraw plant in their kitchen stove, to keep from freezing. And he wasn't even 'fired,' he was just 'laid off'! You'd better ask Fred, if you think McGraw's is the answer to your prayers."

"But they've got their own place now, they can fix it up, it'll be nice someday, and anyway it's *theirs.* Look at me, Charlie." Her twisted hands floated in front of her like an angry prayer. "I'm thirty-nine years old, and what have I got? What have I ever had in my whole life but debts and worries and insults?"

Paul pitied her hands, her swollen knees, the faded house-dress.

"It's hard times for everybody, Nora, you know that. I can't just push 'em over anymore, they're misers now in those drugstores, they lock up the order books when they see me coming."

"But tell me, what have I *had?* In all these years, what have I ever got but arthritis? And kids! All I've had is *kids!*"

Paul shriveled in his chair. He should have left the room when he could, like Jim. Way to go, Ace.

Weeping, Nora didn't say anything for a minute, and in the pause, a bouncy voice on Betsy's radio jingled away: living-in-luxury-on-a-pocketful-of-dreams. It was the last straw. *"Betsy! Turn off that trash!"*

The sound stopped abruptly.

"Pocketful of dreams! Idiots! *Idiots!*" Nora limped to the back staircase and started up. Paul could tell from the way her back moved that she was crying. He hurt all over.

Paul and his father sat there for a minute or two; finally Charlie revived. "Affiliated Hardware in Grand Rapids. United Drug in Fort Wayne. Have to get a new investor, expand the lab, bring in some hotshot salesmen, Walt Krim, Sandy Lesser, work up some good radio spots, no reason it can't work, it worked for the others, they're Carnegies and Rockefellers now, they were nothing, once, immigrants. Get the damn dollar behind you, get some push into it, the old one-two."

Paul waited. "But—what *are* we going to do, Dad?"

Charlie looked startled, as if he'd forgotten Paul was there. He bustled. "We're not going to lay down and play dead, I can tell you that. Everybody has slow periods, but we'll lick it, we always have."

He seemed embarrassed. "I'm sorry about your dime bank.

Jed cut off my credit. I needed gas for that trip tomorrow."
He sighed. "When we get this thing going, I'll make it up to
you—to her. I'll make it up to all of you. We'll forget about
all this when we're on easy street, we'll laugh at it."

Charlie turned to go upstairs, but Paul couldn't leave it
there. "Dad . . ."

One foot on the steps, he paused. "Yes?"

Paul didn't even know what he wanted to ask. The whole
world was a big question mark. "Dad, I . . . I just . . ."

Charlie suddenly looked wary. "Has this got anything to
do with—sex?"

Paul was astonished. Grown-ups—they had only one thing
on their minds. "Worse than that. It has to do with life." He
could still hear Nora's sobbing.

"Life?"

"I can't figure it out. Nothing fits. What's it all about?"

Charlie was obviously tired. He sagged a little, then spoke
very slowly. "You don't figure that out, Paul. You work it
out. You take it a step at a time. One thing leads to another.
Eventually things sort of fall into place."

Paul waited, but apparently his father was finished. They
stood there a moment, looking at each other. "That's it?
That's all there is to it?"

"OK, I know what you mean. You want the big picture,
right? All the answers?"

"Well . . ."

"All I can tell you, Paul, is that if you beat your head
against that wall, what you're going to get is a headache. I
know, I know, you're going to do it anyway, nobody believes
his old man."

"But what should I do?"

"I told you. Work. There's always something. For me it's
Ligonier, Nappanee, Goshen, Grand Rapids. For you at the

moment it happens to be English, civics, biology, history, basketball. Well, do it right. Do it all right and you'll come up with something. Something you can depend on."

"But that's so—helter-skelter."

"Yeah, that's just what it is. Haphazard. Wildcat. Pig in a poke."

"So, just—work?"

"Best thing in the world. Step by step, no formulas. Anyone tells you he's got the magic answer, better put a hand on your wallet."

"Work . . ."

"Just keep on, keeping on." Charlie seemed more tired, more discouraged, than Paul had ever seen him. Finally he turned and went upstairs, lifting each foot like a burden, and in a minute Paul could hear his voice in the front bedroom, trying to comfort Nora—and her sobs. She'd feel better in the morning; she always did. But that didn't help Paul now.

"Love," he said aloud. "We never say love."

And then: "Mom."

And finally, after a minute or two: "Dad."

Slowly he became conscious of a familiar smell, and went to the kitchen. On the table were two Mason jars of string beans and red beets, unopened. A kettle of navy beans was cooling on the kerosene stove. He lifted the lid and picked one out with a spoon. Done. He should have been hungry but wasn't. He put the lid back on the pan.

His father's tormented visions of Carnegie and Rockefeller, Ruthie's disastrous scruples, Jim's misery, his mother's pain— Paul felt smothered by it, and all of a sudden he hated the smelly kerosene stove, hated the soggy beans, hated the old wooden icebox, hated the copper tubs where his mother scrubbed at their clothes with bars of Fels Naptha soap, hated the worn paint on the linoleum floors, hated the ancient smell of the whole dilapidated house. He dashed out to the back porch, letting the screen door slam. The breeze chilled his forehead: he hadn't realized he was sweating. A single cricket was saying a long goodbye to summer. He wondered if Ruthie could hear it, too, some lonely cricket outside her bedroom window. The shadows of maple leaves floated down the wind: October sixteenth, the most beautiful, most ominous day of the year. The rain had stopped, and the stars were bright. Paul thought of Sally Crothers, Silly Sally, who claimed she really believed in horoscopes. He gazed at the random scattering, suns to a million other tragic worlds, and tasted the salt of anger stinging his throat.

"If there's anyone up there running this show," he said out loud, "do me a favor, OK, and from now on, just keep out of my life."

<hr>

When Elaine visited her father on Sunday afternoon, as usual, she shook her head at the sight of his driveway, full of shiny new garbage cans. Cleaning up after his vindictive neighbors had become a weighty responsibility. Using her own key, as usual, she let herself in the front door and enjoyed the oven smells in the hallway, the inevitable leg of lamb.

"Papa, I'm here."

"In a minute."

She raised the blinds in the living room and looked at the only picture in the room, an old photograph of her mother, black-and-white, soft-edged in the manner of the twenties.

Younger than I am now, Elaine thought, and suffered the familiar pang of bereavement. The photo occupied a whole bookshelf all by itself, a conspicuous consumption of space, while all around it were crammed in hundreds of volumes of history, philosophy, and politics.

Saul greeted her as always with a bear hug, quietly, though silence was not his natural gift. His wiry beard roughed up her cheek.

"You look more and more like her," he said. The three years since her death had not reconciled him.

"Not as pretty."

"No modesty in this house, young lady. It buys no hotels on Indiana Avenue."

"Are we really going to play that awful game again?"

"We have to learn the spirit of this great country, don't we? Buy. Sell. Profit. Build. Destroy."

"I was born here. Monopoly comes naturally. But you, an immigrant . . . All these weird books—Jefferson, Madison, Tom Paine—what kind of good American reads that stuff ?"

She used to love it when he laughed, but now he guarded everything; his low chortle yielded as little as possible to good spirits.

"Just look at your library—you're surrounded by deists, agnostics, atheists—where's your Jewish heritage, your Law, your Prophets, your Talmud? Whatever became of your yarmulke?"

"Don't ask. Saving the Jews from Hitler is hard enough. Saving the world from God is a labor of Hercules."

She had taken the wrong tack; he was sardonic again. If there was a right tack, consistently right, she hadn't found it since her mother died.

"Anything especially shocking in the next *Rationalist*, Papa?"

He did his Papa-trick, staring at her with one eye wide

open, the other closed. She giggled, obligatory since childhood.

"Do you mean another 'Labyrinth'? No, I'm afraid I must
disappoint my hordes of faithful readers this time. Pressing
matters—Japanese government resigned, Moscow evacuated,
six million Russians dead, it staggers the mind. Six *million*
dead! How can your brain cope with that, your feelings?" He
slumped in his chair.

She put an arm over his shoulders for a moment. "Getting
gloomy in here." By midafternoon in late October the sun
was already low. She turned on lamps. Weekends were always bad. As the week went on, building to the pressure of
the Friday deadline, Edelman gradually became energized,
animated, a semblance of his old firebrand self. But after the
Rationalist was off the basement press, carried upstairs, and
carted to the post office, a gray depression always settled over
the little house. That was why Elaine always visited on Sundays.

"Why don't you listen to the football games? I.U., Purdue,
Notre Dame—that'd teach you to be a good American a lot
quicker than Tom Paine. Get tears in your eyes for the Old
Oaken Bucket."

He did his grudging laugh again, then settled back, pen-
sive. This was even harder than usual, and Elaine knew why:
the anniversary of her mother's death was getting close: December 6. She remembered the quick hilarity of the old days,
Mama and Papa always interrupting each other, compulsive
raconteurs, their boisterous shouts. She turned on another
lamp. "So, would you like to try your luck, or should I fix
the vegetables right away?"

It roused him. "Isn't it reassuring, how we go on appreciat-
ing food?"

"Come into the kitchen, we can talk there."

"And maybe I can find a bottle of good wine somewhere."

He liked to tease her with this make-believe uncertainty. In fact, he was very old-world and meticulous with his wines, good Bordeaux, the occasional Burgundy: "proletarian discernment," he used to say with his exaggerated wink. She watched him enjoy choosing a bottle, enjoy using the corkscrew, enjoy breathing it in and tasting.

"It's OK?"

"We won't send it back." Enjoying is one thing, admitting is another.

She looked at the label and held her ruby goblet to the light. "Wasn't this Mama's favorite?"

He sighed.

They touched glasses and sipped, and sat down at the kitchen table. She stared at the old linoleum, with its paths from sink to cupboard to stove, worn by years of her mother's cheerful bustling. She decided to risk a little. "Papa—do you think we've talked about it enough? About Mama?"

"What's the use? She's gone. Three years she's gone."

"But we're still here. And we have to keep on. Religious people . . ." She wasn't sure what she was trying to say.

"They're consoled?"

"They say they are."

"But you've been to their funerals. They weep, they moan. Some take to sackcloth and ashes, some throw dirt on their heads. That's comfort?"

"Well, it's organized. Maybe that's a comfort."

"Exactly." That humorless laugh again. "The organization is comforted."

"But if they think they'll meet again? In another life?"

"Do they believe that?"

"They say they do."

"Yes, they say they do. But still they weep. Their mouths believe it, their minds don't."

"Are you sure?"

"Are they sure?"

"They say they are."

"The priests and preachers say they are. But the people weep."

"Well, so do we."

"Of course. We've had a terrible loss, and we know it's forever. We're not fooling ourselves."

Forever: Elaine felt a familiar flip in her chest, her heart making a small protest against that terrible word.

"Still," she persisted, "if it's all they've got . . . I mean, even if they're mistaken, maybe it makes them feel better. So is it right for your Minotaur to undermine their happiness? Isn't that cruel?"

She realized: maybe she was undermining him.

"But *do* they feel better?" Saul's fingers rubbed his goblet like a gypsy with a crystal ball. Under the kitchen light, the Burgundy reflected on his cheeks, and he was young again. "Have you ever noticed how the preachers declare their happiness, that tone of voice, that professional sincerity, like radio commercials?"

"But that's just enthusiasm, they think it's a virtue. A sign."

He looked at her directly, something he rarely did, a long, silent look, and, gazing back at him, she understood how her mother had fallen in love.

"Not just enthusiasm, Elaine, something a little more than that. Sometimes a lot more. It's desperation—ordinary, everyday desperation."

She thought it over. "But what about their consolation, the hope of meeting their departed families, their loved ones . . ."

"Child," he interrupted, and she felt like a little girl. "You're toying with me, just like your mother."

A strong sense of *déjà vu* told her they had had this conversation before. "I just wonder if we've talked about it enough. Have we dug deep enough? Overlooked anything . . ."

As if impatient, he interrupted. "I've never told you about George Bridges, have I?" She shook her head, but he was already talking. "We worked together in New York, years ago, at the library, in the reference department. He was a Christian, but not pushy, so we got along fine, helped each other on the tough requests, on nice days ate our paper bag lunches together on the steps outside. I got to know him very well, and we ended up telling each other our secrets, our hopes. If you could draw up a recipe for friendship, we had all the ingredients. And what I know about George is that he was a genuinely good man."

He sipped. She waited for the point.

"One day at work he was obviously depressed. Over our sandwiches, I asked him about it. It turned out that he had had a physical, and the doctors were afraid he had cancer. Testicular. Extremely dangerous, often fatal. The biopsy wouldn't be ready for two days, but he was already scared to death."

He sipped again, and cleared his throat. Elaine pitied him the pain of this remembering.

"Well, it was fatal. And it didn't take long. I was with him a lot at the end, and it was not pretty. But the worst part was in his head. He was terrified, absolutely convinced—this mister nice guy, practically a saint compared to the rest of us—he was sure he was going to hell. 'The Lord won't forgive me,' he'd say, 'I've done wicked things, and the Lord won't let me rest.' He'd say that over and over. It was the last thing I ever heard him say."

His voice didn't actually break, but it faltered, and he cleared his throat and waited a moment.

"You talk about cruelty? Think about it—the Minotaur,

even the original Minotaur, was never as cruel as this Lord who promises the ultimate happiness but who gives us in this life only desperation, and, at the moment of death, stark terror. As far as comfort and consolation are concerned, poor George would have been better off if he'd never heard the name of the Lord."

Elaine reached out and covered his cold hand with hers. Moments ticked by, the grandfather clock in the dining room distinct and inexorable.

She was tired of this, physically tired out, but she had to say something, he seemed to be waiting for it. "Well, then," she murmured, her voice almost a whisper, "for us, maybe, for us the survivors? Funerals, masses for the dead, yahrzeit candles, the Kaddish—ways of remembering, of keeping alive . . ."

"Toys. All toys. The only real afterlife for a dead person is here, in your family, your friends, *here, here* "—he slapped his chest, then his head. "When that dies out, life is gone, finally gone, gone forever. Your family, your good friends, your children, maybe their children—beyond that it's all paper piety, nothing else. Nobody else cares. County records, entries in a genealogy somewhere—but nobody really cares."

He was staring into his goblet, his voice droning on steadily, sadly, as if by rote. "All we can count on is what we've built, what we've endured, what we've made with our hands, our sharing of feelings, ideas."

He went to the window and stared out into the dusk. "Marriage—you live with a person all your life, you make gestures, adjustments, sacrifices, and for years those little movements bring you closer together, until finally you can't tell where your own thoughts end and hers begin. You don't become *like* her, you become *her*—a hangnail on her finger gives you pain. And then, one day, when you're suddenly alone, alone forever—well, it's a terrible loss, yes, but you have a privilege, too, the privilege of giving her a little immortality, because she's still alive in your chest, in your head. And you keep her alive in this little enclave of the body that's more real, more honest than a marble monument."

Alone forever: her heart did its little skip again. She was as skeptical as Saul, and yet somehow she didn't want all of those people, with their prayers and their preachers and rabbis, to be just a cosmic mockery—not with all that obvious good will, their institutionalized good intentions.

But what else could she think, after all? He was right, as usual. They had settled for too little in their churches and synagogues—because, Saul would say, they were not serious people. Solemn, yes; serious, no.

Coming out of his own reverie, her father smiled at her. "And someday, when I'm gone, maybe family and friends will give me a little immortality, too?"

The flip in her chest continued. Again. Once more. It scared her.

"Of course, Papa. For a long, long time." She got up and kissed him on the nose and took ten deep breaths before putting on her mother's apron.

❧

THE DAY PAUL was exiled from Ruthie Peters' life, Radio Moscow had cried havoc: "Comrades, the enemy is at the gates! The hour for the supreme sacrifice has arrived! The people of Moscow must fight to the last breath!"

Banished from heaven, Paul recognized apocalypse. Or thought he did. And yet a week had passed, and then ten days, and nothing in the outside world yet mirrored the wreckage of his own life. The black arrows of Rommel's tanks and Von Runstedt's panzers had not stabbed any farther across the front page of the *Daily Herald;* Moscow and Leningrad were still locked in siege, the Nazi cannon mired down; diplomatic talks with the Japanese were stalled in Washington; and Kenton itself seemed suspended in the amber sun of late October. The maples were losing their crimson glory, elms and oaks going dead brown. Paul practiced his foul-shooting, endlessly ran the gymnasium bleachers, top to bottom and back, checked out his growing family of Drosophila every day, read Jane Austen for Miss Eva without skipping a paragraph, and kept his distance from Ruthie, in an anguish unlike anything he had ever known.

Thursday nights at choir practice he sang the ringing tenor of "Soldiers of the Cross" and the Fred Waring arrangement of "Onward, Christian Soldiers," and watched the arching eyebrows of the Reverend Tucker and the pale blue eyes of Miss Huron sending their guarded signals to the organ mirror. Once he followed Tucker to Miss Huron's house again, just to be sure he hadn't been mistaken that other time. But no, it was the same as before, and he decided never to follow him again. The pain of his own exile had made him sympathetic to the erring pastor.

On Sundays, though, no one in the congregation would have dreamed of patronizing Reverend Tucker. Tall in the pulpit, his earnest baritone rich with passion, he was a warrior for Christ, with no chinks in his armor.

"For His name shall be called Wonderful," the sonorous voice rang out, "Counselor, the Mighty God, the Everlasting Father, the Prince of Peace, Isaiah Nine. We are children in His sight, beloved but fallen, sinners in the wrath of the Almighty."

Paul watched the pastor's gaze wander off toward Miss

Huron, rest there a moment, and then, with a sort of wrench, move on, sweeping over the rows of oak benches, past old Mr. Eichhorn, who always snored, to the center section, where his wife was nodding at him, a dark-haired, dark-eyed, watchful presence.

"Only in faith can we find again what we have lost, the greatest gift in the starry universe, God's love."

The preacher's eyes slid back again, briefly, to Miss Huron, who sat quietly, looking at his impassioned face with a trace of a smile—"suggestive," Paul thought, and he felt a little thrill. Just before Sunday school, Ben Stiles, a notorious gossip, had whispered to him that Miss Edelman was carrying on with Dr. Roberts. Paul told him he was crazy, but the news excited him.

"But we will not, cannot have faith in our time if faith itself becomes the victim of Satan. We now find our most sacred beliefs the object of derision. A perfidious people who once betrayed our Lord betray him once again, here in our little town.

"Even in our high school, our temple of truth, those people have mouthed the contemptible lie that men are but dirty animals, sharing the slime of primordial ooze with slugs and maggots.

"We will not tolerate forever the flouting of our principles, insidious attacks on the sanctity of our homes, our faith, and our Lord. We must bring now to our daily lives the flaming sword of truth, we must flog the unbelievers with the scourge of our convictions, we must meet this foe on his own bloody battleground, and we must not pause in our crusade until we sink our heels in the necks of the infidels!"

He stopped and wiped his glistening face with a large white handkerchief, and at that signal Miss Huron struck a chord, and the choir erupted in full force: "Up from the grave He arose, with a mighty victory o'er his foes . . ."

Letting his tenor ring out over the muddy chant of the basses, Paul exulted in a welling of adrenaline: battle, victory—how satisfying it is to be righteous, and to have an enemy!

Walking home after church, he thought of his Drosophila, copulating repeatedly, and he realized: yes, of course, he himself was the enemy.

꙳

T HANKS TO Miss Edelman's class, Paul became more and more drawn to the sound of the President's voice, that hypnotic instrument that sizzled on the little Zenith, and now he stayed on the lookout for the speeches, the fireside chats. Sometimes Betsy would sit on the living room rug with him, uninvited, and repeat scandalous Republican jokes. But he preferred to be alone, listening with quiet agitation as the challenges poured forth. On Navy Day, October 27, he lay on the floor and closed his eyes as the militant phrases flowed and eddied.

"America has been attacked. Our ships have been sunk and our sailors have been killed. Our determination not to take it lying down has been expressed in the orders to the American Navy to shoot on sight. Those orders stand."

Paul felt a rush of outrage in his legs and neck.

"Our American merchant ships must be armed to defend themselves against the rattlesnakes of the sea . . ."

The sonorous voice continued, but not for long. FDR may have been a winner in three successive elections, but he didn't stand a chance in the Anderson house when Charlie was around. Paul heard his father clumping down the back stairs and stomping through the dining room. "Garbage!" he snorted, and snapped off the radio. "Don't they give you kids any homework anymore, you got nothing better to do than listen to that junk?" To emphasize his displeasure, he yanked the plug out of the wall before stalking off again.

Paul sighed and turned on the lamp over the library table. History, English, biology: he was dutiful but bored, and later, when everyone but Nora was getting ready for bed, he went for his nightly walk.

He was sure the sidewalks would miss him someday: the buckled concrete in front of the Staley place, where a huge maple root had subverted civilization; the smooth new stretch at Wiley's Dairy, where kids would come from six blocks away to get that lovely caress under their roller skates; the old red brick block near the New York Central tracks, anathema to skaters but friendly under the soles of sneakers; the gravel section by the widow Patten's, where big snowball bushes forced detours and the birds sang all night in summer.

No birds sang after dark this late in October. A prowling cat tiptoed through the crackling sycamore leaves; a breeze in the barren limbs hushed the darkness. He knew his own neighborhood by the feel of its contours; but he didn't stop there. He went down to the lake where he'd been the substitute summer lifeguard. It was chilly now and bleak, the old pier thunking with hostile waves, the diving board and benches gone, trash cans overflowing: desolation. He walked the length of East Mitchell Street, past the McGraw mansion and past the houses of people he knew: Mr. Collins, editor of the *Daily Herald*; Reverend Tucker; Mr. Hedges, the principal of K.H.S.; Old Saul Edelman. Prim in the moonlight, the respectable front porches made him feel like an outsider in his own town.

A year ago, six weeks ago, he would have gone aimlessly wherever his feet wanted to take him. But ever since he and Ruthie danced to the immortal "Stardust," he always knew where he would end up, drawn to the spot by some infallible homing device in his heart: the dark patch of sidewalk across the street from Ruthie's forbidden house.

He stood there in the crisp autumn night, as he did most nights, in the lingering smell of someone's wood fire, and meditated on forsythia bushes, the big front porch, the squeaky porch swing, the screen door, the entry hall, the piano in the living room, the broad oak stairs and balustrade; and then upon those mysteries beyond his knowledge: the upstairs hall, the neat bathroom and its big white tub, the closed door of her parents' bedroom—and, after a moment of self-denial that amounted to reverence—*her* bedroom.

The knob made a little click when he closed the door behind him. She turned over, sleepily.

"Paul." Only a statement, she wouldn't be surprised; he'd imagined this too often.

"I could hear my name. I kept hearing my name. Everywhere."

"I was saying it in my sleep."

"I had to come."

"You shouldn't have."

"I couldn't help it."

"I'm Jim's girl."

"I know."

"I've always been Jim's girl."

"Yes."

The room was warm. The white sheet was folded down to her waist. Wearing a white nightgown, she was shimmering, like moonlight.

"You have to go now."

"I can't stay away."

"You have to stay away."

"I've tried. No matter where I go, I'm always here. With you."

It seemed perfectly natural that he wasn't wearing anything. He knelt by her bed and pulled back the sheet. Her feet were small shadows, below the nightgown. He kissed them.

"Be good, Paul."

"Yes."

He could see the dim curve of her breasts as he slid into bed. Her warmth caressed him all along his body, the silky gown, silky skin . . .

He sneezed in the chilly air, and looked both ways down the street. Nobody in sight.

There was no way Paul could know what would happen next in that warm bed. There were no books, no magazines, no movies to explain the great mystery. He knew, though, what it must *not* be like. It could not be like Chuck Green's dirty stories, or like the pornographic comic books, or like the drawings in lavatories. He knew it would not be ugly, or hostile, or mean, or disappointing, or guilty. It would somehow be better than all the things he had ever liked, better than songs and sunrise and swimming in summer, better than roses and rain on the roof. It would come to the two of them like a gift, and they would share it forever, and it would be better every night, and every year, and the mystery would come to live inside them, and they would keep it theirs and only theirs, and whenever hard times came, it would mean to them that nobody would ever be as strong and as whole as they were.

Paul sneezed again. He never wore a watch when he walked at night; he didn't want time to make a difference. Still, he knew moonrise and moonset, and he knew that everybody but his mother would be asleep, and even she would be thinking of going to bed.

As he trudged home, he pondered Ruthie's silky skin, and his mother's gnarled fingers. Everything that really matters, he thought, is a mystery: beyond me.

❧

O N WEDNESDAYS, Paul was excused from his last study hall to mind his little job, hiking his bagful of *Saturday Evening Post*s to dozens of front porches before he had to be back at school for basketball practice. Ordinarily he performed this task as if it were only a minor inconvenience, jogging through his entire route, a warm-up before the scrimmage. Since his banishment from Ruthie, though, everything seemed hard: pop quizzes were a wrench to the spirit, shooting fouls was like breaking boulders. By the time he finished his magazine route, he was almost too tired and too late to suit up for practice, and then Unc Ehrhard's bellowing at him was another burden to bear.

Paul dragged himself around town with his shoulder bag drooping, and on Wednesday, October 29, found himself walking, for perhaps the thousandth time in his life, past the employment office at McGraw's, the World's Largest Manufacturer of Windmills and Pumps. This time he had company. Everyone knew that McGraw's had advertised some jobs, without saying how many were available, but Jerry's dad had carelessly let it slip at home that there were no more than three jobs open in the whole plant, and Jerry repeated it in the locker room. So Paul was surprised to see a long queue of men at the factory gate, a line stretching down the street for nearly three blocks. How many were there? Two hundred? He didn't want to count; he was already too depressed. He remembered that his father had once said, sardonically: the best guarantee of high productivity is a long line of men waiting at the gate.

He picked up his pace a little, too upset to face them, lined up across the street for a hoax, for a mirage; but in Kenton nothing passes unnoticed. Half the men in line knew him personally, and most of the others had probably seen him play basketball for K.H.S. If he were a star like Jim, that might make him a minor hero to them, but as it was, well . . .

Still, they kept calling his name and waving so cheerfully that he felt ashamed, and he waved back. Tom Tillinghast, laid off at the foundry last year. Bill Emory, who sang in the church choir with Paul. Old man Moss, whose farm had been foreclosed almost two years ago and who hadn't found work since. Tim Elder, who had been in the WPA, on and off, as long as Paul could remember. Herb Wilks, just back from a hitch in the CCC, planting trees in Oklahoma, and now thinking seriously of joining the Navy. Don Miller, graduated salutatorian from K.H.S. three years ago, still living at home, never could find a steady job . . .

Those faces that he knew, he accepted as they were, the accustomed anxiety, the conventional bravado, visors of their woolen caps tipped at a defiant angle. In the firing squad of the great depression, they had always waved off the blindfold. It was those he didn't know that hurt him the most: the worry lines in the cheeks, foreheads wrinkled by a decade of hungry families, desperate wives, barefoot children, sick parents—the need, the aspiration, the grim denials. At the barbershop he would hear them talking. "You're nobody if you ain't got a job," they'd say. "You're just dirt."

Paul kept walking faster and faster, and he was enormously relieved when he was finally past them. Why did people just accept these things? If they hadn't yet burned down the factory in their accumulated frustration, why hadn't they at least turned on each other? Where were the claws and fangs of these hungry animals?

"Cooperation," Miss Edelman would say, "mutual support among creatures of the same species—these are as much a part of nature as the savage 'war' we're always talking about."

Yes, but was that all? After a dozen years of disaster, of jobs lost, of homes and farms foreclosed, of county poor-relief so stingy it bred rickets and slow-witted children, wasn't there some other explanation? Those docile men at the gate, their respectable wives at the church potlucks—was there some other good reason, or even some bad reason, that kept them waiting in line at the McGraw employment office, kept them in debt to the McGraw hospital, breathing air that smelled of McGraw, drinking tap water that tasted of McGraw . . .

Descended from foraging ancestors, daring and independent, what had brought these two-legged creatures down to this humiliation?

God Is The Answer, said a signboard in front of the Pentecostal Church.

"God is an easy answer," the Minotaur had mocked.

Anyway, there they were, all those men at the gate, loyal, obedient, reverent. Maybe God was the answer, their answer, the Gospel of Kenton being the gospel of good neighbors, of homey friendliness, wholesomeness, cheerfulness, the gospel of the common man, the aproned wife, no pretensions—and therefore the gospel of boosting, not knocking; of accepting, not objecting; of taking bad luck without complaining, of accepting whatever is given: God's Will.

Maybe that was it. Paul stopped walking for a moment and looked at the darkening sky. Alone at the western edge of Kenton, Indiana, Venus shone down at him the orderly promise of the heavens.

If that was it, then the Minotaur was right, after all; God was a convenience. But how much more, besides: throughout this long agony of the depression, God had been the strong right arm of Mr. McGraw.

❧

THE KENTON DAILY HERALD

New York, Oct. 30, 1941
Declaring that "there is no danger to this nation from without" but that "our only danger lies from within," Charles A. Lindbergh charged last night that the American people were being led into war by subterfuge.

Lindbergh addressed a gathering of 20,000 in Madison Square Garden under the auspices of the America First Committee.

"Those who said Germany was bluffing were mistaken. The idealists who shouted so glibly that war must be declared on Germany in order to preserve European civilization, sent thousands of the finest men of France and England to defeat and death . . .

"President Roosevelt and his administration preach about preserving democracy and freedom abroad, while they practice dictatorship and subterfuge at home . . .

"As Americans, we never have, and as Americans we never will, fear any foreign enemy. There is no danger to this nation from without. Our only danger lies from within.

"I appeal to all Americans . . ."

CHARLIE THUMPED the newspaper on the supper table, sloshing coffee into his saucer. "Did you read Lindbergh's speech, Nora?"

"Been washing and ironing all afternoon. I'll get to it later."

Paul knew when: after midnight, with the music turned low on the radio, the freakish airwaves bringing in Atlanta and New Orleans.

"Bonehead warmonger in the White House! Dictator running the country, telling us what we're supposed to think—it's a disease, it's catching—so now we've got the Klan raising its slimy head again, right here in Royal County, and our own reverend moron, Tucker, telling us what we've got to believe."

"Charlie . . ." This was dangerous talk, with the children at the table.

"Who cares what Tucker happens to think about Edelman? Doesn't Old Saul have a right to speak up, even if he is a Jew? Isn't it his own newspaper?"

Paul looked up, surprised. He'd never heard his father talk like that before.

"Give them an inch, and next thing you know, they'll take away everything, including the secret ballot. Just like Lindy says, it's all one big scheme."

Jim concentrated on his history book as always, perpetual dining-room scholar. Betsy stared, taking it all in.

"Miss Edelman says . . ." Paul began, but had to stop and figure it out.

"Miss Edelman says what?"

"Miss Edelman always says what she thinks, but—well, I'm never sure what she really believes. Underneath, I mean."

"Her job's biology, right?"

"Sure."

"Is she any good?"

"Good? She teaches more in an hour than old Graff taught in a week."

"OK, that's it then. You learn biology from her, math and English from somebody else, pretty soon it adds up, you figure it all out. What more do you want?"

"It's just—nobody ever tells us what it all *means.*"

"That's *your* job. You let somebody else tell you that, and pretty soon you'll have a dictatorship, like Roosevelt wants."

"It's so hard."

"Just don't listen too much to Saint Tucker, or to those fireside chats you're so crazy about. Those guys got one thing in common with the Klan, they all want to push you around." Charlie stood up and paced the room. "Now this hullabaloo about evolution, heck, that's nothing new, we had evolution on my old man's farm, all the time. You wanted short-legged steers, you bred for it and you got it, you wanted show birds with big tails, you bred for that—evolution's nothing but common sense with a fancy name. And now Tucker acts like it's his business—I tell you, he's a nut, and somebody's got to say so. Somebody's got to *do* something about him."

"Charlie, eat your beans."

"The Klan, too, everybody in town knows they're out there again, sewing their damn sheets together. They're no 'invisible empire,' everyone knows who they are. I even went to one of their meetings, once, because they seemed to be speaking up for the little guy, but you know what? When I heard what they said, and saw what kind of redneck trash they really were, I just walked out. We don't need those kind of guys pushing us around."

Nora was shocked. "*You?* Went to one of their *meetings?* You never told me that." Even Jim looked up from his book, wide-eyed.

"Sooner or later," Charlie brooded, "they're going to have to be stopped. Somebody's going to have to stand up to them—the Klan, that idiot Tucker, Roosevelt, all of them."

Paul couldn't believe it. His father? At a Klan meeting?

"Sooner or later. Somebody's got to do it."

Paul felt strange: uneasy, or vaguely unhappy, in some way that he didn't recognize and couldn't put a name to. His father working day and night to be a Success, butting his head against the stone wall of the depression; his mother forever cutting down, making do, helping everyone, setting things straight; Ruthie in the porch swing, nervous and upset, the red maple leaves drifting down, *Help me, Paul.*

The stinging feeling in his eyes. He couldn't believe it, he never cried, none of the Andersons ever cried—so why had his mother, just a couple of weeks ago, wept like someone in the movies, and why did he feel like this now? He ducked his head, shoved his chair back, and ran for the backyard.

It was cold and dark, the neighborhood beginning to twinkle with jack-o'-lanterns. Soon little goblins would be roaming the streets, pelting windows with corn and soaping them with naughty words. Those men at McGraw's gate, Bill Emory, Tim Elder, Don Miller, Herb Wilks—they'd all been kids in funny masks a few years ago, rattling windows and sometimes daring the newest and boldest prank of all, walking right up to the front door and demanding a treat in lieu of a trick—pure blackmail, but sometimes they got handouts.

And now they're all lining up at employment offices, waiting for handouts . . .

Wiping his eyes on his shirtsleeves, he looked up. The big Halloween moon was low and pumpkin-orange, and clouds were drifting across it. He was just beginning to realize how cold he was when his mother came out, wrapped in a shawl and holding his jacket. He put it on quickly and zipped it up.

"What's the matter, Paul?"

"I don't know." That was the wrong thing to say. She'd think he was lying to her, and she hated that. "It's the truth, Mom, I really don't know."

She put a hand on his arm. "There must be a reason."

Was there a reason? He thought again about Bill and Tim and Herb, standing in line, about his father and the new tennis racket, about Betsy's made-over dresses. He didn't dare think any more about Ruthie—but suddenly he felt tears. He turned away, quickly. She caught his hand and gave him her hanky.

He blew his nose. "Everything is so hard, Mom."

"Yes."

"There were a hundred guys at McGraw's employment office the other day. Maybe two hundred. And there aren't any jobs."

"I know. It's been like that."

"It's not fair."

"No."

He remembered her own despair—her tears, her keening, the flail of her crippled hands. "Mom, what keeps people going?"

He could almost see her arthritis striking, the pain of the night air. He wanted to tell her to go inside, but he couldn't; he needed her.

"You won't ever know that, Paul, until you find it out for yourself."

Hadn't *anyone* figured it out, then? Teachers, parents, preachers, all the grown-ups in town, set down here for their little lives, surrounded by hardships and aching with need and desire, loving and hating, condemned to prey on each other—why have they stayed as decent as they are? Tagged for failure like something in Charlie's worst nightmares of Success and Failure, how do they hold up their heads and carry on?

"You can't ever give up, Paul, that's all there is to it. We need each other even more when times are bad."

Need each other? Old Saul Edelman, dumped on by his neighbors; Lindbergh and FDR, titans at each other's throats; Elaine Edelman, trying so hard to teach her indifferent students; Don Miller, three years unemployed . . .

A breeze picked up. Cold. If you've been cold inside through years and years of depression, would you ever feel warm again?

His mother shivered. "You'd better go in, Mom."

"Aren't you coming?"

"Guess I'll walk a while."

"Turn off the lights if you're late. I don't think I'll stay up tonight." She started in, then turned and hugged him. "You feel it more when you've been hurt yourself. But we . . . We all love you, Paul."

As she went inside, he stood there breathless. She'd spoken the embarrassing, magic word. Love. Finally, in wonder and in pain, he permitted himself to think again about Ruthie. Breathing a little thank-you to his mother, he set off to commune once again with the lurking shadows of night.

NOVEMBER

THE *DAILY HERALD* featured Lindy's speech on the front page of its Friday edition, and added a sympathetic editorial which noted that all the radio networks had refused to carry the words of the fallen hero. Tyranny was just around the corner, the *Herald* asserted, and the great aviator's warning of dictatorship came not a moment too soon.

The townspeople had little leisure to develop this theme in its stark clarity, however, because down at Mesler's Drugs, *The Hoosier Rationalist* was on the stands again. After three weeks' silence, "The Labyrinth" once more assaulted their ragged sensibilities. Nothing was too grand for the Minotaur's contempt; nothing so small that it escaped his notice. The cruel logic of the alien beast tormented the citizens: rebuking God, juggling fate and free will, tantalizing readers with "the meaning of life." By now, people had learned to brace themselves for these onslaughts, and were reading them not only with shock but also with dudgeon, with vitriol, with truculence.

That same night, little goblins did indeed slip through the darkness of Halloween, and windows were soaped and rattled, and in unruly neighborhoods outbuildings were overturned, and fires burned late in many jack-o'-lanterns. There was a fire at Old Saul Edelman's house, too, but it was not inside a pumpkin, and the white-sheeted goblins who set it were not small ones. Actually, the fire was not in the house at all, but out on the front lawn, the very lawn where his neighbors had recently taken to depositing their garbage. Edelman did not call the fire department, and neither did his neighbors. So the fire burned brightly for a while, with a smell of hot oil, and finally went out, and by dawn's early light the citizens of Kenton beheld in the Edelman lawn a charred cross, twelve feet high and six feet wide.

There should have been a moral to draw from this unusual event, but on Sunday, November 2, 1941, no local minister of the Gospel was yet prepared to volunteer one, and by the next Sunday, more urgent matters in Moscow, Berlin, and Tokyo had diverted their attention, and by the Sunday after that, the little blaze belonged to history. So the only sermon drawn from the fire was the one implicit in Saul Edelman's own act. From Potter's Hardware he bought four steel fence posts and a roll of turkey wire, and he fenced in the blackened cross like a public monument.

In the Edelman household there were, among other things, the photographs, names, and birthplaces of Edelmans and others, relatives and family friends, who had last been seen bound east from France and Germany in boxcars, off to some dark destiny. One by one, Saul gathered these up. At noon each day, he climbed his little fence and wired a new photo to the blackened trunk of the cross: Max Ullmann from Strasbourg; Michel Edelman from Lyon; Suze Pollak, Bremerhaven; Gerda Singer, Toulon; L. Berman, Hamburg . . .

One evening when the cross had bloomed with about a dozen pictures and nameplates, Edelman, unyielding atheist, brought out a yahrzeit candle and wired it to the base of the cross, and every evening thereafter, weather permitting, brought a fresh candle, lighted it, and let it burn down to nothing. It was too early in the holiday season for front-yard crèches, so Edelman's shrine was the only local attraction: burning candle, burnt cross.

The neighbors were not happy. The cross, originally an admonishment to the devil's apostle, had been appropriated, co-opted—and now stood in the enemy's camp, a reproach to the citizenry, as unrelenting and sardonic as Edelman himself. Consultations were held, strategies discussed, but no clearly legal solution was available. Calls were made to Edelman, some cajoling, some threatening, all anonymous, but that hardened unbeliever was beyond the reach of reason or intimidation. The charred cross was in town to stay.

At last a perfectly natural solution was found: those who brought the cross took it away. On Thanksgiving eve, white-hooded men from a pickup truck swiftly dismantled the fence, uprooted the cross, heaved it into the truck, and roared off, peeling rubber. Old Saul Edelman gave no more sign of witnessing their public humiliation than he had the burning itself.

The next day he found his nameplates and photographs in the frozen grass, trampled.

❦

AMONG THE TEEN-AGE BOYS, there was an active trade in pornographic comic books: Maggie and Jiggs doing unspeakable things; Popeye and Olive Oyl acrobatically engaged; Little Orphan Annie out of her faithful red dress at last and performing with Daddy and Sandy. In those well-thumbed little volumes, nothing at all was sacred. Battered copies traded about rapidly or sold out-right for schoolboy fortunes in hard cash.

But for a brief period in the autumn of 1941, as German tanks massed at Tobruk and the outskirts of Moscow, the dirty comics were superseded, in the affections of many teen-agers, by the passions of the Minotaur. Not to say that myste-rious, leering sex was any less fascinating than before, but it was by no means as original as these newly public sins: irrev-erence, blasphemy, atheism. The shock of "The Labyrinth" was nothing like the cheap thrills of cursing or masturbating; it exuded the tantalizing scent of the Unforgiveable Sin, the denial of the Creator, the Almighty, the King of Kings, the Ancient of Days. Conscientious parents absolutely forbade their children even to look at the infamous paper, thus guar-anteeing it a wide readership. When *The Hoosier Rationalist* was on sale at Mesler's, stacked up enticingly near the pinball machine, teen-agers accounted for a substantial percentage of sales.

So it was natural that Paul would have come early to "The Labyrinth." In one way or another, he got copies of every one of the Minotaur's pronouncements, pondered the stern dia-lectics of the heretic beast, and spent some part of all his days and nights trying to reconcile those harsh doctrines with the comfortable faith learned at his mother's knee. He even raised some of these worrisome issues in Sunday school but soon found that nothing was to be gained by that; his questions were greeted with shock, or ridicule, or an affected indiffer-ence.

The "meaning of life." Beyond sex, beyond worldly am-bition, the meaning of life is supremely seductive to the young. Paul couldn't stop thinking about it, even after he had been told emphatically that the meaning of life is the Good Book, the Gospel of Jesus Christ. But the Minotaur's earnest skepticism led Paul to question the Biblical miracles—first Noah's ark, then Jonah and the whale, then Joshua and the sun, the loaves and fishes, the curing of blindness, the raising of the dead. And yet, if we take away so much, where do we stop, how do we limit our disbelief, and what is left of our childlike faith in the Scriptures— and, at last, in God?

He knew Charlie's answer to all that: just work, and things will fall into place. And he knew Reverend Tucker's answer, too: hold fast in the faith, even when men shall revile you, and persecute you, and say all manner of evil against you, for great is your reward in heaven.

But none of that was enough; it just didn't satisfy him, and finally, having nowhere else to turn, he decided to do the unthinkable. He would discuss it with a schoolteacher. After all, it was Miss Edelman's father who published (and presumably wrote) "The Labyrinth." So, even though she scared him a little, he decided—staying late after lab one Tuesday afternoon—to risk it. She seemed more relaxed than in class, which encouraged him.

"Thanks for helping clean up, Paul." She was putting the last beakers in a cabinet.

"You're welcome." He couldn't think of a way to get started. It was so important.

"About ready to call it a day?" She picked up her coat and purse and a satchel full of books and papers.

"Oh, I have to go to basketball practice now. But it won't matter if I'm a little late, it's just a warm-up at first, free-throw shooting."

She smiled at him sideways. "You mean you're trying to be late?"

There was no fooling her. A conference with Miss Edelman was like a continuous pop-quiz. He felt himself blushing.

"I really would like to talk to you for a minute. Ask you something." He sat down on a lab stool.

She hesitated a minute, then briskly put her things on the counter and sat on the stool next to him, still smiling. "What is it, Paul?"

He didn't know where to begin. "Your father . . ." Her smile disappeared, and she put her hand to her chest. "He writes 'The Labyrinth'?"

She seemed to nod, so he went on. "What I wondered . . . He's always bringing up the meaning of life, you know, and—it just bothers me. I'd like to know what he means by that."

She looked at him, as if sadly. "Maybe it's—well, philosophers have put whole lifetimes in on that one. Maybe it's something that can wait a while. You're still pretty young."

The disappointment suffocated him. "Young? What's that got . . . I mean, age isn't the point, is it?"

She seemed about to say something, then didn't. She took a couple of deep breaths, got up and walked to the blackboard and back, and sat down again.

"What I'm saying is that we, all of us, work these things out for ourselves. And sometimes it takes a while."

He knew, he'd figured on that. Still . . . "That's what I want to do, work it out. But I'm not getting anywhere by myself."

"Have you talked to your parents?"

He nodded. "They give me back the same answers that I'm questioning. It's not much help."

She was shifting on the stool, apparently edgy. "Sometimes you can only figure out your life by seeing where you've been. That means having to live a while—do your best—get from day to day—maybe make some mistakes—try things out. Then see."

He hated her sounding so much like his father, one-step-at-a-time, keep-on-keeping-on. He rebelled. "But that's so aimless. It doesn't lead anywhere."

She leaned closer to him, and he thought he could smell her musky scent. Miss Edelman—Miss Edelman's naked body . . .

"I can say this much, Paul, that one thing we need, all of us, is to be willing to see things honestly for ourselves. That's part of what my father is getting at, I think."

No help, no help. He felt like a fool. She leaned closer and put a hand over his hand: the warmth, the softness, the sweet smell of her body. He realized: she was only six or seven years older than he was. What was she thinking? What was she really thinking? Miss Edelman. Elaine Edelman. Elaine . . . Lancelot . . .

"Elaine," he breathed, hardly knowing he was speaking.

It startled her, and she drew away as if waking up. "We'd better go now, Paul, it's getting late." And added: "I'll think about what you said, and maybe we can talk about it more, later."

She left quickly. He followed her out the door in a daze, then wandered down the hallway to the gym. Having dared to ask for enlightenment, he was more confused than ever. In scrimmage, Walter Stone, a second-string guard, easily held him scoreless.

Walking the silent streets that night, Paul pondered sin, his own abundant sins. Lust: he was driven and haunted by lust, the feel of Miss Edelman's hand, Ruthie's breasts warm against him at the dance, a desire that almost smothered him even as he recalled it. Envy: sometimes it seemed he envied everyone in town, his own life so pale and limp; but mostly he envied Jim, the ideal, the model, the flawless paragon. Covetousness: he did indeed covet his neighbor's house, the McGraw mansion full of worldly satisfactions, and oh God, how he coveted his brother's girl—and there, he'd just taken the Lord's name in vain. Blasphemy: not only had he read every "Labyrinth" he could get his hands on, he'd read them with intense interest, with wonder, even with a guilty touch of delight—and now he had to admit, he was eager for more. Hatred: his viscera churned at every memory of Fox Lake and the smirking Stokes' intentional fouls. Wrath: whenever he thought of the line of shabby men at McGraw's employment office, he seethed again with a frustrated, impotent rage.

Was there any sin he hadn't committed? Well, he hadn't killed anyone yet or made any graven images. And he was not puffed up. If there was one sin he was safe from, one sin he was sure he would never be capable of, it was pride.

That certainty, riding the yellow November moon, did not make him feel any better.

❦

THE THURSDAY QUILTING CLUB met in the basement of the First Church of Christ, lunched on an extensive potluck, and, over fine stitches, talked. And talked. There had been dry seasons in the history of the Thursday Quilters when conversation had suffered from a certain sameness in their daily life, small nourishment to the potluck of news. But on November 6, 1941, the basement air was rich with events and revelations.

"It's this war," Mrs. Potter said. "It's the times. If things were more settled, we wouldn't have all these crazy goings-on, right under our noses. That woman!"

"You're right, Flo." Hulda Mesler always talked with three or four pins in her mouth, sometimes even when the patterns were already tacked and beyond pinning; it gave her remarks a tough, no-nonsense quality. "We've heard too much now about her and Dr. Roberts."

"And poor Edna, working so hard for the church. You'd think the man would have a little . . ."

". . . respect!" Jane and Rosie Hill, the twins, had always lived together, and wore identical dresses and identical flowered hats; and for forty-five years, Rosie had been finishing Jane's sentences. On the rare occasions when Rosie was not with her, Jane left most of her sentences unfinished.

"Well, I may not know much, but love and honor, to have and to hold, means till death do us part, where *I* come from." Abby Shriver was the youngest quilter—she admitted to thirty-eight, but still wore dresses from the Junior Department at Penney's—and she had a tendency to phrase the eternal verities as if she'd just thought them up.

Katie Rathert nodded along with everybody. "I don't know what the world's coming to."

"What can you expect from a schoolteacher who tells children . . ." Jane began.

". . . that they sprang from a monkey!" Rosie added.

"Well, my Carl is looking into that," Mrs. Potter stated. "He's going to see about that." Whenever she spoke, she peered over the tops of her reading glasses and stabbed a needle in the air for emphasis.

"So good of Mr. Potter to give so much of his time to the School Board."

"Too bad the Board members aren't all good Christians like him."

"Oh, I think Dr. Roberts is a Christian . . ." Jane began.

". . . because," Rosie continued, "if he wasn't a Christian, what *would* he be?"

Fine stitches perforated the quilt as six troubled heads pondered the alternatives.

"Well, *she's* no Christian," Hulda finally said through her mouthful of pins, "and God knows her father isn't. Imagine, keeping a black cross in his front yard. The impudence."

"I may not know *much,*" Abby announced, "but I know *blasphemy* when I see it."

"They shouldn't have let her come back here to tell our kids the Good Book is a pack of lies."

"My Carl is looking into that. The Board hires, and the Board can fire. My Carl will settle it."

"I hope he gets it settled . . ."

". . . before more harm is done."

"I may not have been to college, but I know sacrilege when I hear it."

"I wouldn't be a bit surprised," Katie mused, "if *she* was writing those awful things he puts in his nasty little paper."

"They sound like her, all right." Hulda spoke the next word like a curse: "Biology!" Inadvertently she spat out a pin.

"She may be behind a lot of things around here."

"Those articles are so awful, I couldn't even bring myself to read them."

"My Carl reads them. He says they're unconstitutional."

"Well, my goodness, Hulda, how can Bob sell that paper in his store?"

Hulda Mesler took the pins out of her mouth and gave Katie a straight look. "I told him somebody was sure to ask that. But all he'll ever say is, 'Business is business.'" She put the pins back.

"Well, everybody's reading it now, that's the truth."

"I wouldn't dirty my hands with it."

"Mark my words, *she's* behind it. He may be a devil, but he never wrote such awful stuff till *she* came back."

"The truth is the truth, that's what *I* say, and once you twist it out of shape, anything can happen."

Hulda removed the pins again and glanced around the quilting frame. "Can happen to anybody. Even a minister of the Gospel. You know what I mean?"

This was dangerous territory. Quick glances darted from face to face.

"That woman may be a good organist, but she's put him under a spell."

"Something funny going on, all right. He was a saint, but he's been led astray."

Katie came back to her theme. "It's all been happening since that schoolteacher came back. You can't tell me it's all just a coincidence."

"That awful paper . . ."

"Dr. Roberts . . ."

"The Reverend . . ." Jane began; but this time neither she nor Rosie could finish.

A little silence settled over the quilt. Not a needle stirred.

"It's as though they're all . . ."

"Bewitched?" Rosie asked.

"That's it," Katie said.

"The Board of Elders should do something."

"The Ministerial Association."

"We should talk to our husbands."

"I'm certainly going to speak to Bob again about not selling that nasty paper anymore."

"I may not know much, but I know when something funny is going on."

"Bewitched," Katie breathed.

The quilt was nearly finished. Crimson with heroism, white with purity, blue with truth.

I<small>T HAD BEEN</small> a long war already, but only someone else's war, ever since that cool September morning, way back in 1939, when Bobby Newton bicycled around the neighborhoods with the only extra edition the *Daily Herald* had ever produced: <small>HITLER BOMBS WARSAW</small>. Americans had watched it all from the sidelines, those two years of disaster, the fall of France, the bombing of London, the swallowing-up of Europe, Rommel sweeping across Africa, the Japanese pushing through China toward the glory of the Greater Prosperity Sphere.

People weren't entirely without a strategic sense in Kenton. Tracking the black arrows on the newspaper maps, they were capable of imagining Von Runstedt's arrow, edging around the Caucasus, meeting up with Rommel's arrow, piercing the Sahara, and then both of them pushing on eastward to join up with the arrow that was pointing south and west through Asia.

It had been a long and far-off war, and now it seemed to be approaching a critical moment. Moscow was being evacuated, civilians sent somewhere east. The Soviet government had slipped away to a secret hideout, probably in the Urals. The Nazis were claiming breakthroughs on all fronts: Moscow, Leningrad, Rostov, six million Russians dead, eight armies destroyed, the Red defense "evaporated." And yet, mysteriously, the battles continued, and on alternate days came reports that the panzers were mired in endless mud or stalled in a grip of ice, that the Russians were counterattacking, the Germans encircled. As winter came on, people began to mention Napoleon. Gradually that war, that far-off war, became a part of Kenton. In Newport News, Virginia, they were building the world's newest and best battleship, the U.S.S. *Indiana.* Regardless of the nation's official neutrality, everyone in town had seen the new movies—*Dive Bomber* and *A Yank in the R.A.F.,* and *Sergeant York*—and everyone knew what the dreadnought was intended for, who the enemy was.

THE DAILY HERALD WORLD NEWS ROUNDUP

Evansville, Ind., Nov. 11, 1941
Sergeant Alvin York, World War I hero and Medal of Honor Winner, attacked the America First speeches of Col. Charles A. Lindbergh and other isolationists here today. Sgt. York, who captured 132 German soldiers single-handedly during World War I, was the featured speaker at Armistice Day ceremonies, sponsored by the American Legion.

"America cannot avoid this new war," York said, "unless, like Lindbergh, we value our present security more than we value liberty and freedom and democracy."

The 53-year-old Tennessee mountain farmer said that this time "we are going to have to take Germany off the face of the earth and put all the other little warring nations under a protectorate of the democracies."

Arlington National Cemetery, Nov. 11, 1941
In an Armistice Day speech, President Franklin D. Roosevelt said here today, "We know it was, in literal truth, to make the world safe for democracy that we took up arms in 1917.

"The men of France, prisoners in their cities, victims of searches and of seizures without law, hostages for the safety of their masters' lives, robbed of their harvests, murdered in their prisons—the men of France know what a former victory of freedom against tyranny was worth.

"The Czechs know the answer too. The Poles. The Danes.

The Dutch. The Serbs. The Belgians. The Norwegians. The Greeks.

"We know it now."

Indianapolis, Ind., Nov. 11, 1941
Miss Luella F. McWhirter of Indianapolis and Miss Nancy Biddle of Bloomington have been selected as maids of honor for the launching of the new battleship *Indiana* at Newport News, Va. A large delegation of Hoosiers, headed by Governor Schricker, will leave Indianapolis by special train on Nov. 20, to attend the launching.

St. Louis, Mo., Nov. 11, 1941
Paul V. McNutt, former governor of Indiana, declared here today that democracy is destined either to sweep over all the earth, or to be abolished everywhere.

Totalitarian forces and the democratic way of life are locked in a death struggle, he said in an Armistice Day speech.

"The showdown is daily nearer. In a world of total war, neutrality is an illusion."

Charlie Anderson must have held some kind of record for sheer resilience. Paul had often seen him in weary slumps after tough and futile days on the road, but he had never seen him defeated. Charlie had natural strength and extraordinary stamina, and beyond that, inexhaustible supplies of adrenaline. Even when tired, he was a dynamo.

As well as he knew his father, Paul could still be surprised by him—and the new flag was a real surprise. He had lived through sixteen Fourth of July celebrations without the Stars and Stripes on the front porch, and now, on Armistice Day morning, as Paul reached for the milk bottles by the front door, there was his father, standing on the spindled railing, working screw-eyes into the ceiling. The flag was folded up, lying on the porch swing that Charlie never took down before Christmas.

"Where'd you get this?"

"Potter's. Traded some Slayzall for it."

"How come?"

"I don't know—you go along all your life, figuring you're about as patriotic as the next guy, no need to brag about it, and then you wake up one morning, and the next guy's got himself a flag and a gun, and you find out you're some kind of outcast in your own country."

Paul began to feel uneasy. "What happened?"

"Nothing special. Just a feeling that's been coming over me lately. They—those guys—they're taking over the flag, wrapping themselves up in it—and trying to make out that some people don't deserve to even own one. So, I'm letting them know."

"Who's 'they'?"

"You know who. The warmongers. The Klan. The holier-than-thou's at church. The old loudmouth belting it out every Sunday, like he was some kind of saint."

"Which he's not."

Charlie looked at him. "You know about it, too?"

"I guess I was the last one to find out."

"The lousy hypocrite. Jumping on old Edelman now, just to get the heat off himself. There may be a lot of guilt around that church, but there sure as heck isn't any shame." Charlie gave the screw-eye one last fierce twist and jumped off the railing. "Now let's see how she looks."

Paul and Charlie each took a corner of the flag and held it up carefully while they eased themselves up on the railing.

"Blue field on the left. From the street side."

"How'd you get to know so much, kid?"

"Scout camp. Did this every day. My end's OK."

"Mine, too. Drop her."

They jumped down and trotted out to the sidewalk. It

looked good, hanging perfectly straight, silky-new—and then a breeze rippled it, and Paul shivered with a chilly joy.

"You cold?" Charlie took off his battered felt hat and held it awkwardly.

"Not really. It's just . . ." Paul felt embarrassed.

Charlie smiled. "Feels pretty good, doesn't it?"

After a moment of silence that Paul dedicated to Armistice Day and Old Glory and America the Beautiful, Charlie cleared his throat. "Something else I want to show you before you take off for school. Showed Jim yesterday."

It was mysterious, following his father upstairs, past the bedrooms, back to the attic stairway, rarely used. In the cold attic, Charlie opened a big box and dug under some old quilts. When he pulled out the shotgun, Paul was astonished. He had never touched a gun in his life, and had no idea that there was one in the house.

"My old man's. From the farm. It's older than you are, but I've always kept it oiled, in shape. It works. These, though, are brand new." He pulled out a red cardboard box, full of shells. "Twelve gauge. Big enough, don't you think?"

"What's this all about?"

"Like I said, nothing specific yet, just a feeling I've been having. I want you and Jim to learn to use this thing. We'll go out to the dump some day, everybody shoots out there."

"Twenty-two rifles, not cannons."

"They won't mind if we disintegrate a few rats instead of just ice-picking them between the eyes."

"Dad—I don't get it."

"Not sure I do, either. Just a feeling."

Paul nodded. Feelings. Sometimes he wished he'd never had any.

Dr. Roberts kept evening office hours on Tuesdays for the benefit of working people, and his waiting room was always crowded then. Elaine arrived just before closing time; there were still three people in the room, all reading magazines. The receptionist, a slim, pretty woman, told her to fill out a file card: date of birth, childhood diseases, parents' health history, symptoms.

Perspiring in the warm office, Elaine took off her coat and wrote on the card. When Dr. Roberts came out and saw her, he stared, as if trying to fix his eyes on something out of focus. She looked away, stepped to the reception desk, and handed in her card. He called his next patient and disappeared without looking at her again.

She still felt too warm. She took off her jacket and looked around: an impersonal room, simple chairs, bare desk, a big wall calendar with a trout fisherman on it. November 11 already, and two Thanksgivings coming up, old and new, both of them indicated in red. On a small table, some ancient magazines, *Collier's, Liberty* (" 'I Am Innocent,' Swears Bruno Hauptmann"), and more recent copies of *Life:* Harry Hopkins visiting Stalin, Hitler meeting Mussolini, Roosevelt and Churchill on the deck of the *Prince of Wales,* the Duke of Windsor calling at the White House—a world of rendezvous. And here she was, having one herself.

She tossed the *Life* back on the table, stood up, and paced the room, aware of the glances of the receptionist, then went back to the same chair and picked up the next magazine, *Social Justice.* She had heard of it, the print version of Father Coughlin's Sunday-afternoon sermons. But what was it doing here, in Tom's waiting room? "Roosevelt Should Be Impeached" was the lead editorial. With the queasy fascination of looking under a rock, she began to read.

"Without the knowledge or consent of Congress, the President has denuded this country of thirty-six flying fortresses, either selling or giving them to Great Britain.

"By this action Franklin D. Roosevelt has torpedoed our national defense, and he has consorted with the enemies of civilization, through the continued recognition of Soviet Russia."

Elaine looked around to see if anyone was aware of what she was reading. Only one woman ahead of her now, leafing through a copy of *Good Housekeeping.* The receptionist didn't look up.

"Let the citizens of America recognize what this Executive has done to the country.

"Let them rise in protest—now if ever—against this power-mad dictator who would place upon his own brow the crown of World Messiah."

Messiah: at the subtle anti-Semitism in that final thrust, she felt a rush of familiar, impotent rage. Her heart gave the scary little flip. She dropped the magazine in a wastebasket and settled back in her chair, breathing deeply, concentrating, as she did in bed, on flowers, nothing but flowers: the sweetness of roses, the curve of a tulip, apple blossoms, phlox, iris, gardenias, marigolds . . .

When something touched her arm, she opened her eyes and straightened up; her neck hurt. Dr. Roberts was standing over her, smiling. Had she been asleep? The wall clock said nine-thirty, and the receptionist was locking her file drawers. Dr. Roberts said, "Why don't you go ahead, Joy, I can handle things by myself now." Joy looked pleased, said goodnight, and left quickly, smiling a little dubiously at Elaine.

"Nice reading material you keep in your library, doctor." She pointed to the wastebasket.

Dr. Roberts looked puzzled, pulled out the magazine, and stared at it. "Funny—I used to hear his voice on the radio, every Sunday afternoon, all summer, booming through people's screen doors. Do you think this country is ready for freedom of speech?" He laughed and tossed the magazine back in the wastebasket. "Somebody must've left it behind. I don't screen my patients for political views. Or is it religious?"

"Do you screen them for IQ?"

"*Mens sana* is their business. I have plenty else to take care of."

She stood up. "Well, aren't you going to ask me in? Like the others?"

"In? In my office?"

"This is really a business call."

He looked surprised, but took her hand and led her into his examination room. "Is something wrong?"

"That's what I came to find out. It's beginning to worry me. Funny little kick in the chest. Right here." She opened the top of her blouse.

He picked up a stethoscope. "Breathe normally." He listened for what seemed like a long time, then leaned back. "Sounds OK to me."

She was irritated. "I guess it's decided not to perform now."

"No one ever has a toothache at the dentist's. When does it usually happen?"

She had to think. "Well, sometimes when I'm teaching. Sometimes when I talk to my father."

"And when you're with me?"

"No, never."

"I'm the opposite. Sometimes I get a bumpy heartbeat just thinking about us."

Somehow she hadn't expected this. They were so complete together, so much alike. "You mean—guilt?"

"I'm afraid so. Good old-fashioned guilt. I was brought up a Presbyterian, you know, and stayed one until I reached the age of reason. And I guess it's true—once a Calvinist, always a Calvinist. I think about Edna and—well . . ."

"My God. Then how did we ever get this far?"

"I don't mean I want to undo anything we've done. It's just that—she's so lost. And—you know . . . Despite everything . . . I love her."

She found her voice saying things she didn't want to hear. "I understand, Tom. It's all right. Just—don't leave me."

"Never. But you'll leave me, you know."

"Only if Cary Grant shows up in Kenton."

"It's probably already started. Some lucky single guy has been watching you—some handsome young lawyer or McGraw exec. And soon he'll be pursuing you, holding out a diamond like a carrot on a stick."

She laughed, a waterfall of a laugh. "I should get so lucky, here in this outpost."

"And you'll fall in love with him, for his golden youth and his Midwestern charm and his Kenton wit and his Purdue culture. And that'll be that. Poor Dr. Roberts will be spending all his evenings at home."

She laughed again. "You know, you make it sound irresistible. I wonder where the guy's been hiding for the last two months."

Tom wasn't smiling. "Elaine, did you know your father's been coming to see me, too?"

"For what?"

"Routine . . . I wondered if he knew about us."

"Fat chance I'd tell him, but . . . Is he OK?"

"Running some tests on him. Lab work. Takes time. So you think he knows about us?"

"Don't be silly, Tom, this is Kenton."

"Meaning?"

"Meaning everybody knows, including the blind and the deaf."

"Edna, too, you think? Good God." Why hadn't he faced up to this before?

"Especially Edna. You don't suppose her best friends would miss a chance to give her the good news, do you? I'm sure we're a regular topic of discussion around here, like Tucker and his favorite musician."

"I guess I already knew that, somewhere at the back of my mind." Depressed, he considered his hard-earned reputation: the years of dedicated service, the selfless midnight house calls—and now . . . He let his finger trace her cleavage, the delicate curves. She lifted his hand and kissed the daring index finger. Then she remembered: "Another time I feel that tremor—do you know a boy named Paul Anderson? A junior at K.H.S.?"

"Sure. One of my patients—physical exam for basketball. He's OK."

"Physically, maybe. But psychologically—I mean philosophically—he's got problems."

"Really? Not exactly a common affliction in our student body, is it?"

"Not when I was in school. But now, my father . . ." She didn't like saying this, any of it.

"Got them to thinking, has he? Bad for the soul and the digestion, everyone knows that." His finger traced her cleavage again.

"It's not funny, Tom." She pushed his hand away and pulled her blouse together. "It's that damned 'meaning of life' business . . . Well, you know how my father thinks."

"I'm beginning to. We're all beginning to."

"And Paul—he's troubled. In this little town, he's never heard anything more heretical than a Roosevelt fireside chat. He hasn't any notion of the abysses out there. No, he does have some notion, that's just the problem."

"And he asked you to fill him in?"

"He was so bewildered. And he's so sweet, and—well, good-looking, with his brown eyes and those dimples. And he looked at me, and he was so unhappy. I couldn't help it, I just had to touch him. It was awful."

"Awful?"

"I mean I . . ." She felt so warm she opened her blouse again, unbuttoned it halfway down. She was blushing all over.

"Beautiful." He was gazing as if he'd never seen skin before.

"I have to tell you, Tom. I have to tell someone—he called me by my name, my first name, and I . . . Well, this is terrible, just crazy, but I—I wanted him, right then. Just for a minute, but—a lot." She felt the humiliation rush over her, a heat wave.

Dr. Roberts held her gently, like a father. "Healthy animals," he said, sounding sad. "Healthy young animals. You're a lot closer to his age than to mine, remember."

"But he's my student! A kid!" She breathed in quickly. "Oh! Now it's doing it!"

He seemed to be expecting it, slid the stethoscope quickly to her chest, and listened. She waited, trying to calm herself. Finally he pulled away.

"Listen to me, Elaine. Your heart is perfectly all right. You don't have to worry about it."

"Then what's that scary feeling?"

"It's only a premature atrial beat, nothing important—it happens because you're under some stress. But it's not a disease."

She felt a little better. "What should I do?"

"If it's going to worry you, I could turn it off. With pills. But that's treating the symptom, not the cause. It'd be better if you could reduce the stress."

"Reduce the stress!" Her laugh was a bitter sound she hadn't ever heard herself make. "My father. My student. You. What it all comes down to is just plain old stress. Living is stress."

"That's about it, sometimes."

"Well, now I know what to tell Paul if he asks me again. The meaning of life is stress." That strange sound in her throat again: not a real laugh.

"Elaine." He seemed more and more like a father. "Elaine, I know this sounds sort of simple-minded, but—sometimes you just have to accept some things. Otherwise . . ."

"Otherwise there'll be a crazy lady teaching biology at K.H.S.?"

"Otherwise you'll never turn off that erratic beat."

"Just—accept things?"

"That's it. For example, if you were to invite me over for an hour or two tomorrow . . ."

"Oh, I do."

"Well, then—I accept. You see how easy it is?" He smiled, and didn't seem so fatherly anymore. "I love you, Elaine."

He had never said that before. She gazed at his earnest face, memorizing the way it looked at this moment, on Armistice Day of 1941 at 9:45 P.M. in a Main Street office in Kenton, Indiana. Her fingers reached out and touched his lips.

"I love you, too, Doctor Thomas Edward Roberts."

And suddenly she couldn't wait until tomorrow. Leading him over to the examination table, she was already pulling off his necktie.

⚜

◆◆"WHAT WENT WRONG?" the Minotaur had demanded, and by Friday, November 14, 1941, it began to appear that something very basic had indeed gone wrong in Kenton. The city water department had burnt out the motor of its main pump, and in some neighborhoods the backup pump brought forth mere trickles. The *Daily Herald*, symbol of stability, missed an issue because of a malfunctioning rotary press. Twice in one week the electricity all over town went out at suppertime. State inspectors, long critical of its struts and joists, finally condemned the old elementary school building, erected in 1897, and the taxpayers were now faced with the imminent expense of a new one.

Katie Rathert and the Church of Christ Quilting Club were keeping watch over all this. Now, whenever they said *Bewitched*, a little hood of darkness settled over their eyes.

The problems seemed more than mechanical. Civility itself had diminished. Editorials in the *Herald*, sermons in the churches, and even sidewalk conversations had taken on a shrill quality. The tension in the raw November air was more than merely nervous. Dr. Roberts thought he recognized its clinical properties: sexual, he told Elaine, a sexual expectation. Frustration. "It's the war," he would say, "the hunger for war, a real-for-sure nympholepsy . . ." But when she pressed him to explain further, he shrugged it off.

It was not the most hospitable environment for a new pronouncement by the Minotaur. Bob Mesler, under skillful and prolonged psychological pressure from his spouse, had dropped his contract with the devil. But more people were subscribing to the *Rationalist* now, not wanting to miss anything scandalous, so the new issue, on November 14, circulated quickly, and secondhand reports hit the telephone lines all over the county. The general malaise intensified.

THE LABYRINTH

A Jewish iconoclast, heretic, and breaker of the Sabbath once announced to his followers: "You shall know the truth, and the truth will make you free." We are preoccupied with our "God-given" freedom, here in the home of the brave.

But what kind of freedom? The rich are as free as the poor to sleep under bridges. Laboring men and women are free to work at wages set by their employers. Laboratory animals are free to run mazes. A freedom not based on knowledge, reason, and truth is the freedom of a rat in a box. So we depend upon our schools, our books, our newspapers, and our well-informed leaders for the basic tools of responsible freedom.

But search the pages of your local paper for news of anti-Semitic violence by the Nazis. Listen to your priests and pastors for moral leadership against racial discrimination. Wait for your local politicians to crusade for the academic freedom of our schoolteachers. Look, listen, and wait: you will hunger and thirst in a desert.

It begins in our schools. Look at your children's textbooks. Why, in 1941, are there no Negroes mentioned in those pages of enlightenment? Why, after a dozen years of our country's deepest depression, is there no word of poverty? Why is there no mention of instructive American blunders or atrocities, or eminent free-thinkers, or monopolistic business practices? No serious discussion of Marxism, no women, no Jews or Latins, no Hoosier nonconformists like Theodore Dreiser or Eugene V. Debs? "While there is a lower class, I am of it. While there is a criminal class, I am of it. While there is a man in prison, I am not free." There speaks your garden-grown American philosopher, but you will not find him anywhere in your schoolbooks.

For all of our prattle about freedom, we fail to nourish it with truth. So it is that we have masses of people acting out their collective neuroses: proclaiming freedom but practicing intimidation; worshiping free choice but supporting the Klan; praying to a dead Jewish radical but burning crosses in the lawns of living ones.

And so it is that we still have, in the year 1941, biology textbooks which fail to mention the most basic principle of that science, organic evolution. And when a teacher rises up in our midst, bringing us the biological truth, she is told in no uncertain terms that for every bearer of truth, there is a cross in waiting; for every Giordano Bruno a flaming stake; for every John Thomas Scopes a grand jury and indictment; and for every honest teacher, dismissal.

That's what has become of truth, here in the land of the free.

—The Minotaur

ON SATURDAY EVENINGS the farmers of Royal County took hasty baths in chilly bathrooms, put on clean shirts, loaded their scrubbed wives and children into the Hudson sedan or the Ford pickup, and drove to Kenton. They parked diagonally to the curb on Main Street, and the kids ran off to the Strand Theater to see Abbott and Costello, and Mom and Dad went into J. C. Penney's to buy heavy work shoes and striped overalls and long johns and housedresses, and sometimes a white shirt or a pretty hat with a veil, for church.

If the weather was good, they'd walk to the corner popcorn wagon, spend a nickel on a bag of buttered popcorn or peanuts in the shell, and then go back to the car and sit there, munching and watching the people stroll by on the sidewalk, until the movie was over and the kids came running down Main Street and piled in, and they were off to the farm again.

That routine had gone unchanged within recent memory, although before there were cars in Royal County, not so long ago, the streets were lined with buggies and wagons, and horses were tied to the hitching rails that were still in place, and Main Street itself, recently blacktopped, had been red brick. In the days of buggies, Kenton had not needed its four stoplights.

The unexpected was not a part of this life. And yet, on Saturday, November 15, 1941, the unexpected happened. Whether or not it had anything to do with that week's provocation from the Minotaur, the message was clear.

They came from somewhere east of town, out on Murray Pike, crossing the city limits at nine o'clock, the peak hour of Kenton night-life, all of the stores still open, the first show at the Strand just out. Cars, pickups, panel trucks, they kept close together, bumper-to-bumper, headlights on bright, horns blaring without a letup, right through the red lights like a funeral procession, the scream of their horns an eerie night music, down Main Street to Oak, then U-turning back through Jed Shinover's Sinclair station and up Main Street again to Mitchell, a shrill chorus, then down Mitchell Street until the lead car was at Saul Edelman's house, where they paused, horns blaring, for a full five minutes before they cruised on, down to Birch Street, U-turning back again, once more full chorus for a few minutes at Edelman's, up to Main, another turn through the town, and then out east again, their license plates muddied over, illegible, and in every front seat, two figures hooded and robed in white.

Charles Anderson must have been waiting for this event, or something like it, because he didn't hesitate. Coming out of Potter's Hardware, he saw the grim parade entering Main Street. He sped home immediately, took the attic stairs two at a time, both directions, and then raced off again in the little blue Ford. That is why the Klansmen, blaring their horns in front of Saul Edelman's house, saw, dim in the streetlights, a solitary man in a gray overcoat and a battered felt hat, sitting on Edelman's welcome mat, with the gleaming barrel of an old twelve-gauge lying across his knees.

Afterward, Charlie was uncharacteristically reticent, apparently a little embarrassed by his impulsiveness. "Maybe I shouldn't have done it," he told Paul later, "but when the bastards start pushing you around, somebody's got to push back." He shook his head, as if puzzled. "How come it's getting so a man can't say what he thinks anymore?"

And shaking his head again: "Somebody had to do it. But what if I'm not around? Who'll be there the next time?"

Miss Edelman had asked him to stay after lab, so Paul sat there in the empty room, waiting and nervous. She had hardly looked at him in the last two weeks, since he'd been crazy enough to call her Elaine. Sometimes he did things so dumb he couldn't believe he'd done them. It humbled him, and kept him from making too many harsh judgments on dopey Chuck Green and nitwit Walter Stone.

"Your lab work has gone sloppy, Paul." Her voice was sharp.

He jumped. She had come up behind him without a sound. "I'm sorry about that test tube, Miss Edelman."

"It's not the broken glass that matters, it's those generations of Drosophila, down the drain. You may have been just on the verge of something. Who knows what mutations might have been taking place—and now . . ."

"I still have nineteen tubes of them left. I won't let you down."

"It's not *me*, Paul. Why do you keep going off on these tangents? You're not stupid." Her irritation scared him. He wanted to contradict her, to plead ignorant, dumb, downright feebleminded—anything to escape this stern accountability.

"You're not working the way you used to, not paying attention to what you're doing." She was pacing back and forth, two tables away, talking louder than usual. Paul had the impression she was talking to an audience, and he wasn't even in it. "There's no excuse for it. You're a bright boy, and you always used to be hardworking and careful. What's happened?"

He couldn't tell her about Ruthie. "I'm sorry . . ."

"It's such a waste. Kids with college potential, good records, capable of doing something with their lives, making a career—a *career*—and then coming up to their junior or senior year and just—giving up." She couldn't seem to stop scolding. Paul's capacity for guilt was considerable, but he began to wonder if she wasn't overdoing it, picking on him. One lousy test tube, out of twenty.

"So you just let go, and instead of making something of yourself, you drop out, get married at seventeen or eighteen, sign up at the foundry, and by the time you're twenty, you've got two kids, a rifle, and a pickup truck . . ." Her voice broke, and she turned her back to him, and at that moment he caught on.

"I'm sorry about what they did at your father's house, Miss Edelman." He stressed the "Miss." "I think everyone's ashamed of it. Especially that black cross."

When she turned around, tears were running down her cheeks, although her face was otherwise composed. Her voice was a little too calm, Paul thought. "You think they're ashamed?"

"Well, my dad is, anyhow. You know what he did, sitting out there with a shotgun. He's never done anything like that before."

"Your father's a good man."

"My mom said those paraders should've been arrested."

"But who'd do it? Haven't you heard—one of those Dodge pickups with the muddy license plates belongs to the sheriff."

Paul had heard it. Everyone had. He picked at his fingernails. "Miss Edelman . . ."

"Yes?"

"Is it true what Old—I mean, what Mr. Edelman said in his last paper? Are they trying to get you fired?"

She walked to the end of the long table, came around to his row, and sat down on the stool next to his. It took a long time for her to answer. "I hear it's true."

"But you're the best teacher at K.H.S. Kids are really learning something in here."

"Well, maybe that's the problem—do you suppose?"

He thought about it. "I see what you mean. So is that why your father decided to write all that? About freedom?"

"Maybe. Partly."

"Then—I know you don't want to talk about it, but—does that mean he's saying that freedom is really the meaning of life?"

She smiled, and the late afternoon sunshine caught the tears in her eyes. She looked so young, so vulnerable, that Paul was reminded again—she'd been a student here herself, in this same classroom, just a few years ago.

Her smile faded. "The reason I'd rather not talk about it isn't that I begrudge you anything I happen to know, or think I know. It's only . . . Well, it's personal. Strange, isn't it—if life has any 'meaning,' you'd think it'd be public. Universal knowledge. But as far as I can tell, it isn't. That's why I said the other day that you have to, somehow, figure it out for yourself."

She put her hand to her chest, as if she couldn't catch her breath. She was obviously agitated, and Paul felt responsible. "You don't have to talk about it. I'm sorry I asked."

But now she wouldn't stop. "You see, my father came here from a country where freedom was undermined and then lost, for everybody. But it was worst of all for Jews. Freedom can be a big thing in anybody's life, even if you're lucky enough to be rich and powerful. But if you're poor, if you're powerless, if you're in an unlucky minority—then freedom is the very air you breathe, because it's all you've got."

She was sitting on the same stool as when she'd touched his hand, and Paul wondered what she'd do now if he reached out and touched hers.

"Anyway, Paul, remember about the work. Do it right. Every time. I know you're upset about things, about Ruthie, about . . ." She stopped abruptly and grinned at him. "All this lecturing, good grief! Anyway, I hope it helps." Her hand came forward a little, as if she meant to touch him again, but then it stopped.

"I'll do better," he said, unable to look her in the eye. "I'll try."

So Miss Edelman knew about Ruthie. Still awake past midnight, Paul felt himself blushing against his pillow. Of course she knew. Everyone knew. Kenton functioned on party lines, family dinners, barbershops, church socials, teachers' lounges, Rotaries and Lions, quilting bees, card parties, candy stores, sewing clubs, sororities, Benevolent Orders of Moose and Elk, family reunions, bars and taverns, slumber parties, coffees and teas—hushed voices, nudges, secret smiles, whispers, knowing glances—a whole apparatus of discovery undreamed of by Galileo or Newton or Darwin and never known to pause or rest. "They say, they say . . ."

> *They say that love is blinder than a bat,*
> *And I love you, so put that in your hat.*

His mother's couplet jingled in his mind. He was sweating through his pajamas, through the sheets. He tossed off the bedclothes and listened: from the other twin bed, Jim's breathing was regular. Paul got up and tiptoed out of the bedroom, along the hall past his parents' closed door, and down the creaky stairs. In the living room he switched on the dim lamp over the library table, rummaged through the drawer for pencil and paper, and scribbled, as if it were somebody's birthday.

> *They say that love is blinder than a bat.*

He crossed it out. What was he trying to say?

> *They say that love is always deaf and blind,*
> *And anyone who buys it must be dumb.*

It had to rhyme, of course. He pondered it.

That "dear" and "darling" mean you've lost your mind,

OK so far, but then it stalled. Birthday poems were a lot easier than this.

And "sweetheart" is a . . .

He tried "proud" and crossed it out. Where was he going, anyway? Crossed out "clown's," crossed out "fool's." His grandmother should be doing this, or his mother; their stuff always meshed with a neat little click.

Then, ah:

. . . is a sad delirium."

Sad? Wild? Hot? Gray? No, sad is right, when had he ever been sadder?

He was cold. He wasn't wearing his bathrobe, and Charlie had banked the coal for the night and closed the damper. Should he go on? He had to; the lines kept coming.

They say a sigh's a sign . . .

Of insanity, that's what, lunacy, distemper, he knew it all too well.

. . . a sign of silly sickness.

So sigh he did, and went on, crossing out words, fumbling for rhymes, changing his mind and scratching out lines, and finally working out the closing couplet. He grabbed a fresh sheet of paper and, with a shaking hand, copied it out as neatly as he could.

> They say that love is always deaf and blind,
> And anyone who buys it must be dumb,
> That "dear" and "darling" mean you've lost your mind,
> And "sweetheart" is a sad delirium.

They say a sigh's a sign of silly sickness,
And once upon a time I'd have agreed:
Your head is better led to shed its thickness,
Your heart, unless it's smart, can break and bleed.

But since I felt your fingertips, I've tasted
A kind of sweetness nothing else can touch:
Being together. Everything else is wasted.
Heaven might be better, but not much.

I'd give up seeing sun and stars, whatever,
If I could feel you close to me forever.

He read it over. Would Shakespeare like it? Don't ask. Miss
Eva? Who cares? There was only one opinion he cared about.
He sneezed; he was freezing. He'd put the page in his biology
book and slip it to Ruthie in study hall tomorrow. Maybe she
wouldn't walk home with him anymore, but she hadn't made
any rules against sonnets.

Back in bed, he shivered in a sudden icy happiness, and
then, haunted by his old partner, guilt, began to feel sorry for
his sleeping brother.

❧

K H.S., having the largest gymnasium in the area, was
always host to both the county tournament at
Thanksgiving and the state sectional tournament
in February. So the Fox Lake Raiders had invaded
Kenton again. The gym was a fluttering forest of colors, the
garish banners and crepe paper streamers of Ligonier and

Albion and Avilla and all the other high schools of the county sharing the rafters with the Comets' crimson and gold. School bands squealed and brayed their way through fight songs all day Tuesday and Wednesday, and by Thursday, gangly losers from the neighboring towns were benched in the grandstands, their letter sweaters with the big purple L's or blue A's or orange M's proclaiming a thankless Thanksgiving.

Fox Lake, playing in one bracket, had overpowered its share of the losing teams. K.H.S., in the other bracket, had run the legs off its quota of victims. The destined Thursday-night final was getting closer, and everyone was hungry for it. The semifinals were not expected to be interesting, and they weren't. Fox Lake breezed by Columbia City in the Thursday-morning game, playing its second-stringers most of the second half, saving the starters' strength for the final with Kenton. K.H.S. had a little more trouble with a fired-up Cromwell team in the afternoon game, and Unc had to keep the first-stringers in, all the way, taking no chances.

In the locker room afterward, Unc was already nervous about Fox Lake. "I want you all home in no less than thirty minutes. Walk, don't run, don't go near the drugstore and those damn pinball machines and comic books. When you get home, sit down, relax, lay on the bed, read something dull from your English class, *Ivanhoe*, something like that. Don't eat much before the game, you can fill up later. No milk, remember, gives you cottonmouth. Sleep if you can, but make sure somebody wakes you up in time. Be back in this room by eight on the dot, ready to suit up." He chewed a fingernail, pacing. "And don't think about tonight's game. Think about *Ivanhoe*. That's an order." He belched, a long deep belch that made Paul think of death.

Why does he do it? Paul wondered. He didn't have to coach, he could just teach his civics classes and be comfortable. Why do people take on jobs that kill them? Why did Charlie leave Potter's Hardware and that safe and steady fourteen dollars a week? What made Miss Edelman keep trying so hard with a bunch of kids who, most of them, didn't give a hoot about genes or cells or leks?

Unc belched again as he stalked out, leaving reverberations in the locker room. Behind Unc's back, Gopher waved his hand in front of his nose, and some of the guys snickered. Jerry snapped his jockstrap at Scrap's bare butt and was rewarded with mock screams.

Jim was already dressed and on his way out, first as usual. Paul pulled on clean socks. Unc had been a good athlete once, all-state in high school and first string at Earlham, where he set a conference record in the high hurdles. Paul tried to imagine the lean young man inside the potbellied old coach, barreling down the cinders, taking the highs in easy strides.

But all he could see was the Unc they'd always known, who began every school day with a big mug of black coffee from the teachers' lounge and an earnest pledge in his civics class: *one nation, indivisible, with liberty and justice for all.* Second and third mugs of coffee between classes kept him in good spirits until noon. But then he began to get noticeably edgy, and then testy, and, by the time basketball practice started, downright snappish, directing the passing and lay-up drills like a top sergeant. Nobody crossed him then, not openly, although some of the clowns on the team, like Scrap and Gopher, spent a lot of time mocking him behind his back. So nobody ever dared to say anything when he occasionally told them to play dirty, or when he made snide remarks about the colored boys at Fort Wayne Central.

When Paul left, he noticed Unc sitting at his desk in the glass-doored cage that passed for his office, a thumbnail in his teeth, staring at the wall.

Jerry gave him a ride, so Paul was home in five minutes. Jim rode home with Charlie, and was already there; and so was Betsy, trying to tune the static out of "Bewitched, Bothered, and Bewildered." "You guys were pretty good today," she croaked, hoarse from cheering. Her little gang of freshman girls always sat together at big games and screamed until they lost their voices. She twitched her pleated skirt: "Gimme a K!" she rasped, "Gimme an H! Gimme a K-H-S!"

"Hi, Mom." Paul waved at his mother, who was stirring yellow coloring into a bowl of waxy oleomargarine. Real butter was forty-five cents a pound now, unthinkable.

Charlie came in from the front porch and stomped into the living room, unfolding the *Daily Herald*, snapping its rubber band toward the wastebasket, and missing as usual, already reading the headlines.

" 'Guns on Our Merchant Ships'!" he called out by way of greeting. "How do you like that? One more step to war, just exactly what they're after." He plopped down on the couch, studying the paper.

"Supper will be ready in a minute," Nora announced from the kitchen, her voice a little higher than usual, and musical.

Betsy was switching stations on the radio, dialing past Jack Armstrong, the All-American Boy, and past the news—"Rostov is now encircled by Nazi tanks"—then pausing at the yearning violins of Artie Shaw's "Stardust." Paul glanced over at Jim, who slowed down a little on his way to the kitchen, like a bird floating, then went on as if he hadn't heard.

"Japs in Washington, still talking. Still bombing China, too, killing defenseless peasants." Charlie insisted on informing his family on matters of national and international interest, like it or lump it. "Got a new boss, name of Tojo. Will he be able to talk to our idiot, you suppose?"

Paul looked out the window, listening to the rest of "Stardust," then followed Jim into the kitchen. Nora wiped her hands on her apron and put plates on the table. "Betsy said you won, that's nice. Dad and I are both coming to the game tonight. I made hamburgers so you can eat right away, and then rest up."

The table was decorated with orange cardboard turkeys, but Nora was postponing their Thanksgiving dinner until Sunday, since the boys weren't supposed to eat much on a basketball day.

Jim was chipping ice off the block in the icebox. Paul filled five glasses with water.

Charlie called in from the living room. "Limeys and Aussies doing OK in Africa now, giving old Rommel a taste of his own pumpernickel . . . Well, it's their war, they declared it, let them fight it out."

He came into the kitchen, still holding the paper. Jim, between ball games, was contentious: "Unc Ehrhard says don't wait till they're on your goal line to make some yardage on them."

Betsy croaked, "Hit 'em again, hit 'em again, harder, harder!"

"Yardage!" Charlie slammed the paper on a chair and sat down. "Goal line! Why does everybody talk about war like it's a schoolkids' game?" He snorted and reached for a hamburger.

Nora tried to change the subject. "Betsy, come in here this minute! Supper's ready. Let's see, do we have enough pickles and onions?"

Charlie was brooding. "I'll tell you this, if we go over there and get into it, we'll see some games we've never played before. That was a honey of a block you made there at the end, Jim. The only thing to do is make yourself strong at home, so they don't dare attack you. Good foul-shooting this afternoon, Paul, nice work. Listen, they've got women and kids digging trenches around the whole city of Moscow. And I'm telling you, if the Germans or Japs or anyone else ever came over here, we'd do a lot better than that—we'd beat them off with broom handles."

The radio was playing Cab Calloway now, and Betsy jitter-bugged into the dining room, snapping her fingers and rasp-ing, "Hi-de-hi-de-hi-de-ho," and then stopped. "Jeepers, my voice! And I still gotta yell my dumb head off tonight!" She wheezed out a hoarse giggle and smeared globs of ketchup and mustard on her hamburger.

"No more yelling, young lady," Nora scolded. "You'll do your voice permanent damage, *then* you'll be sorry."

"You kids can't remember Mayor Cermak of Chicago," Charlie put in. "Pretty good mayor, even if he was a Demo-crat. Anyway, he was riding with Roosevelt in a parade, and somebody took a shot at Roosevelt and killed Cermak in-stead."

It was one of his favorite stories. Everyone waited for the familiar punch line.

"The two most hated men in America are the man who shot Lincoln and the man who missed Roosevelt."

Betsy giggled, and Jim and Paul laughed politely as their father chortled. Nora smiled. "Charlie, I hope you don't ever tell that story in public."

"You think that's bad? Listen, you should hear what they're calling Lindbergh—and anybody who agrees with him. Fascists, tools of Hitler, fifth-column. When it comes to name-calling, the Democrats have us beat by a country mile."

Jim and Paul finished supper and went upstairs. Jim got out his prized yellow cord trousers to wear to the dance, and Paul fell on top of his twin bed, in his clothes. He heard Jim setting the alarm.

"Hope we can sleep," Jim said, pulling back his bedspread. "We've got to be way up for this one."

"We can do it, Ace."

"Darn right we can."

Paul knew he meant it, and he felt the sour comfort of having a big brother who could do anything.

And then the pure physical tiredness seeped through him and he slept, without benefit of great literature.

The Kenton Comets were good that night, but for the first three quarters barely good enough, just keeping even with the Fox Lake Raiders. Jerry was holding Stokes amazingly well, given the height disadvantage. Stokes had scored only three times from the floor and once from the foul line, and he hadn't used his elbows yet, but Paul felt the old hatred, anyway, remembering the bruises and welts from their last encounter. Jim was all over the place as usual, a crimson and gold whirlwind, stealing passes, hitting from thirty feet, giving them a noisy hustle in the backcourt. He was leading both teams in scoring and doing a lot of rebounding, too.

The problem was fatigue, weariness from the afternoon game. Everyone knew it would hit hard in the fourth quarter, slowing down their fast break, loosening their grip on the hard passes, making them careless on defense. They expected it, and it came. Unc didn't dare substitute much; the subs were too short. So he'd pull the starters out one at a time for a minute or so, give them a drink and a toweling, and send them back in. He couldn't spare any time-outs yet—they'd be precious in the final minutes.

The Fox Lake coach knew it, too, had obviously been

planning on it ever since the tourney pairings came out, showing Fox Lake headed for the Thursday-morning semifinal game, Kenton for the afternoon. His tall first-stringers had hardly worked up a sweat since yesterday, so he uncorked a surprise at the beginning of the fourth quarter, a sort of gawky fast-break game of his own. K.H.S. was caught flat-footed the first time, and Stokes scored easily, gloating as he trotted back up the court. Kenton was ready the next time, but being ready meant running hard in both directions, and that was expensive. Paul began to feel the jelly in his legs. Unc called time.

"You can't keep this up all quarter, we'll have to switch games on them. Forget the fast break, play every point like you're guarding a lead. Hang back and be set for them on defense, then bring it up slow, pass it around, keep their zone moving, run them good, but don't shoot till you get a real shot. Don't dribble much, just pass it around, crosscourt, keep them running. You got that? Whenever Jim or Jerry can get open underneath, bounce it in there and take the good ones. But don't hurry. We've got ten minutes yet, plenty of time."

It worked well enough to keep the Comets even, and they weren't dying from the pace anymore, but they weren't popular with the crowd, either. The fans liked razzle-dazzle, grew impatient with the stalling, and began to boo. Fans from the smaller towns, beaten and disgruntled, resented the cowardice of a slow game, especially from K.H.S., the biggest school in Royal County.

Fox Lake wasn't really much good at the fast break. They weren't all that fast, for one thing. Besides, it wasn't their kind of game, and they kept throwing the ball away. That kept the Comets in the running and soon put them ahead by three points. K.H.S. fans were screaming and stomping in unison, the wooden bleachers resounding like drums. With four minutes left, Fox Lake called time, and when they came out again, they dropped the fast break.

What they substituted for it was pure roughhouse, the stuff that sent the Kenton boys home black and blue in their last game. On the first rebound off their basket, Stokes and Peewee Hosler went up with Jerry, and when they came down, there was a flurry of elbows. Stokes went back up with the ball and scored. As he loped up the court, he was smirking again; Paul felt a rush of blood in his temples.

Jerry was lying flat on his back, and Unc was yelling at the refs. They whistled an official time-out. Unc came out on the floor and eased Jer up and down by the waist a couple of times. Finally Jer got up and stumbled over to the huddle, muttering curses.

On the way back to the bench, Unc said something to the ref, who ignored him and whistled the teams into play.

Kenton brought the ball up and passed it around. In a minute Jim was free, a step ahead of Black. Paul bounced it to him and followed it in. Jim faked a shot, then bounced it back to him. On a dead run, Paul fed it to the backboard and it fell through. Three points ahead again. He heard his mother's happy shriek, his father's triumphant yip.

When they got back down the floor, Paul noticed Jim was limping. He was playing Spencer close, and went after the rebound when Spencer missed. This time it was Tiny Hosler and Stokes who worked Jim over, and the gouging was too obvious for the refs to miss. There was a whistle and a foul on Stokes.

Unc was off the bench, yelling at the refs. It had obviously been more than an ordinary foul, but the ref on Unc's side poked a finger at Unc and yelled back, and Unc called time. He was purple around the nose, and his eyes were bloodshot. "How are you, Jerry? Jim, I saw that hamstringing they gave you back there. Well, two can play that game. Get in there with them and make sure your fists are tight and your knees are in action! Two of you on one of them, that's the ticket. Get Stokes first! Take him out of the game, get a knee in his nuts if you can, an elbow below the belt, *crush* the bastard!" He stared around the little circle, as if it were all their fault. Paul stared at the shiny hardwood floor. Even though he hated Stokes's guts, he felt sick. He let his eyes wander, hoping he'd see Ruthie in the bleachers. Losing track of the noise, and Unc, and the game itself, he called up the feel of her body dancing against his. He wondered: did she find the poem he'd left on her desk? Did she like it?

The warning buzzer sounded. Unc was pounding his back. "Now get out there and do some damage!"

Jim stood at the foul line, bouncing the ball and looking groggy. He raised his arms for the single shot. It pushed off too high and fell a little short, bouncing off the front rim, straight back at him.

Everybody went after it, Jim, Jer, Paul, and three of the Fox Lake heavyweights. Elbows and knees were going everywhere; in a moment Jim was down on all fours, Jer had a hand to his nose, Paul felt a sharp stabbing in his thigh—and Fox Lake had the ball down the floor, three on two against Scrap and Gopher. In ten seconds, they were only one point behind.

The home side of the gym was raging, the other side screaming approval, and K.H.S. was down to the final minute, guarding a lead that suddenly felt like a loss.

Scrap brought it up slowly and they tried to hold on to it, passing as sharply as they could, Scrap to Jim, Jim in to Jerry. But one bad one was all it took. Jer lofted the ball back from heavy traffic in the foul circle, and it floated along a little too slowly. Before Paul could reach it, Stokes had it and was ahead of him, going fast. He bounced it to Black, who dribbled once and shot. Stokes and Paul went up for a possible rebound, Stokes a little too early. He was coming down already when the ball swished through the basket, just above Paul's fingers, putting Fox Lake ahead by a point.

Paul fell back down on top of Stokes, feeling the frustration of that basket and the memory of Stokes's nasty smirk and the pain of the beating they were taking. They were falling together in slow motion, and Paul saw the giant go off balance when he hit the floor, and felt his own elbow hit Stokes across the shoulder, exactly where he had hit Paul in the first game of the season. With a sudden eruption of rage, Paul put his whole body into that fierce blow, every falling pound he could muster, landing more on Stokes than on the floor, and he saw the leering face break into shock as Stokes doubled up, holding his right shoulder, his body a tight circle of pain.

Strike . . . Crush . . .

Close up, it may have been the most obvious intentional foul of the season, but when the ref's whistle blew, far behind them, the call was out of bounds, Comets. No foul. Revenge! Paul felt like singing.

The Fox Lake coach was off the bench, shouting obscenities. The hostile crowd, as if governed by the coach's anger, broke into fury. Programs, popcorn bags, storms of confetti, and streamers of toilet paper cascaded onto the floor. The referees looked startled for a moment, then stern. They consulted, and signaled. Technical foul on the Fox Lake coach, same on the crowd.

The collective rage increased. The ref called an official time-out and ordered janitors onto the floor. Big brooms swept along like snowplows through a blizzard; they had to cover the floor twice before the stands ran out of ammunition and the mess was finally cleaned up.

Waiting on the bench, the Kenton team drank sips of water, toweled off, and rested, rested, rested. Fox Lake ahead by one, 50–49. Unc told them: five seconds left, and two foul shots. Paul knew he'd have to go to the line, his penalty for being their most consistent foul-shooter. He wished he were anywhere else in the world. Guilt dragged at his shoulders: his body had followed orders, and what did that make him—Unc's stooge?

But it was even worse than that. Beneath the surge of guilt, he still felt the pleasure of revenge.

When the crowd quieted down a little, they lined up at the foul circle, and Paul noticed that Stokes had been pulled out of the game. He felt another rush of shame, and the hoop, as if in punishment, looked smaller than usual, while the Fox Lake team, on both sides of the lane, loomed larger and larger. Paul bounced the ball and tried to relax his quivering arms. The home side of the gym was hushed, but the other side began a steady, antagonistic wail, like an angry siren.

Paul put the ball up jerkily, too hard. It hit the backboard, fell back, bobbled around the rim, and dropped through. The groan of the hostile crowd was drowned out in the shrill triumph of the K.H.S. fans. Paul bounced the ball again, studied the basket, and pushed. This time it hit nothing but net.

With the home crowd shrieking incredible decibels, the Comets harried the giants, careful not to foul. Four seconds, three, two—from forty feet out, Peewee Hosler hurled the ball. It caromed off the backboard into the crowd as the buzzer rasped. Kenton by one. County champs!

The band blared away. The fans were all over the team, screaming and slapping them on their painful bruises, until finally they got Unc up on their backs and off the court and into the locker room, where they hustled him into the shower and cooled him off good, all of them laughing until they felt tears.

THE AFTER-GAME DANCE at the country club was a glorious Thanksgiving victory revel, the jitterbugging to "In the Mood" a frenetic celebration of being seventeen or sixteen or fourteen and, for that single night, utterly happy. The Melodaires were in top form, exuberant; kids kept running up to the Comet heroes and pummeling them in sheer joy; and Paul was perfectly miserable.

There is, he discovered, a pain worse than a love you can't touch; it's a love someone else is touching. He nursed the agony of watching Jim hold Ruthie through six consecutive dances, while he danced with Sally Crothers once, and Mildred Elderman once, and finally just sat out the rest.

There was a moment, a particular moment he must have been waiting for, but he didn't realize it until it came, breathing its gentle torment: the Melodaires eased into "Stardust." Paul quickly looked away from Jim and Ruthie, and scuttled to the counter for a chocolate Coke.

"Nice game tonight, Pug." The kid behind the counter was a skinny sophomore, someone Paul didn't know very well. Paul grunted thanks and carried his drink to a dark corner

window, where the night air streamed in, cooling his forehead.

He'd been there only a few seconds when he felt her presence behind him. She didn't have to say anything; he knew
she was there. He put down his Coke and turned around.

"May I have this dance?" She was smiling, but she didn't
look happy.

"I'll check my tally." His hands went out, almost touching
her, and her arms came up slowly to his shoulders, and hovered there for a moment, and then she snuggled against his
body and they moved to "Stardust," drifting in that dark
corner, light-years from Jim and the other dancers, waiting
for the world to end.

It was "Stardust" that ended, and they stayed right where
they were for "It's Always You," happy to be away from the
others, happy to be in the sheltering dusk of the rosy shad-
owed lights.

"Welcome home," he murmured at last.

She put her cheek against his.

Paul had no idea what had happened, but he knew enough
not to ask—not now, not yet. It was enough that she was
there with him, that she wasn't going back to Jim. When the
band played Peggy Lee's new hit, "Somebody Else Is Taking
My Place," Paul felt a twinge of his accustomed guilt, then
was surprised by how easily he suppressed it. He looked
around; Jim seemed to have left. So they went on dancing
until at last the Melodaires played "Good Night, Sweetheart"
and began packing their instruments, and the harsh lights
came on. Then they reluctantly put on their coats and walked
the long stretch of West William Street, hand-in-hand in the
warm Indian Summer of their own Thanksgiving, Paul reso-
lutely asking no questions. When they got to her house, she
turned at the door and hugged him around the waist.

Now, he thought. Now she'll tell me. But moments slipped by in silence.

"I'm sorry." She wouldn't look at him. "I don't mean to be mysterious."

"Oh, go ahead, say something inscrutable."

She wouldn't play. "I can't say anything right now, it's all too new. Could we talk some other time?"

"Day or night. Night and Day. Blues in the Night. My Blue Heaven."

Finally she let herself smile at him. "Heaven might be better," she said, "but not much."

It took him a moment to realize she was quoting his poem.

She smiled again: "I'd give up seeing sun and stars, whatever, if I could feel you close to me forever."

She'd memorized it! He grinned back at her, feeling as if he'd been miraculously cured of some dreadful, lingering disease. "Can you come over Saturday night?" she said. "Take me to the movie, and afterward we can talk. I do have a lot to tell you."

❧

THE NAZI JUGGERNAUT, code-named "Typhoon," had blasted the Russian armies across a thousand-mile front, as *The Kenton Daily Herald* had faithfully reported, and Hitler was said to have commanded that Leningrad be wiped off the face of the earth, razed to the ground by artillery and continuous air attack. But when the fall rains began, the German soldiers slithered in Russian mud, pulled their tanks back from the front to use them as tractors for their mired artillery pieces, and, with keen humiliation, urgently requested plow-horses.

The resistance stiffened. Red partisans were ambushing supply columns: warm German clothing, heavy boots and wool socks, never arrived. When the snows began, the ghost of Napoleon's Grand Army and the winter of 1812 began to trouble the sleep of German generals. Now it was below zero on the Moscow front, and frostbite was claiming thousands of casualties, ice was immobilizing the German tanks, telescopic sights were not working, machine guns would not fire, fuel froze.

Nevertheless, the German troops were in sight of the city, and on November 22, 1941, the greatest tank force ever assembled on one front slowly, arthritically, converged on Moscow from the north, south, and west, ready to take the city.

On November 22, 1941, the *Daily Herald* carried the banner headline, 10,000 SEE U.S.S. INDIANA LAUNCHING. Under a large photo of the ship was the caption, "Mightiest Warship Joins U.S. Navy."

" 'Uncle Sam rolled up his sleeves one more turn today,' " Nora Anderson read out loud, sounding chipper. Charlie, who was busy repairing an old electric fan, snorted. Paul, holding the fan steady, smiled. Nora's arthritis and her spirits always improved on those rare occasions when the humidity was low and Slayzall was selling well.

"Listen to this. 'Mrs. Margaret Schricker Robbins, daughter of Governor Schricker, crashed a bottle of champagne against the steel hull with the cry, "I christen thee *Indiana.*" The jacks were stricken away, and the great ship slowly slid into the river.' "

"They'll raise our taxes again," Charlie snarled, pliers at the wiring. "Get us so far in debt to their fancy war machine that we'll have to use it to justify its existence. Lindy has them pegged, all right."

Paul thought of the aviator in Fort Wayne, the Gospel Temple, the crowds, the Typical American Girl with the German name.

" 'After fitting up, the pride of Indiana will take her place on the front line to fight for all the liberties Americans everywhere hold dear.' "

That was too much. Charlie threw down the pliers. "Front line! *What* front line? Since when has Congress declared war? We're at peace, damn it, we're *neutral!*" He plugged in the fan to make sure it was working all right, then yanked the plug out and carried the fan down the cellar steps. Nora followed with the paper, and Paul went last, giving his mother a hand when the arthritis made her pause on the stairs.

At the center of the basement crouched the old coal furnace, huge-bellied, its big heat ducts reaching out in every direction, an inverted octopus. In the biggest of these, where it was running horizontally, Charlie had cut a large hole and made a metal flap for it.

"Hold that flap open, Paul."

Nora sat on a stool, reading in the dim light. " 'Indiana,' the governor said, 'the first seat of government in the great Northwest Territory, is justly proud of the new honor which comes with the christening of this great ship.' "

"Horse feathers," Charlie muttered automatically, not really paying attention. The fan was anchored in the hole now, its cord fed through a padded cutaway. Charlie slammed the flap shut and began driving in screws. "Well, they may be going to starve us to death with their blasted war taxes and lead us by the noses into their blasted foreign war, but at least this winter we're going to have forced-air heat in the blasted living room."

❧

As Charles Anderson was fitting the fan into the big furnace duct, the upstairs radio was announcing that the Germans had finally taken Rostov, and the British had knocked out a record number of Nazi tanks at Tobruk, and Indiana University was beating rival Purdue for the Old Oaken Bucket. And at the same moment, farmers all over Royal County were taking their chilly baths and getting their families ready for the Saturday-evening ride to Kenton, and the Reverend Stephen B. Tucker was visiting shut-ins in the neighborhood of Miss Marsha Huron, and Ruthie Peters was practicing a Chopin scherzo on the baby grand in the family living room, and Dr. Thomas Roberts was on Elaine Edelman's double bed, resting up.

He was lying on his side, half in a doze but still aware of Elaine's undraped loveliness, the gentle taper of her back, the tuck of her waist, the thrust of her hip. He snuggled against her warmth, spoon-fashion, heard her sleepy murmur, and was instantly aroused. He felt so strong, so complete, that some demon of perversity couldn't resist roughing up the corners of his happiness.

"Elaine?"

She murmured again, not words but a sound so comfortable it would put babies to sleep.

"Elaine, have you ever . . ."

She made a throaty noise, an animal disturbed.

"I mean . . . Have you done this often?"

She stiffened. The silence was suddenly brittle. She turned and faced him. "What?"

"I was just wondering. I mean, I know I'm not the first, but, well . . ."

"Not the second, for that matter. Am *I?*"

"I'm sorry, I didn't mean it to be offensive." He began to feel like a D-minus student in one of her classes.

"Really? What did you mean it to be?"

"I'm just interested in you. In your life."

"I'm flattered."

He could feel his body tensing up, but he had to ask. "Did you have many—friends—in college?"

She rolled away from him. "Tom, why are you doing this?"

"Because I'm so happy."

She got out of bed. When she spoke, it may not have been anger exactly, but her precision put a chill in the room.

"Perhaps we should compare notes, doctor. If you insist, I'll tell you everything. But maybe you shouldn't insist."

He shivered. "I don't insist."

"Then I'll tell you. To make a long story short, I did a little experimenting in high school, most successfully with a very nice boy you'd remember from the basketball team, who later left here for Indianapolis and married someone with money. At Purdue I dated around a lot, sort of aimlessly, and ended up going steady with a very intense and handsome mechanical engineer, for our entire senior year, toward the end of which we managed to find ourselves sexually incompatible. Don't ask me why. I know why, but don't ask."

"Do you ever wish you'd married that guy on the basketball team?"

She looked at him as if she were ready to flunk him. "God, you won't give up, will you?"

"It's your life, it's important to me."

"*Marry* him? We were kids! I happen to like *mature* men. Which reminds me, doctor, when are you going to grow up?"

Shamed at last, the bulldog in his mind relented, and his whole body relaxed. "OK, Elaine, I'm sorry . . ."

"Oh, you're sorry." She pulled on a chenille robe and sat down at her dressing table. "Well, let's see how *you* like it. Your turn. The whole file, doctor, your complete sexual dossier. Take your time, it's early yet."

He felt excruciatingly foolish. Why hadn't he, addled with happiness, anticipated this? "Let's forget it, OK?"

"Five more seconds. Four. Three . . ."

"You see . . . Well—Edna is all there is to tell. She's the whole story." He felt himself blushing.

"You were a virgin when you married Edna?"

He nodded. Elaine smiled. "I love you, Tom." She got up and left the room. All the way down the hallway to the kitchen, her laughter sang to him like wind chimes.

Relieved that her anger had vanished, he lay back and almost dozed off for a moment. Then she was back again, carrying a tray of wine and cheddar and the folded newspaper from the front porch. She threw off the robe, sat down on the bed, and opened the paper. "Hear about the new battleship?"

"Heard it on the radio. Six hundred Hoosiers in Washington. Rare chance for the politicians' wives to wear mink."

"Cynic. Don't you know there's a war on?"

"Someone did mention it." He sipped the wine and passed a hand over her red hair, feeling the silkiness of it, then the smooth skin, the latissimus dorsi, the iliocostals, the provocative gluteals. He felt the excitement thickening in his throat.

She turned the pages. "Not like the others, this Hitler fellow. Not like good old Kaiser Bill, or Napoleon, even."

"Genghis Khan, maybe?"

"Something like that." She flipped the pages. "Bread, up to twelve cents a loaf now. Where will it end?"

There was a pause, and her eyes crinkled a little, a symptom the doctor had learned to diagnose. "What's the matter?"

She read a while longer, then handed him the paper. On page four, opposite a full page of photos of the battleship launching, was the lead editorial.

LIBERTY, OR LICENSE?

Today, as we prepare to send our young men out to defend our nation in the proud new vessel bearing the name of our state, we dedicate ourselves anew to the principles that made our country great: freedom of speech, press, and religion, the right to a free man's conscience.

However, our great country is now being undermined by a fifth column of blasphemers and skeptics. The "Hoosier Rationalist" has strained our patience far too long; and in the schools of Kenton, the atheistic theories of Charles Darwin are poisoning the minds of our young children.

These things must be stopped, and stopped now. It is all well and good to prattle about "rights" in ordinary times, but these are not ordinary times. The "Hoosier Rationalist" should be shunned by right-thinking people, and those who teach blasphemy in our tax-supported schools must be rooted out.

Liberty is one thing, license is another. America must be saved. Otherwise, it does not matter how many battleships we launch—the battle will already be lost, here at home. The danger, as Col. Lindbergh truly said, lies from within.

Wake up, America. Wake up, Royal County. Wake up, citizens of Kenton. The time is short.

Thomas Roberts gave a low whistle. "Well, at least they didn't come right out and advocate a public stoning."

Her voice was almost a whisper. "They must be saving that for next week."

He stared at the paper. November 22. The weather was turning cold, said a box on page one. The easy autumn was about over.

❧

AFTER THE THANKSGIVING dance Paul hadn't slept much, or the next night either, nervous about what Jim was thinking there in his quiet twin bed and anxious about what Ruthie would say on Saturday night. At breakfast or supper or waiting for the bathroom or helping set the dinner table, he edged around Jim like a polite stranger, and Jim never acknowledged his presence at all. Two long days of this holiday pussyfooting.

The memory is a slippery friend; you never know when it will turn traitor. Did it have to keep reminding Paul, all day Saturday, of the time, first day of kindergarten, when Jim taught him how to tie his shoestrings, and the time he rescued him from Dick Shrike, the fourth-grade bully, and the time he pulled him out of deep water at Long Lake?

You're my brother. Someday you'll do me a favor.

At six-thirty Saturday evening, Paul walked, then ran, over to the Peters' front porch. Ruthie was already there, at the door. She came out before Paul got up the steps, and they headed for the Strand Theater.

Except for the thirteen different Protestant churches, there was little luxury of choice in Kenton. The movie you saw in a given week was whatever happened to be playing at the Strand. If you wanted something else, you either committed the extravagance of driving thirty miles to Fort Wayne, or you waited a week, until the show changed. So the Andersons and the Peters and everyone else all waited, and somehow managed, once a week, to come up with a quarter apiece and a dime for the kids, and interrupted the depression blues with new movies: *Road to Zanzibar, How Green Was My Valley, Citizen Kane, The Lady Eve.*

What was playing at the Strand this week was the usual salty popcorn in buttery paper bags, and a new movie called *The Maltese Falcon,* so full of menace and treachery that afterward Paul and Ruthie emerged into the cool night air and simultaneously yanked up their jacket collars like trench coats and glanced around furtively, on the lookout for Kenton goons and desperadoes.

Walking down Main Street, Paul gave her a Bogart squint and spoke through his teeth: "You ever notice, kiddo, when you come out of a movie sometimes, you feel like you're still in it?"

"After *Gone With the Wind,* I talked with a Southern accent for two whole days. Made everybody in my family sick."

They turned left on William Street and went on walking.

"If you were in the movies, who'd you like to be?"

"I don't know. Jean Arthur. Ginger Rogers. Carole Lombard. Somebody not too ishy. How about you?"

"Depends. A tall guy, with creases in his face. Square-jawed. Cary Grant? Joel McCrea, maybe. Did you see *Union Pacific?*"

"Missed it." She snapped her fingers.

"I saw it three times. Three and a half. All the same day. I was just a kid. Went in at two o'clock on Saturday afternoon, and at about nine-thirty that night my Dad came down the aisle and took me by the shoulder. I was pretty hungry by then, so I didn't mind too much."

"Got your dime's worth, anyway."

"If I'd had a nickel for popcorn, I'd have talked him out of it and stayed for the whole last show."

They strolled the fourteen blocks to the end of William Street and the entrance to the country club.

Paul stopped. "Want to go in? I'll race you eighteen holes—even give you a handicap."

"I already have all the handicaps I need."

Her gravity unsettled him. They walked across the grass, still springy underfoot, in the lingering Indian Summer. At the first tee they stopped and looked up at the big orange moon low in the sky, and Paul took both of her hands.

"You said you had a lot to tell me."

She pulled her hands loose and hugged him hard. He breathed in her familiar smell. Innocence.

"It isn't easy, Paul."

"I can see that."

"Jim and I—well, you know—we've been going steady since we were freshmen. Three years. It started so early, I never even had a date with anyone else. Until tonight."

"I don't think he has, either."

"But is that right, do you think? I mean, is it smart, to be so ignorant? So limited? About the biggest thing in your life? About love?"

"Doesn't it sort of depend more on how you feel about it than how you think?" Paul's guilt nagged at him, and he tried to be fair, but he didn't really want to be fair. He wanted Ruthie.

"That's the problem—how I feel." She dropped her arms and turned around, looking out over the dark golf course. "I don't feel like just being Jim's girl anymore, just going steady and just getting engaged and then just getting married and just having kids and bringing them up to get married and have kids to bring up and get married and have kids . . ." She trailed off.

"I know what you mean."

"There has to be something more." She looked at him—almost, he thought, angrily. "Don't you want to go to college, Paul?"

He laughed. This was not what he'd expected her to talk about. It was Miss Edelman all over again. "Sure I want to. But that's not the problem. Tuition, books, room and board, where would it come from? Half the time my dad can't pay our rent, not even a crummy twenty-five bucks a month."

"You could work."

"Oh, I'll work all right. At McGraw's or the foundry, probably."

"You can do better than that, Paul. A lot better. You're smart, you work so hard already, with school and sports and your job and helping your father. You could get through I.U. on a scholarship, and then you'd have a future."

A future. The word charmed him; it had a strange ring to it that tinkled in his head. Like Miss Edelman saying, "a career."

"Just never thought it was in the cards for me. For Jim, maybe." Paul considered it. "They say only about one kid in ten from K.H.S. ever gets to college."

"You're that one, Paul. And Jim, too. And me. All we have to do is decide to do it."

All the bitter years of the depression, the only years he had ever known in his life, rebelled at this simplicity. A job, that was what people aspired to, not a "career," not a "future." Just forty hours of work and sometimes meat on the table.

"Ruthie, is that what you wanted to tell me?"

"Part of it—the second part. I'm going at it backwards. But you already know the first part, don't you?"

"Jim?"

"I told him, at the dance. Sometimes, even if you think you know what you're doing, even if everyone expects something of you, sometimes it just won't work out, and you know it won't."

"It's hard to believe you actually broke up. After all this time."

"We had to. Not because Jim isn't nice—and smart, and talented, and all that. Sure he is, he's King Arthur himself. But Paul, after you've been going steady for over three years, and when you're going to graduate soon, and when your family and your friends *expect* you to get married . . . Well, you have to ask yourself—do you really love this person?"

Paul let her pause hover in the cool night air. She cleared her throat. "And when I did ask myself, I realized that I've just been drifting. For a while, when you drift, it's OK—you just drift along. But then, later, you realize that you're drifting *into* something. I don't want my life to be like that, Paul. And it doesn't have to be."

"No." She made it all seem so simple.

"And yours doesn't, either." She was walking the edge of the tee-off green.

"Ruthie, why are you telling me this?"

She came up to him and hugged him again. He hugged her back, and, without knowing exactly what brought it about, he was kissing her, feeling for the first time the softness of her lips, unlike anything he had ever known, the first real kiss he had ever clung to. He felt good all over—in his lips, in his arms, in his thighs, in his toes. He felt good in his heart and lungs and stomach. His ears felt good, the skin on the back of his neck felt good. All the other good feelings of his sixteen years, put together in one instant, wouldn't have been as good as this. "In love," he thought. "This is what it's like. Love."

Her cold tears brought him around. Slowly they eased off, backed away a little, and they weren't kissing anymore.

"Why am I telling you?" she whispered. "Don't you know, Paul?"

He wiped a finger across each cheek and tasted her tears. "Ruthie," he said, marveling. "My God. Ruthie Peters."

"Paul and Ruthie," she said, "Ruthie and Paul." All of a sudden she grinned and gave him a little poke in the tummy, and suddenly they were running downhill, through the moonlight, over the fairway, down to the brook, across the bridge, around the sand trap, and onto the putting green, where they collapsed on the cold grass, panting and laughing. She pulled him against her, and when they could breathe right again, they kissed and stretched out on the ground and permitted themselves to feel ecstatic for a while, just kissing, and there was no one in the world Paul envied anymore.

After a while he felt her shivering, and he got up and gave her a hand. They locked arms around each other's waists and walked slowly back to the first tee.

They kissed again, there on the spot where he had first been really kissed, and Paul couldn't keep from saying it any longer: "I love you, Ruthie."

"I love you, Paul."

His head swelled with triumphant music, and he picked her up and whirled around and around until dizziness made him stop and put her down. She was breathless and dizzy too, and they clung to each other to stay upright. "That was fun," she breathed. "Oh, I love you."

"I love you."

"I *love* you."

"I love *you.*"

Then they were running again, flying, out of the country

club, down the fourteen blocks of William Street, past a hundred sleeping houses, past yellow patches of streetlight, and they didn't stop till they got to Ruthie's porch and plunked down in the porch swing, with a satisfying *sprong* of the chains. They panted, exhausted and happy.

It was late, and in Kenton, even on Saturday night, most people went to bed early; for the first time ever, Paul found it an attractive custom. This was an entirely different kind of night from any he had ever had alone, walking the quiet sidewalks in the moonlight.

After they were rested, they kissed, and then kept on kissing. He had no idea what time it was when he finally heard someone stirring inside the house. Ruthie broke away. "It's Mom. I'll have to go in now."

He didn't want this joy to stop, even for a short while. "Tomorrow, then?"

"Sure."

"I'll try to get the car after dinner. We'll go somewhere."

"Anywhere."

"Three o'clock if I can get it then. Or else I'll let you know."

"I'll be waiting."

A quick kiss, mouths barely touching, and then she was inside.

The three blocks home were not enough. Paul ran to the park and then walked a while to cool off before he had to go home at last and try to appear normal, in case anyone was still up.

Nobody was, and he was not normal at all. He was a lot better than normal. And he knew that Jim, lying there in his quiet twin bed, understood just how much better, and how much worse, you could be.

Paul had been lying awake for at least half an hour when he heard Jim clear his throat. When he spoke, it was a whisper so soft that if Paul had been asleep, it wouldn't have wakened him.

"You having fun, Pug?"

Paul felt a chill, as if he'd heard a ghost, and he thought of the saying: "His blood ran cold." He knew Jim didn't want an answer, any answer, and he knew he wouldn't go to sleep for a long, long time.

❧

ALTHOUGH THE REVEREND TUCKER devoutly believed in hell, he had never been an arm-waver. His scourging was earnest but not fevered. Even after he scolded his flock with a straight-from-the-shoulder sermon, people still shook his hand at the church door, smiling. "That wasn't preachin', Reverend," they'd say with a little laugh. "That was meddlin'."

Recently, his pastoral fervor had become a kind of exaltation, and he forsook brimstone almost entirely, in favor of grace and charity and love. He now gave a strong new emphasis to forgiveness and the quality of mercy. He no longer veiled his messages in the Greek, *themis, thanatos, agape,* but laid it out in a flurry of King James and Revised and Hoosier English.

"If I speak with the tongues of men and angels, and have no love, I am a tinkling cymbal, First Corinthians Thirteen." His resonant baritone caressed the scriptures. "If I feed the poor but have no love, I am nothing."

Watching carefully, Paul caught the preacher's quick glance into the organist's mirror.

"There are eunuchs from their mother's womb, and eunuchs made by men, Matthew Nineteen, and some have made themselves eunuchs for the kingdom of heaven's sake. But not all can accept that sacrifice, and so, to each of us, the divine commandment is, to love thy neighbor and even thine enemy."

A certain restlessness stirred in the congregation. Paul could see that the women in their heavy winter dresses and the men in their wool suits and starched white collars were feeling itchy.

"Even when Jerusalem is surrounded by an army, you must love your enemy, for there will be days of vengeance, and God's wrath shall descend upon the people, and a great harlot will sit upon the waters, and men will fall by the edge of the sword—and yet love itself will be the end and the beginning."

Because slothful comfort was known to imperil devotion, the oak benches of the First Church of Christ had never been covered with cushions, but now the hard seats had clearly become intolerable.

"In the winter of the spear and the sword, the voice of the turtle is heard in the land, saying, behold, you are beautiful, Solomon One, you have ravished my heart with a glance of your eyes, in spices and raisins and pomegranates, in a garden full of fountains, on a mountain of myrrh, we are sick with love, the scent of your breath is like apples, and your kisses like exquisite wine . . ."

Paul was sweating now as if it were a blazing August Sunday. The cardboard fans with their blue-eyed Jesus, tucked in behind the hymnals winter and summer, began to flutter through the sanctuary. Women shed woolen scarves, men took off their jackets. Bessie Rimmel, one of the altos sitting in front of Paul, was breathing in harsh, audible gasps.

The Reverend Tucker's forehead was gleaming, and he

paused a moment before continuing, his voice low and insinuating. "You have been told that lust is adultery in the heart, and I tell you, yes. But I tell you again to judge not, lest you be judged."

Murmurs rippled through the congregation.

"And I tell you likewise, ask and it shall be given you, seek and you shall find, take up the sword of righteousness and the spear of salvation—and this day, sinners, *you shall be with me in paradise.*"

The Reverend Tucker stopped talking, his mouth still open, eyes staring ahead, as if he were looking right through the big stained-glass windows into some overwhelming vision.

Miss Huron took her cue from his silence and struck a chord, and the choir and the whole congregation, at the bidding of their mimeographed programs, swelled into fortissimo: "The Son of God goes forth to war . . ."

By the fourth fervent verse, the congregation had worked off some of its agitation. After Reverend Tucker pronounced the benediction and they all sang "Blessed Be the Tie That Binds," people left the church uneasily. Only a few of them paused to shake hands with the preacher.

◆❧◆

"WHOLE WORLD'S GOING to hell in a handcart," Charles Anderson announced by way of a Sunday blessing, and the family pitched in, dismantling their belated Thanksgiving turkey, postponed because of the county basketball tournament. Jim and Paul went for the drumsticks, Charlie a big slice of breast, Betsy a thigh, Nora her peculiar favorites, the neck and the part that goes over the fence last. The mashed potatoes and sweet potatoes went around, the inevitable string beans, the cranberries, the biscuits in gravy. The silence of eating was an act of reverence.

But Charlie couldn't stop talking for long. "Lend-Lease to Russia now, the Reds will be shooting it all back at us one of these days." He had just taken a quick look at the headlines, but that was enough. "Harvard eggheads giving orders to the U.S. Army, they'll have us in the trenches again, just like the Wilson war all over, blasted Democrat wars, pass the cranberries."

Charlie was perpetual Greek chorus to the world's tragedy, and no more effective. Betsy went right on forking up food with her right hand, softly snapping the fingers of her left to the beat of an unheard boogie. Jim had his history book at the table, reading while everyone else talked—valedictorian in the making, the only permissible form of antisocial behavior in the family. Nora kept an eye on details: here's the bread, Charlie, Betsy, eat your beans, don't gulp air, Paul, Jimmy, chew every bite ten times.

"And now half the state is off in Washington, D.C., or Virginia somewhere, sloshing champagne on battleships, and nobody's here minding the shop. No wonder the water pressure's bad and the electricity goes off halfway through Eddie Cantor, beggars at the back door every day, and no wonder the mail is always late and the potholes never get fixed and grass is growing in the streets, just like Hoover said it would if that jackass got elected." Charlie assaulted the mashed potatoes. "And no wonder you can go to your own church on Sunday morning and see the preacher turn into a nut right in front of your eyes . . ."

"Charlie." Nora's warning tone. "Pass the sweet potatoes, please."

"Dad, could I use the car this afternoon?" Paul knew his timing wasn't right, but he had to work fast.

"Family man, pillar of the church, shepherd to his flock—why are we letting him get away with it?"

"Charlie, don't forget, I need seven dollars for tomorrow."

"About three o'clock, Dad? You won't be using it, will you?"

Betsy interrupted her private concert. "What do you want the car for, Pug? Got a big date?" She laughed as if that were a joke.

Jim looked up from his book. "What's so funny about his having a date? He's a big boy, isn't he? A junior in high school? He might even have a date with a senior." He glanced over at Paul, his face perfectly expressionless, then began reading again.

Charlie's train of thought always ran on a single track: "I'll tell you what I'm going to do about that jackass, Tucker. I'm going to get hold of Moss and Iddings and Carter, and make sure the Elders take this up, next meeting."

"Charlie, would you like some more turkey?"

"Dad, do you need the car yourself?"

"What kind of a preacher is he? Everybody knows what he's doing on the side."

"What's he doing?" Betsy was immediately interested. She hated being left out, especially if it was something she knew she shouldn't know.

"If you don't really need the car, Dad, I could use it this afternoon."

"Jed Shinover down at the Sinclair station knows, and he's not even in the church. Bob Mesler knows. Pete Jacobs at the barbershop was kidding me about it the other day. The man's making us a laughingstock, our whole congregation's a flock of patsies. We must be crazy to let this go on."

"Let *what* go on?" Betsy insisted. "Come on, Daddy, tell me."

"Charlie, that bill collector's coming again tomorrow. I've got to have the money this time."

"What happened to the ten dollars I promised you yesterday?"

"Don't kid around, now, I've got to have it. I'm not putting up with that man's insolence again."

"All I can say is, you keep a rotten apple in your barrel, you end up full of worms."

"Why is Reverend Tucker a rotten apple?" Betsy squealed.

"Be quiet, Betsy. Now before you forget it, Charlie, give me the seven dollars."

Charlie was digging in his pockets: "OK, here's five ones. And a silver dollar. And, let's see, a couple of half-dollars, two bits, a nickel, two dimes . . . How's that?"

"That'll help." Nora scraped the money together and put it in her apron pocket. "Now how about some nice warm mince pie?"

"While you're in your pocket, Dad, could I have the car keys?"

Jim looked up again. "For God's sake, Dad, *give him the keys!*"

Paul was confused and grateful and apprehensive. What was Jim up to? But when Charlie slid the keys down the oilcloth to him, Paul scooped them up with an overwhelming sense of relief and good will, gobbled a big piece of pie, and even helped carry some dishes to the sink before rushing upstairs to brush his teeth and change into his cords and letter sweater.

✖

D R. ROBERTS never went to church, and consequently suffered the assiduous attentions of the
faithful, who hoped to save him. Not his wife,
however; Edna had long since given him up, and
now contented herself with a steady, mute reproach, which
he accepted as a given of their daily life. Other believers,
undiscouraged, continued to ply him with pamphlets, but Dr.
Roberts only nodded and smiled, and remained unredeemed.

Since her auto accident, Edna was afraid to drive, so the
closest Dr. Roberts ever came to church was delivering her
to her devotions on Sunday morning and picking her up at
noon. As often as possible, true to his own devotion, he spent
his Sunday mornings in Elaine's bedroom, a shrine from
which he was finding it harder and harder to disengage himself. By noon, though, his residual Calvinism always triumphed.

"I'll be late."

"Kiss me."

"Yes . . . Have to hurry now."

"Once more."

"She can't walk home, Elaine."

"Oh, go, then. Go on." But she held him captive: three
more kisses.

"Why are you still here? Go, go!"

And finally he was off, the green Nash exceeding the resi-
dential speed limit and pulling up at the church just as people

began to emerge, only a few of them shaking hands with Reverend Tucker at the door, others just pulling on coats and hurrying out into the cold. Tom was surprised when Edna, usually so talkative with the preacher, brushed by him with only a quick nod.

He held the car door for her and closed it firmly but without slamming it, the way she liked. On the way home, he could tell something was different. "Problems?"

"What?"

"Anything wrong?"

"I don't know what you mean."

"Well, I mean by the time we get to Oak Street, I usually have a briefing, a rundown on the sermon . . ."

"Oh, you don't care. You don't really care." She blew her nose reproachfully.

She wouldn't say any more. He let it drop.

Sunday dinner was always a casserole, contrived on Saturday and put in the refrigerator, to be warmed up after church on the day of rest. Tom set the table and helped with the salad, still wondering why Edna was so quiet. As they ate, his old habit of seeing things from a distance flashed him an image of the two of them sitting there, an attractive woman and a presentable middle-aged man, well dressed and dining politely together, the image of contentment. How little we know, he thought, how little we can tell . . .

She pressed her napkin to her lips and then quickly, almost surreptitiously, wiped her eyes, a gesture that left a cramped feeling in his chest. Sometimes he couldn't tell if what he felt for her was guilt, or pity, or love, or what, his feelings so confused he couldn't begin to sort them out.

But he knew he wanted to help her. He tried again. "What is it, Edna?"

She remained silent for a moment, and when she finally

spoke, it was cautiously, as if on tiptoe. "Do you hear much gossip at your office?"

Gossip? He was instantly alert: Elaine, was that it? Was she going to say it at last, point an accusing finger, make it official? "Sometimes," he said. "Not much, though. Too busy getting people in and out, trying to keep up with the waiting room."

"But you do hear things, don't you? Have you heard about our organist, that young Huron woman? Isn't she one of your patients?"

He let himself relax. So that was it: Reverend Tucker. He might have known. "She's old enough to know better."

"But is it true what they're saying? I thought it was all just gossip, spiteful people . . ." She put down her fork and wiped her eyes again. "But the sermon today . . . Well, is it true?"

"I guess I've heard the same things you have."

"But a minister? *Our* minister?"

His guard went up again. She *must* be trying to tell him something. He made his voice sound normal. "I guess ministers are like everyone else."

"Some people aren't supposed to be like everyone else. They're supposed to be *above* it." She lifted her eyes heavenward, and, as he always did, he fell in love with that gesture of hers.

"You're right, Edna, sure—but, well, people aren't perfect. Even preachers."

"People could try! They could act like grown-ups, not schoolkids! Oh, it makes me sick to think of it! Poor Mrs. Tucker, she's such a wonderful woman, such a servant of the Lord, such a perfect lady."

Mrs. Tucker came to Dr. Roberts' office for an occasional prescription. She was so ladylike she had never consented to a complete physical examination. "Maybe," Tom murmured, "that's the problem."

Soft as his voice was, Edna heard what he said, and began to cry. "Why do you say things like that?"

Everything had a double edge now. Seeing her tears, he squirmed in his chair.

"If anything like that ever happened to me, I wouldn't be able to bear it! I'd kill myself! Really, I would!" The tears turned to anger. "It's such an outrage, what people have to put up with! Civilized people! Good Christians! And for a woman like that! What's the matter with people, anyway?"

She pushed her chair back and stalked off to the bathroom, and soon Tom heard the water running in the tub. Exhausted, he left the neglected dinner on the table, flopped on the couch, and, despite the afternoon sun shining on his face, immediately fell into a profound but troubled sleep.

WITH CAR KEYS in his pocket, Paul always felt lucky, and, as luck would have it, Charlie had just treated the Ford to its customary five gallons of gas. November was still on its golden best behavior, pretending to be a day in October. Ruthie was waiting on the front porch when Paul drove up. She came running down the steps, jumped in, slid across the seat, and settled into his right arm. Paul was instantly so overwhelmed with love that he could have just stayed there at the curb the whole Sunday afternoon. But he began to feel the oppressive nearness of her parents, so he reluctantly pulled away from Ruthie and started the car.

Beyond the city limits, he put an arm around her again. They drove like that, along the county roads, narrow gravel lanes bisecting the flat cornfields. The slanting sun of Indian Summer was trying to fool them, but they could tell by the dead farmland—the ghosts of cornstalks, stubble of wheat-fields, gray grass in the pastures—what season it really was.

"Where are we going?" she asked after a while.

"Where do you want to go?"

"Into the sunset."

Aching with love, Paul pulled off the road onto a grassy berm, stopped the car, and held her tight. She slipped a hand under his jacket, and they lived that way for a while, watch-ing the sky.

November 23: only a month to the shortest day of the year. By four-thirty the sun was already settling into the low wispy clouds, and the sky was turning pink, crows scolding past the cornfields, headed for the woods just in time. As the moments passed, the clouds turned violet, then dusky purple, and even-tually pink again in an afterglow, and Paul and Ruthie sat there in each other's arms, not wanting it ever to end.

It was almost dark when he finally thought of Jim, off somewhere by himself, bereft. She must have felt his mood. "What is it?"

"I was just thinking about Jim."

"Jim understands, Paul. We talked. He knows it's over."

"But he's so miserable. And I'm so happy. It makes me feel terrible."

"It's your Church of Christ training." That was a Method-ist joke. "You'll never have the least bit of fun without paying for it. Church of Christ guilt. Church of Christ remorse."

"I'm afraid you're right. Still, Jim's alone out there . . ."

"I'm sorry for Jim, too, really sorry, but there's nothing I can do about how I feel. People change. We can't live in yesterday or last year. This is now. This moment. Here, shut your eyes, and think—*this moment.*" She kissed his nose, his eyelids.

He sighed happily. "This moment."

"And nothing is your fault. Repeat after me: It's not my fault."

"It's not my fault." He kissed her earlobe.

"That's better. Jim will take care of himself, he's a survivor. You, you're different, you need all the help you can get."

She laughed and kissed his neck, and a thrill went chasing through his legs. He put his hands under her coat and felt her soft sweater, her slender body. When they kissed again, his hands slid along the pink cashmere, and he realized how very little of Ruthie Peters he could legitimately touch: that part of her back from the waist up, nothing lower, nothing in front. It made him feel a little claustrophobic. Still he was grateful for that much. More than he ever expected, more than he deserved.

When they kissed now, it was with a kind of seriousness, an earnestness that amazed Paul, who knew very little about kissing. They learned the feel of each other's cheeks, eyelids, foreheads. It was suffocating, the excitement, so they'd take little holidays, sitting back in the car seat and letting November cool their faces—brief intervals of self-denial. And they talked.

"Have you been thinking about college?"

"A little."

"Good! Where are you going to go? I.U.?"

"Hey, not so fast. It depends on a lot of things. On how Dad's business goes, and whether they need me here, helping out, earning some money."

She touched his face impulsively. "I love you. But listen, Paul, they'll be all right without you. And you don't have to ask them for anything. You can manage it by yourself. Get a scholarship, and a part-time job. You have to think of yourself, on your own, if you're ever going to have a future."

A future. The word set off chimes in his head again. Would Pug Anderson have a "future"?

"Everything's so fouled up, Ruthie. Not enough jobs, not enough money. And the war—Dad's afraid we'll get dragged into it, even though nobody wants it."

"My dad thinks so, too. Pretty soon, maybe. He hates it, but you know what he says? He says we'd better get it over with."

"Your father has three daughters. Mine has two sons. It makes a difference."

"Daddy was in the last war. He hates war. But he thinks Hitler has to be stopped."

"Well, it looks like the English and the Russians are slowing him down."

"Paul . . ." Their eyes had adjusted to the dark, and he could see her silhouette, brooding. "If we do get into it, maybe you should consider not going."

She was full of surprises. He felt as if he'd just heard treason. "I'd *have* to go, Ruthie. You'd be ashamed of me if I didn't. Besides, there's the draft now."

"Not if you were a—whatcha-call-it? An objector. They had them in the last war, Daddy said."

"I'll bet he wasn't too crazy about them, was he?"

"They're still alive, though. And this new draft, they're getting out of it, too."

"You have to be a Quaker or something. Jehovah's Witness."

"Well, you go to church every Sunday."

"I go to an 'Onward, Christian Soldiers' church. Even if my dad is against it, if there's a war, I'd have to go."

"*I* wouldn't."

"If you were a boy, and everyone else went, you'd have to. I'll have to."

"But you don't even believe in it."

"I haven't figured it all out, that's all. But I know Hitler's a dictator. Mussolini, too."

"So's Stalin. Lots of others. Are we going to fight them all?"

"But Hitler wants to conquer the world. And he might, if nobody stops him."

"Well, still—it's something to think about, Paul."

They didn't talk anymore then, but as he kissed her again, Paul realized that Ruthie Peters was a lot more complicated than he had imagined.

It was black outside the windshield. He clung to Ruthie, and she hugged him tight, and they kissed again. But there are limits to frustration, and eventually she did him the painful favor of sliding across the seat and suggesting that it was time to go home. Paul suddenly felt hungry; they had missed supper.

He started the car and turned on the headlights. She slid back across the seat to him, and he held her warmth close, all the way to the Candy Castle, where Paul spent the last of his *Saturday Evening Post* nickels and dimes on cheeseburgers, before taking her home.

After he dropped Ruthie at her house, Paul drove around her block twice, peering into the Peters house each time, reluctant to let the evening end. When he finally drove home, he cut the motor halfway down the block and slid up to the curb without a sound. Getting out, he eased the door shut, then saw someone sitting on the porch steps, in the dark. He knew who it had to be.

Jim was looking at him, his head cocked a little to one side.

Paul knew he was squinting, the way he always did when something was bothering him. "Late hours for a ballplayer, Pug."

"Not even midnight yet. People go to bed in the middle of the afternoon around here."

"Mom wondered where you were. I told her I'd wait up."

"Nice of you, Ace."

They left it there for a moment, Jim still sitting on the steps, head cocked, Paul standing there, legs apart, like a guy ready to run for it.

"Ruthie and I have been going steady for a long time— since we were freshmen."

"I know."

"Since Thanksgiving, 1938. That's when Thanksgiving was still the last Thursday of the month. Who'd have thought that would ever change?" Jim's hands were clasped, elbows on knees. "Everything's changing. It's—damn it, it's—historical, what Ruthie and I've been through together. We've been going steady through the whole European war."

Paul hadn't thought of it that way. He felt a sad little twinge in his chest.

"Jerry tried to break us up once. Last year. Had a new car, new for him, tried to date Ruthie."

"I didn't know that."

"She laughed at him. She's polite, you know, but she told me she just couldn't help it, she had to laugh."

Paul didn't know what to say.

"Lots of guys have made their moves on Ruthie."

"I'll bet."

"But she wouldn't give them the time of day. She's my girl, Pug. Always has been."

"I'm sorry, Ace."

"We learned to dance together. When she learned how to

jitterbug, she taught me. Always used 'In the Mood.' Almost
wore out that record."

"I remember."

"Junior class play together, co-stars. Junior-Senior banquet
together. At the Candy Castle, kids get out of our booth when
they see us come in."

"I've seen them." Jim's voice stabbed little holes in Paul's
conscience.

"One of us'll be valedictorian. Our grades are so close we
don't even know which one."

"Yeah." Smart Jim, talented Jim, all the virtues. Paul's
automatic envy made him feel even worse.

"We studied 'Evangeline' together in Miss Eva's class. Lab
partners in old Graff's Biology I. Chemistry lab, too. Thirty,
forty trips to the movies in Fort Wayne, Berger's Burgers on
Road Six afterward. Skating at the Silver Moon. Out at Long
Lake, our own special place to park."

Paul hadn't known how many ways he could feel bad at
once: guilty, scared, envious, sneaky, unworthy, defensive.
But beyond all that, eclipsing it all, was the sudden terrible
fear of losing Ruthie. "Why are you going through all this,
Jim? I mean, I know it all already."

"Because, damn it, she's *my girl.* "

Jim's voice rang in his ears like an echo, and Paul kept
hearing it in the quiet street.

"Look, Jim, I know this is hard, but . . . Well, Ruthie has
a right to change her mind if she wants to."

"She hasn't changed her mind, she's been stolen. Kid-
napped."

For the first time Paul had a glimpse of what it would be
like to be driven crazy. He felt so sorry for Jim that he could
almost have given Ruthie up. Almost. He spoke very softly,
as if at a sickbed. "Jim, Ruthie's a free person. She can do

what she wants, go where she wants, with whoever she wants. She's not yours, Jim, she's free.".

Jim just sat there. "She wouldn't have done this by herself. You did it. You did it to her. To me."

Someday you'll do me a favor.

Paul was desolate; he knew he couldn't help Jim now. "You're forgetting one thing, Ace." Jim wouldn't ask him what. "Ruthie doesn't love you anymore. She must have told you. Didn't she? She just—doesn't—love you."

The way Jim moved, hunched over, made Paul ache. His brother. His only brother. "I'm sorry, Jim." He was panting, as if he'd just run a race. "Do you want to pop me or something? I wouldn't blame you."

It was a long time before Jim answered. Finally he stood up, holding his arms out as if he were afraid of falling.

"Oh, no, I wouldn't do that. Not to my own brother." He started into the house. "I've got something else for you, instead. For all of you. A little surprise. You'll see."

❧

SOME MOMENT IN the lives of heroic figures fixes them forever in the amber of history or legend: Antony at Actium, Roland at Roncesvalles, Joan at Orléans, Nelson at Trafalgar. For the Reverend Stephen B. Tucker, that moment came in the pulpit of the First Church of Christ on Sunday, November 30, 1941.

The Board of Elders had met in closed session the previous Thursday, and, although there were no public announcements following the meeting, a current of rumor hummed along the telephone lines of the congregation. The Reverend Tucker had been warned. Some said the Elders had threatened to send him packing. In any case, by Sunday the spirit of ultimatum was in the air, and the faithful of the church were understandably excited.

The Reverend Tucker who preached the sermon on November 30, however, was no chastened schoolboy, but a tower of strength unto the Lord and a scourge to the heretic. Using as a text Matthew 21:21, "Have faith, and doubt not," the man of God went on the offensive.

"We have manifested from this pulpit acts of love and toleration, yes, even to the mercenaries of the Prince of Darkness, and we have called upon the hirelings of Satan to repent and go their ways, healed and saved. But we have raised our voices in a wilderness."

Apprehensive, Paul listened from the choir stall. The congregation was unusually attentive.

"There is a time to plant and a time to harvest. The battles we have fought against this enemy will never be won except by faith. *Have faith, and doubt not.* We have been told by the skeptics that our Holy Bible is not the Word of God but only the ramblings of a primitive and barbarous tribe of desert people, inscribed by authors unknown, in vague and misleading language, subject to error and whim and erasure and alteration and outright fantasy. And we are told that this holy book contradicts itself all the way from Genesis to Revelation."

Reverend Tucker held the black book over his head like a trophy. "And what do we say to such allegations? We say that the spirit triumphs where the letter faileth, and the miracle of the Word will shine forever, above the carpings of pedants and heretics. *And we believe.*"

Paul thought about that for a moment while Reverend Tucker breathed heavily and moved about the podium. Not once had Paul seen him glance over at Miss Huron.

"What does it matter that the infidel assaults our holy Word?" He held the book aloft again, briefly. "Shall we cower because they tell us it is absurd for a woman to be made from the rib of a man? Do we doubt that an omnipotent Creator was obliged to rest on the seventh day, or that a snake could speak Hebrew? Do we worry when atheists complain that a million animals could not have been squeezed into a four-hundred-foot ark?

"Of course we don't worry, because we know that faith is counted for righteousness. *And—we—believe!*"

Someone in the congregation shouted "Amen!" It startled Paul; he had never heard that in his church before, and supposed that only Pentecostals did it, or maybe Baptists.

Reverend Tucker's voice became confidential for a moment, and he patted the black book reverently. "We are not deceived, brothers and sisters, by the voices counseling 'reason'—we know from bitter experience that 'reason' is a dark mirror, and only faith is perfect. So we are not surprised that in a world of faith, a woman could be turned into salt, Genesis Nineteen. We know that human beings, full of faith and free from the curse of science, could live to be nine hundred years old, Genesis Five. We know that God can turn rivers to blood, turn rods into serpents, and turn dust into lice, Genesis Seven and Eight. *Have faith, and doubt not!*"

He thumped the Bible. "We know that everything denied to us by 'reason' is possible to the Lord. We know that He was right to command slavery and mass murder and starvation and human sacrifice and public stonings—not from 'reason' but because all things are possible to an omnipotent God. And the power of the Lord beyond all other power is what justifies our faith. *And we believe!*"

This time several voices shouted "Amen!" and it surprised Paul all over again. He looked around. It wasn't like the usual service, people sitting vacantly in the pews fighting off sleep through the sermon. They were bright-eyed, all of them, nodding approval, elbowing their neighbors: more like a political rally than a church service. Even old Mr. Eichhorn, who always snored, was still awake. There was a low buzzing of excitement in the choir stalls: now it must be coming.

"We know it is written, put on the breastplate of faith, for the day of the Lord cometh as a thief in the night, First Thessalonians Five. And shall we now stand by, girded in our swords and bucklers, while thieves in our schools steal away the souls of our children?"

Mutterings swept through the congregation like wind in a wheatfield. Paul felt more and more uneasy; he too knew what was coming next.

"The woman who teaches agnostic evolution to our children, the woman whose heathen father pollutes our newsstands with his malicious falsehoods, is a so-called 'public servant,' drawing precious dollars and cents from the pockets of the hardworking, churchgoing people of this town, from you and from me. And now our children are bringing her corruption into our homes and dirtying the very air we breathe. I ask the people of this church, the people of Kenton, to stand up and testify. *Have faith, and doubt not.*

"If we act in our faith, we must prevail, and will then say to each other in grace, We have fought the good fight, we have kept the faith, Second Timothy Four. There is a time to gather stones, and a time to kill, Ecclesiastes Three, and when we are finally triumphant in the good fight, we can say to ourselves, in the very words of the Lord God himself, Exodus Twenty-Two, *Thou shalt not suffer a witch to live!*

The organ did not break forth in triumph, as it usually did, on Reverend Tucker's last word. Miss Huron had been slow to respond all morning, her rapport with the preacher strangely impaired. So there was a long silence in which the agitated congregation seemed stunned, and the final exhortation resounded in Paul's head: *not suffer a witch to live.*

He could hardly believe what he had seen or heard. As the verses of "Onward, Christian Soldiers" marched by, he tried to sort out his confused thoughts and feelings. What had he become? A dozen years of the Church Militant, Christian Soldiers, the Good Fight, the Blood Red Banner, a Mighty Fortress, Soldiers of the Cross—what had he become? What might he yet become, his adrenaline triggered weekly by mystery, confusions, enigma? Was it too late already? Was his life forever caught in the grip of that tidy and lethal smugness?

Before the anthem was finished, Paul put down his hymnal, yanked off his black robe, and, as everyone stared, strode up the center aisle. He knew that it was for the last time.

As the militant hymn came to a close, he stopped at the church door and turned around. The elders and deacons were crowding onto the podium, congratulating Reverend Tucker, who was holding his Bible and smiling. The congregation bustled with excitement, pulling on coats and scarves. Miss Huron, her face reflected in the organ mirror as she played the muted recessional, looked subdued.

Paul wanted to leave, to free himself from all this, but he just stood there at the door, staring at the jubilant congregation, feeling angry and betrayed.

Years of Sunday school. A lifetime of sermons . . .

DECEMBER

THINGS WERE TOUGH all over. The frigid Russian
front was still in a state of massive carnage and
endless confusion; the Japanese negotiators in
Washington were apparently stalling, and their
new premier, Tojo, was reported to have said he would
"purge" Asia of the British and Americans; the radical labor
boss, John L. Lewis, was threatening to call a coal miners'
strike, just as the snows began; and connoisseurs of tree bark
and animal furs were predicting a long, cold winter.

At home, Paul suffered an inner cold that never let up. His
parents, though they hadn't been harsh with him, were
clearly unhappy about his sudden break with the church.
Worse than that, though, he kept wondering what Jim's
threatened "surprise" was going to be, and lately the thought
of it kept waking him up in the middle of the night, sweating.
He tried everything he could think of to make up with Jim.
Every morning he'd say something conciliatory, or put a
question, or ask for advice—but Jim would never even look
his way or acknowledge his presence. Ace Anderson was
freezing him out.

Still, he didn't give up. Monday, December 1, was Jim's
eighteenth birthday, and Paul had set his mental alarm clock
to wake up early. He wanted to wrap Jim's present and write
a poem for him, and then he had to get to school early to study
for a big history test.

He had been wondering for weeks what he could give

Jim—a real problem, since he didn't have enough money to buy anything nice enough for such an important birthday, and he didn't own anything Jim would want.

Except one thing. If it had been August, he'd have thought of it sooner. Jim had never said so, but Paul knew he envied him the fancy Don Budge tennis racket his father had given him last summer.

So the problem was solved. He knew where his mother kept the leftover gift-wrapping paper and ribbons. But wrapping a tennis racket, he found out, wasn't easy. He finally managed it, even though there was no disguising the shape. A Hottentot or an Eskimo, confronted with that red and gold package, would have had no trouble guessing what was in it.

Harder than wrapping the present was writing the obligatory poem. Paul tried and tried, but the words wouldn't come, and he knew why. Finally he decided to eat something first and try again afterward.

It had turned much colder overnight, and a deep and fluffy snow had smothered William Street, but Gustave Jaeger's reliable mare had tugged the milk wagon through it. Paul brought the bottles in from the porch, their cardboard caps popped open, frozen cream standing an inch above the bottle top. He set both bottles on the kitchen table and spooned off the icy cream, his prize for being the first one up. It was still dark out, and nobody on the whole block seemed to be awake yet. In the cold house, isolated in snowbanks, Paul felt a kind of purity that relieved his unhappiness about Jim.

After he downed a bowl of the Breakfast of Champions in ice-cold milk, he felt better, and hacked away at the poem.

> For Jim,
>   Who is nobody other
>   Than my favorite brother:

When you take those swings
With these classy strings,
You'll want to sing:
It's the sport of kings.
    Happy Birthday, Ace,
    From Funnyface.

Not his best, or even his third-best, but it had to do—he was late for his big date with the history book. Feeling a pang of loss, he stood the racket up on Jim's chair, a red and gold surprise, carefully folded the poem, and propped it up against the package.

Everyone else would give Jim his present after supper at Grandma Jerrold's house, when they sang Happy Birthday in barbershop harmony and devoured Jim's favorite: Nora's famous devil's food cake with chocolate frosting, the big three-decker ablaze with eighteen candles. But Paul wanted Jim to have the racket first thing in the morning, because he hoped it would make him feel good all day.

Maybe, maybe it would make them friends again.

Nobody else was stirring yet upstairs. Paul pulled on his four-buckle arctics and red plaid mackinaw for the long walk to K.H.S. By the time he got to school, old man Riley had unlocked all the doors. Paul began to make his daily check of his Drosophila bottles, carefully isolating the newly matured females. The tiny creatures had been breeding since right after Labor Day—"copulating repeatedly," Paul couldn't forget that phrase. It summed up the state of nature for him, competitive, sexy, extravagant. And now, from a few hundred original flies, there were thousands. There had been five generations of them, families of one hundred or more at a time. It had been a lot of work for the students—feeding, isolating, examining, keeping data—but Miss Edelman insisted it would be worth it.

And it was. The veins of the wings of some flies in the second generation had developed abnormalities in their second longitudinal vein. The students, under the teacher's careful direction, had isolated and inbred these, so that the abnormalities kept on being inherited, until, by the fourth generation, they had become dominant.

"Now," Miss Edelman had asked, "what has happened to our word 'normal'?"

Paul fed bits of overripe banana to his flies and observed one of the new generation that had just emerged from the pupa state. As he examined it under the microscope, he caught his breath: for the first time, abnormalities had appeared not only on the second longitudinal vein but on the third vein as well. A brand-new variation!

He war-whooped his excitement, the musical howl echoing through the empty lab. He was Gregor Mendel at work in his garden—variation, inheritance! His mind conjured the heady syllables: mu-ta-tion, ev-o-lu-tion!

He couldn't wait to tell Miss Edelman the news, but he'd have to come back after the history test and tabulate the data on the new abnormal veins. Calming himself down, he carefully stoppered the Drosophila bottles and went off to study hall to read about the Bill of Rights, until the bell rang for his first class.

He didn't see Jim at school all day. He found out why at three-thirty, when the principal's secretary told him he'd had a call from his mother, telling him to skip basketball practice and come right home.

Jim was gone.

The Pennsylvania Railroad ran a single track from Fort Wayne to Kenton and beyond. Twice a day, in both directions, a short train chugged through, with a few mail and baggage cars and a passenger coach. This morning Jim had started out as if for school, turned the other way at Main

Street, waited an hour at the depot, bought a one-way ticket to Fort Wayne, walked to the post office there, and enlisted in the Navy.

When Jim phoned, he told his mother he wouldn't be home to blow out the eighteen lucky candles. Pug could do it for him, he said. Pug was lucky at everything.

Coming in the back door on a run, the first thing Paul saw was his birthday present on the kitchen chair, still wrapped in red and gold, a reproach. His poem was open on the table. Nora told him the whole story, weeping softly and steadily. "All I ever had was kids," she cried, "and now they're taking them, too." She sobbed so pitifully that Paul found himself cradling her like a child. "Just like the last war. My brother Ed with his stiff leg. Poor Bob Hickey gassed so he couldn't ever talk right again. Donnie James missing, never came back . . ."

She seemed to recall for a moment that she had spent twenty-one married years comforting people. She smiled briefly at Paul and patted his cheek. But then the grief came over her again, and she sobbed into his shirt.

A minute later, like someone switching stations, she turned it off deliberately, stood up, rubbed her painful knees, and pulled Paul to his feet. She smiled at him again, the wrinkles of her eyes making do for cheer. "I'll go get supper started."

On his way upstairs, Paul passed Charlie coming down, and they hugged each other for a moment without a word, and then broke away, embarrassed. His father hadn't hugged him since he was a little boy.

Lying on the bed with his clothes on, Paul heard Betsy crying in her room. He watched the shadows on the ceiling, wishing Jim were there in the other twin bed, wishing he'd been able to talk to him, and almost wishing that he hadn't been so lucky with Ruthie.

He got up and looked in the bureau drawers. Jim had taken

the stuff he always carried in his pockets, and his secret four dollars out of the cracked vase, and even the worthless rabbit's foot, but nothing else. In the closet, the crowded merit-badge sash still draped Jim's Boy Scout uniform. Pioneering, Path-finding, Exploring—a little lifetime of doing everything right. Jim's desk was eloquent: a place for everything, and everything in place. The only thing missing was Jim's old photo of Ruthie.

❧

THE BIWEEKLY MEETINGS of the Kenton School Board had become chilly, then frosty, and some-times stormy, and ended by adding a new ugliness to Mondays. Dr. Roberts had taken to gritting his teeth a lot on Monday mornings and tensing his abdominal muscles.

On the Monday that Jim ran off, there was an unusually rowdy session, Reverend Tucker shouting at Wendell Keller, who shouted back, Lucinda Jacobs sputtering at Carl Potter, who vented his rage at Joe Berry, who was trying to finish a risqué anecdote but was interrupted by Tucker's thunder-ous motion, seconded by Potter, to fire their disruptive biol-ogy teacher.

That evening it was Dr. Roberts' wretched duty to report the proceedings to the teacher in question. She listened in silence, walking nervously back and forth across her living room. "And that was it—I couldn't put off the vote any longer. Well, I played my flimsy trump. Reminded them how many years I'd served on the Board, and told them straight out that, as chairman, I might not get a chance to vote, but I wanted them to know that if they passed the motion to dismiss you, I'd resign."

Elaine glanced at him quickly and walked to the window where he couldn't see her face.

"I knew we couldn't do any better than the last time, Potter and Berry and Tucker with their minds made up. Well, Wendell stuck with me, and Lucinda, of course, but Millard—Millard's a strange bird, never says much, you never really know what he's thinking. Unfortunately, he's a member of Tucker's congregation. An Elder, in fact. And finally his hand went up with the ayes." Tom stopped talking, as if he couldn't control his voice. Elaine waited. "So—we lost it."

She had lost it, he meant.

"They're directing Hedges to terminate your contract, effective immediately—end of this week. I don't know what else they did, because I resigned, then and there, and walked out."

She looked through the window at the moon, waxing and gibbous, the stars pale around it. Out there the Drosophila were buzzing under blue laboratory lights, copulating repeatedly, exhibiting, like Galileo's telescope, the truth of nature to anyone willing to observe.

"So that's it," he said. "Not as spectacular as a stoning or burning at the stake—but it's how we handle our witch-hunts nowadays. It's ironic, but I suppose I could have helped you more if I loved you less. If the whole town didn't know we were—keeping company."

A moment passed before he went on. His voice kept wavering. "A small thing, firing a teacher. It doesn't throw a hundred men out of work or lower property values or raise the tax rate. All it does . . . All it does is put a little warp in the hearts of the executioners, and in the hearts of those who stand by and let it happen. All it does is stunt the minds of their children, so that they grow up to match their lucky parents." For the first time, he sounded really angry. "You know what pisses me off the most? When I was walking out on them, I turned at the door, and old Potter was smiling. Smiling!"

"A man may smile, and smile, and be a villain."

He didn't know what else to say. He had never felt so helpless. "Elaine—what will you do now?"

She didn't turn around. "It was my first job . . ." she murmured. "And I was working so hard at it."

He couldn't tell if she was crying or not. "You were the best teacher in the school, everybody said so. Maybe you should get a job in Fort Wayne. Some bigger place."

She kept her back to him, watching the moon. "Not easy to get a job in midyear, Tom. Anyway, I imagine it'd be about the same there. I can't just cover my eyes and teach a lie. Maybe there's some Old Saul in me, too. So I guess I'd always be a target, wherever I went."

"Well, then . . ."

"Maybe I'll go back to school—to I.U., to grad school again. Dr. Kinsey said he could get me a scholarship—I was sort of his protégée last year. I could get a Ph.D., and then I wouldn't have to put up with another high school job in another Kenton." She was really crying now. "Oh, God, Tom, I'll have to leave town—but I can't leave you!"

At the thought of losing her, something shriveled inside him—still, he wanted to help her, no matter what. He managed a cheerful voice. "So, then—Dr. Edelman?"

She turned around at last, trying to smile. "Yes, Dr. Roberts?"

"We'll see each other often, won't we? Promise me we'll see each other."

"I promise."

But he was drowning in dismay. How could he live without being with her every day? Talking to her? What would become of his life? What would become of hers?

And what about her father?

Even in deep trouble of her own, she could still sense his anxieties. "There's more, isn't there, Tom? You haven't told me everything."

"Well, everything about the Board."

"What else, then? More bad news?"

He hated this. "I . . . I just wonder if this is the time and place, that's all. But I guess it is."

She stood quietly, waiting for the little hop in her chest. It came. "What is it, Tom?"

"You remember, your father's been coming in for tests."

"Yes?"

"Well—we thought there might be something suspicious in the neck, in the nodes."

She sucked in air. "And there is?"

"Yes. I mean, no—it isn't just suspicious anymore. He went to Fort Wayne for a biopsy last week."

"He told me he was going to meet someone from the CIO."

"He didn't want to worry you. But he can't keep this to himself, not for long."

"Tell me right out, Tom."

"It was positive."

She cried softly. He held her. "Just like my mother—three years ago . . . Have you told him?"

He nodded. "He didn't act as if it was a surprise."

"How long will it . . ."

"It's a type that develops fast. Maybe a few months."

Moments crept by. She wiped her eyes. Moonlight made a square on the carpet. "Do you know how old he is, Old Saul Edelman?"

"It's in his records, but I don't remember."

"Forty-five. Behind that gray beard, Old Saul Edelman is forty-five years old."

"I thought you'd want me to tell you."

"Of course I did."

"They're better at it now, Elaine, the surgeons, the radiation. Maybe . . ."

"Maybe," she said. "Maybe."

"I'm sorry."

"Yes, so am I. We good people, we're always sorry, aren't we? We all *mean* so well, and we *do* so poorly. Think of our two lives, Tom. So ineffectual. So powerless. So jinxed. You're a doctor, and you can't cure my father. You were president of a school board, and you couldn't protect one of your own teachers. I'm—I *was* a teacher. A 'teacher,' imagine! That's a word I've respected all my life. Not just respected, *revered*. And it turns out I can't even hold my very first job. And when we fall in love, we two losers, all we do is hurt your innocent wife."

Tom tried to break in, to stop the self-reproach, the unfairness, but she was talking too steadily.

"All of us 'good' people—what good do we do? My father. My poor father. Champion of integrity. Defender of truth. And for what? To lay waste the precious feelings of a whole community, and end up a target of the very people he's trying to help! And now he gets his final reward, terminal cancer at forty-five! *Good people!*"

She was rigid with anger. When he put his arms around her, it was like embracing a statue. But finally she hugged him fiercely. "Don't leave me, Tom. Stay tonight. All night."

"I wish I could. But . . ."

"Please stay. I can't bear to be alone now."

I'd kill myself. Really, I would.

He felt as if he were going to burst, to explode. "I do love you, Elaine!"

"Then stay. Please."

"It's just that—it's already late, and—it's our silver anniversary this week, and . . . I just can't do it to her, Elaine."

She slipped out of his arms and went back to the window. The moon was half covered with clouds.

"Goodbye, Tom."

He slunk away like a criminal and drove all the way home at ten miles an hour.

❧

OR THE SECOND TIME that week, Paul was called out of class. On Wednesday, just before noon, they told him in the principal's office that his father's lab was on fire. He ran all the way to Main Street, and could hardly bear to look. Cars and trucks were jammed into the blocked-off street, the town's single fire truck pumping water into the Hillmeyer building, crowds of people gawking and shouting.

The demon Slayzall had gone berserk. The deadly stuff had torched the heart of Main Street, and now threatened to spread in both directions. The volunteer firemen looked desperate, tugging at their big hose in the snow. The water supply, diminished by the faulty city pump, was hardly reaching the second floor, where the five-gallon cans of kerosene and carbolic acid were igniting. The Hillmeyers, father and son, were in the street without their coats, screaming at the firemen.

Where was Charlie?

At last Paul spotted him in the crowd, his hands clumsily bandaged, watching the scene through the haggard face of an old man.

"Dad! Dad, you OK? How'd it happen?"

His eyes didn't focus on Paul. The fire seemed to have hypnotized him.

"I don't know, I just don't know. I was heating the phenol, like always, and all of a sudden the crazy stuff was burning— it burns like the devil, I'll tell you." He looked down at his bandaged hands. "I tried to put it out, but there was no stopping it. Finally, I had to run for it, so I tore downstairs to Hillmeyer's, yelled at everyone to get out fast, and called the fire department."

"Why didn't they put it out right away?"

"Yeah, why, why? It took them *twelve minutes* to get here." Charlie indicated his wristwatch.

"To come ten blocks?"

"You figure it out. We've got two firemen on duty, round the clock, and most of the volunteers got here before the fire truck did."

"Oh God, that's awful."

"It'll be awful for Main Street if they can't stop it soon. It's already too late for the lab."

Too late: Paul imagined the wildfire in that upper room, the big mixing vat blazing, the filler tank gushing flames, copper tubing melting in the heat, packed cases of Slayzall— pints, quarts, gallons, all neatly labeled—blowing open and sending showers of glass and volatile oil into the inferno.

Wilhelm Hillmeyer, bloody apron askew, ran at Charlie as if he were carrying a sword. "Criminal!" he wailed. "You've killed my business! My shop, my refrigerators, my chickens, my veal, my sausages! All cinders and ashes! Look at it!"

"I'm sorry, Willie, I'm really sorry. I tried to stop it, but it got out of control so fast, and the damn fire truck was so late . . ."

Wilhelm was out of control, too. He started to pummel Charlie, but his son grabbed him. "He couldn't help it, Dad. He didn't do it on purpose."

"Purpose, purpose, who cares? He's killed my living. Look at it burning! It's all gone! There's nothing left!"

Tag tried to calm his father. "There's the insurance, remember?"

"There used to be insurance. These days who could afford insurance? But I'll get even with you, Anderson! I'll get you! I'll sue you for everything you've got! You hear me?"

Charlie's handsome face looked older and older. "Everything I've got, Willie, is up there."

The fire blustered and roared. Wilhelm cried into his spattered apron like a child. Tag pulled him away. "Come on, Dad, we've got to get you a coat, it's freezing out here."

Nora appeared, pushing her way through the crowd. "Charlie! Paul! Oh, dear God, what happened?"

Staring at the fire, Charlie mumbled, "Got away from me."

Nora hugged him and wept. "You're all right, you're all right . . ."

Charlie shivered in the wind, unable to take his eyes off the fire. His voice was dead. "It's the end of Slayzall."

Paul couldn't believe it. The end of Slayzall? The magic killer, the silver bullet, the most lethal toxin in history? No more trips to meat-packing plants rich in roaches, no more mothproofing of neighborhood carpets, no more day trips to drugstores and hardware stores in the flatlands of Ohio, the hills of Michigan? The end?

Nora couldn't stop crying, but she hugged Charlie as if she were protecting him. Her eyes never left his face as he said again in that stranger's voice that sounded like cold death, "It's the end."

Paul had seen his mother pull herself out of misery before, plenty of times, with a kind of psychic bootstrapping that by now he could almost predict: the way her chin took on a different set, the blink of her eyes that signaled a new look at things, then the two deep breaths. She straightened up, a challenge to her painful knees, and put a hand on Charlie's cheek. "It's not the end, Charlie." She held his face like a child's, and smiled at him, the merest flicker of a smile. "Look at me. We're together. We're all right."

But his eyes went back to the fire, as if he hadn't heard her.

"Listen, Charlie, this isn't the end." She began to inspect his bandages. "Thank goodness you're not hurt badly. Thank goodness you got out all right. So we're OK. We can start over. Do you hear me, Charlie? We'll start over."

He straightened up a little and finally turned away from the fire, as though breaking an evil spell.

"Maybe it's just as well," she said. "Maybe it's a chance to do something better."

He looked at her at last, and his face seemed a little less haggard.

"We'll start over tomorrow. We'll start today." She smiled at him. "You can do anything, Charlie. I know, I've seen you. You can do anything."

His bandaged hands came forward, and he hitched up his pants with his forearms. "You're right, Nora. We're not going to play dead."

Paul was bewildered. "But what are we going to do, Dad? What are we going to do?"

Charlie looked at him. "We'll just have to keep on keeping on."

❧

ON FRIDAY, DECEMBER 5, the *Daily Herald* was thicker than usual—twelve full pages—covering the spectacular local fire and the Christmas sales. Opening the shopping season, the merchants of Kenton were featuring business as usual: at the Toggery Shop, form-fit Oxford shirts, $1.98, pure silk neckties, 98 cents; at Schelhammer's Department Store, a necklace of cultured pearls, $6.98, Tabu cologne, $1.50; at Miss Ivey's Charm Shoppe, a quilted robe and matching nightgown, $8.98; at the Book Nook, William L. Shirer's *Berlin Diary*, $3.00, and the collected sonnets of Edna St. Vincent Millay, deluxe edition, same price; at the Post Office, U.S. Savings Bonds, a $25.00 value, $18.75; at the Strand Theater, *They Died with Their Boots On*, half-price on Thursday.

On the surface all was well, but just below that studied calm, things were going haywire: toasters were burning Kenton bread, potatoes were going moldy in Kenton cellars, and the Kenton Comets, playing without Jim, lost to Rome City. The Nazis went on shelling Leningrad and British bombers were striking back at German cities and the Japanese Imperial Army pushed across China, and along Main Street, which was buried in fresh unplowed snow and haunted by the charred ghost of the Slayzall lab and Hillmeyer's butcher shop, people grew apprehensive and laid small bets on the reappearance of the Minotaur.

That same Friday, the beast did speak again to the offended

but fascinated citizens. People begged or borrowed copies, quoted them over the phone, and ended by focusing their accumulated frustrations on Old Saul Edelman, the monster himself.

THE LABYRINTH

Look steadily into a mirror: you are a dying animal. Your life is a speeded-up film, jerkily passing from childhood to maturity to decrepitude to death, the career of a fruit fly. To the other animals, death is an accident. The large brain makes it a tragedy, and tragedy calls for reasons: Why? Why me?

You realize, there is no time now for anything but truth. And this is it: death is simply a natural part of a natural process. People are, and have always been, a part of nature, just as tigers and termites are.

Priests and preachers refuse to accept this sensible view of things, choosing instead to nourish our collective neuroses: "Eternal life!" they proclaim—and so, by promising glory in a grand but unreal eternity, they disparage the satisfactions of our small but valuable moment.

Imagine yourself religious. You picture God planning all things reasonably and wisely. Our bodies, we are told, are temples, so we treat them with respect and look forward to our threescore and ten years.

But God, it turns out, is not only unreasonable, but also a vandal. After years of our taking good care of our tidy little temples, God abruptly breaks down the door, smashes the windows, rips the paintings, and slashes the furniture. All of a sudden, without any warning at all, God shrieks in our ear: *Cancer!*

Now imagine yourself not religious. Cancer slips up without warning, threatening death. You do not fear death, but you hate it: you hate the loss, and the sorrow of leaving behind bereaved family and friends. What you feel is the proper rage at being mortal: you know you've been dealt a bad hand. Ants and alligators must also die, but they do not confront that fact with rage or regret. Those feelings are human.

Religion says, Console yourself, there will be another chance, another life. Two things are wrong with this. First, there is not a shred of evidence for it. And second, it is intended to blunt our rage and regret, thus dehumanizing us. Our anger at death testifies to the value of life; our sorrow for family and friends testifies to our devotion. Every noble quality we possess depends for its poignant value on our natural brevity. Our final pain is mortal, and our own. We refuse to have it cheapened by the seductions of an alleged immortality.

Doomed to extinction, our loves, our works, our friendships, our tastes are all painfully precious. We look about us on the streets and discover that we are beautiful because we are mortal, priceless because we are so rare in the universe and so fleeting. Whatever we are, whatever we make of ourselves, that is all we will ever have.

And that is the meaning of life.

—The Minotaur

WHEN THE NEW ISSUE of *The Hoosier Rationalist* came out, people's frustrations had inflated like a balloon, with surface tension vulnerable to mere pinpricks. The pale Saturday dawn revealed more than the usual deposits of garbage in the snowy Edelman front yard. Old Saul, who normally cleaned up the mess early in the morning, failed to do so this time. Consequently the neighbors suffered the sight of the stuff all day, and several of them tried to call in complaints against Edelman to the city health department, forgetting that the office was closed on Saturday.

All through that desolate week, after Jim ran off and Charlie's lab burned, remorse and despair kept sweeping over Paul in periodic waves, like nausea. He could tell, by their exceptional gentleness around the house, that his parents were as miserable as he was. Ruthie finally persuaded him to go somewhere special, to try to cheer him up. So on Saturday afternoon, Paul emptied his dime bank, borrowed the car, put in three gallons of gas, and picked Ruthie up at five o'clock for the thirty-mile ride to Fort Wayne, to see Mickey Rooney and Judy Garland at the Paramount Theater.

That is why Paul and Ruthie weren't in town when the balloon burst.

The *Daily Herald* didn't like the way things were going in Russia, or in North Africa, or at the Japanese "peace" talks in Washington. The *Herald* didn't like Elaine Edelman's heretical teaching, or Saul Edelman's unholy tirades. The *Herald* had editorialized before on all of these things, but on Saturday, December 6, it got down to brass tacks, plain talk, spades-as-spades.

The *Herald* said pointedly that outside agitators were not wanted in Kenton, that bestiality in the public schools and blasphemy in the press must be ripped up by the roots, and that if it continued, no civic-minded person could be responsible for what happened. "We have come a long way from the time when witches were hanged and heretics burned at the stake," the *Herald* concluded, "because civilized people have learned to live together with mutual respect. But when that respect is arrogantly violated, then Americans of courage and high principle will rise up to do what must be done. To live by the sword is to die by the sword.

"Wake up, America."

Was it a coincidence, Dr. Roberts wondered, that on the Saturday evening when that editorial appeared, as the early winter darkness was settling in, he heard the fire siren? A volunteer fireman himself, he quickly grabbed his package, handed the correct change to the clerk at Schelhammer's Department Store, and took off. He could still hear the wail of the fire truck, out east somewhere, so he rolled down his car window to the raw weather and followed the sound, north on Main, east on Mitchell. As he proceeded along Mitchell Street, he had a sinking feeling, and when he got to the 800 block, he could see it ahead. "My God," he muttered, "Saul's place."

A dozen other volunteer firemen had got there ahead of him, their cars lining both curbs behind the fire truck. He pulled up as close as he could get and ran toward them. "Where's Edelman?" he yelled.

Charlie Anderson, one hand still bandaged from his own fire, was helping with the hose. He yelled back. "Must have been gone when it started, Doc. We went in the front door, called and yelled around, but no answer."

The house was burning everywhere; front, back, sides, and roof, black smoke boiling up from the red flames. Dr. Roberts sniffed: the smell of burning oil was unmistakable.

"Arson!" he yelled.

Anderson nodded. "You bet! On my way over here, I passed a pickup full of white-hooded guys tearing off down Oak Street. Bastards!"

Holding his coat over his face, Dr. Roberts tried to make it to the side door, but the heat was like a wall.

"Come on back, Doc!" Anderson yelled. "You couldn't get inside there now, and even if you did, it'd be too late! Edelman must be out of town or something. Let's hope so, anyway. If he's in there, he's a goner."

"If he's in there, it's not just arson, it's murder." Dr. Roberts fell back and helped with the hose. They did what they could, but a brisk west wind put the fire beyond control. The house was a firestorm.

It was a respectable neighborhood, but aging, and the lots were small. So when the flames, licking into the night air, sent burning debris aloft in violent updrafts, it was not surprising that some of it should carry eastward on the strong wind and settle down on the shingles of the Carter house next door. Soon that house was on fire, too, and the firemen, knowing they had no chance of saving Saul Edelman's place, dragged their hose next door and tried their luck with the new fire. They might have prevailed there, but now the water pressure was low, and their sorry stream barely reached the second story. Soon that house, too, was a torch, sending its bright debris upward and eastward.

And so it was that the Edelman fire became the Carter fire and the Carter fire became the Tucker fire, and the Tucker fire became the Mueller fire and the Kimmel fire and the Collins fire. The desperate firemen couldn't get the blaze under control until it reached a vacant lot at the corner of Birch Street, and by that time, Saul Edelman's fire had touched the lives of the publisher of *The Kenton Daily Herald*, the pastor of the First Church of Christ, and several other innocent bystanders.

Elaine had to be told. When it was clear that the conflagration had spent itself, Dr. Roberts jumped into his car and roared off. But after two blocks, he paused at a stop sign. He realized that it wasn't just a matter of bringing bad news. She would need him now more than ever. Who knows what had happened to Saul?

Don't leave me, Tom. I can't bear to be alone now.

If he went to Elaine's tonight, could he possibly leave again?

He sat there with the gearshift in neutral. He could see Edna sitting anxiously in the living room, knowing he had gone to fight a fire, worrying about him in that angry, nervous way she had. And it was their anniversary. Their silver anniversary. Dinner would be waiting, a special cake. His package from Schelhammer's, a gift-wrapped silver bowl for Edna, was riding in the trunk of the Nash.

I'd kill myself! Really, I would.

He pounded the steering wheel. The lighted dashboard leered at him—was he losing his mind?

"She needs me!" he yelled at the dashboard. And then corrected himself. "I mean I need her!"

But he sat in his car at the deserted intersection for a long time, the motor idling steam into the cold night air, before he finally turned the corner and headed for Elaine's.

❧

IT WAS NEARLY midnight when Paul and Ruthie, cozy behind the heater of the sixty-horse Ford, got back to town. On Saturday nights they expected to see people on Main Street, but not as many as were there now. Paul saw Scrap and Gopher in front of the Candy Castle, so he rolled down the window and yelled, "Hey, Scrap, we just got back from Fort Wayne—what's going on?"

Scrap peered at the car. "Who's that? Paul? Hey, you missed a great fire! Burned down the whole east side of town, practically! You shoulda been here! Started at Edelman's house and spread like crazy. Go take a look!"

"See you later!" Paul and Ruthie sped off to Mitchell Street, then slowed down to join a line of cars that was creeping past the row of smoldering houses. Firemen with flashlights had the area cordoned off at the sidewalk. When they reached the Edelman place, they could hardly recognize it; it was burned almost to the ground. The smell of charred wood filled the car. Awe: Paul recognized it in his voice. "It's like a war," he said.

Ruthie nodded. "Scrap said it started at Edelman's."

"Did you read the Minotaur thing yesterday?"

"It upset lots of people, I guess."

" 'The meaning of life—is what—we make of ourselves!' " Paul's sudden laugh had a peculiar sound; he stifled it. He felt depressed again.

What had he made of himself?

They drove to Ruthie's house and parked there. It was a long way to the next streetlight, and the clouds had thickened, so the car was as dark as a midnight meadow.

"It's so awful," she said softly, and he realized she was crying. He touched her face, wiping away the tears. "Paul," she said, "what can we do?"

He knew she didn't mean the fire. "We can't change anything, Ruthie. Jim's gone, and it's a four-year hitch. We can't bring him back—but he'll be OK, if we can just keep out of the war."

They moved closer together, awkward in the little front

seat. "You taught me this, Ruthie—we mustn't let Jim, or anybody else, make us feel guilty."

"We won't."

Paul kissed her, and her lips were magic, conjuring stardust visions, and they kissed again, a quick soft touching that made him dizzy with excitement, and then their lips met firmly for a moment, and they finally backed away and waited for a tantalizing minute, and then kissed again, mouths open a little, and Paul was so stirred that he could hardly breathe, and he gasped and backed off again, and they both laughed, and caught their breath for a moment, and kissed again, and her tongue slid across his upper lip, and he trembled all over, and they clung to each other, still kissing, until they had to stop and breathe again.

In pure happiness, Paul unbuttoned her coat and felt her small waist, the fuzzy sweater, and smelled her familiar innocent smell. His sight had adjusted to the dark now, and he could look into her eyes as he broke the rules and slid his hand up to her breast and felt the wonder of it.

Nothing in his life had prepared him for joy. He had been ready for work, for monotony, for losses, but there was no warning and no training for this ecstasy.

"I love you, Ruthie."

"I love you, Paul."

He removed his hand from its enchanted warmth, and they sat there in the cold car, feeling breathless and happier than they had ever been.

In love.

So they felt sorry for everything that wasn't lucky enough to be Paul and Ruthie: sorry about Jim, and sorry about Old Saul and all those charred houses, and sorry about Slayzall and Hillmeyer's and sorry about Miss Edelman and FDR and Lindbergh and London and Leningrad. But they didn't want to think about any of that right now. The future might look bleak, but they wanted it.

"Mom will be coming out after me if I don't go in. It must be really late."

He turned on the dash light and looked at his watch. "Midnight. Twenty after."

"Sunday morning."

Paul would have liked it to go on being Saturday night, but facts are facts. "December seventh." As he said it, he realized it was a date he would never forget; some midnights are indelible.

She hugged him one last time, and he treasured her warmth. Her voice was a whisper. "We have a lot to look forward to."

"It's only just begun," he said.

I
MAGINE.

Not America First, happy ever after, but a spasm in history . . .

Imagine worn linoleum and bright oilcloth, the tall black telephone on its neat doily. Recall the Jack Armstrong ring, the Melvin Purvis Junior G-Man badge, the shelf of Big-Little Books, pin curls and bobby socks, the worn leather bag heavy with marbles: iridescent glassies and steadfast clays. Remember best friends' best friends: Jer's Scots terrier, Scrap's cocker, Margie's St. Bernard. Think of the summer sky after John Philip Sousa concerts at the trellised bandstand by Long Lake: Big Dipper, Little Dipper, Lazy W, Milky Way— background music courtesy of screech owls, crickets, and a thousand frogs. Conjure up the irresistible smells, the splash of hi-test gas at the Sinclair station, bonfire smoke in the October air, fresh bread at the corner bakery, the upholstery of Uncle Ed's new Studebaker.

. . . a spasm in history, insane violence, a vision of One World—and then, in due time, thinning hair and bitter anniversaries: VE Day, the Bomb, VJ Day, all misted in quaintness, here in the song of a sleepless bird sending its liquid keening into a honeysuckle midnight, into the dim moonshadows of maple leaves . . .